P9-CFA-836

Tales from
DEADWOOD

The Killers

Mike Jameson

BERKLEY BOOKS, NEW YORK

THE BERKLEY PUBLISHING GROUP
Published by the Penguin Group
Penguin Group (USA) Inc.
375 Hudson Street, New York, New York 10014, USA
Penguin Group (Canada), 90 Eglinton Avenue East, Suite 700, Toronto, Ontario M4P 2Y3, Canada
(a division of Pearson Penguin Canada Inc.)
Penguin Books Ltd., 80 Strand, London WC2R 0RL, England
Penguin Group Ireland, 25 St. Stephen's Green, Dublin 2, Ireland (a division of Penguin Books Ltd.)
Penguin Group (Australia), 250 Camberwell Road, Camberwell, Victoria 3124, Australia
(a division of Pearson Australia Group Pty. Ltd.)
Penguin Books India Pvt. Ltd., 11 Community Centre, Panchsheel Park, New Delhi—110 017, India
Penguin Group (NZ), Cnr. Airborne and Rosedale Roads, Albany, Auckland 1310, New Zealand
(a division of Pearson New Zealand Ltd.)
Penguin Books (South Africa) (Pty.) Ltd., 24 Sturdee Avenue, Rosebank, Johannesburg 2196,
South Africa

Penguin Books Ltd., Registered Offices: 80 Strand, London WC2R 0RL, England

This is a work of fiction. Names, characters, places, and incidents either are the product of the authors'
imagination or are used fictitiously, and any resemblance to actual persons, living or dead, business
establishments, events, or locales is entirely coincidental.

TALES FROM DEADWOOD: THE KILLERS

A Berkley Book / published by arrangement with the authors

PRINTING HISTORY
Berkley edition / January 2007

Copyright © 2007 by The Berkley Publishing Group.
Cover illustration by Bruce Emmett.
Cover design by Steven Ferlauto.
Interior text design by Kristin del Rosario.

ISBN: 978-0-425-21339-1

BERKLEY®
Berkley Books are published by The Berkley Publishing Group,
a division of Penguin Group (USA) Inc.,
375 Hudson Street, New York, New York 10014.
BERKLEY is a registered trademark of Penguin Group (USA) Inc.
The "B" design is a trademark belonging to Penguin Group (USA) Inc.

PRINTED IN THE UNITED STATES OF AMERICA

10   9   8   7   6   5   4   3   2   1

Prologue

"Yes, sir, it was Wild Bill his own self, big as life," the bartender in the Gold Room said as he wiped the hardwood with a rag and regaled his customers with a yarn. "He came in all the time to drink and play poker, only we didn't know it was him at first. You see, he put his hair up under his hat and wore a pair of spectacles with smoked lenses. That way, folks wouldn't bother him. When they knew he was Wild Bill, you see, they'd ask him a bunch of questions, and some of 'em would even sneak up and try to touch his coattail or his sleeve, for luck, you know. He must've got tired of it. Hell, I'd get tired of it, too, if folks were always makin' a fuss over me."

"Get to the fight," one of the customers said. He held a mug of beer and wore an impatient expression on his face.

"Well, Bill was playin' poker, as per usual, and suddenly he got the notion that one of the other players was cheatin'. Naturally, Wild Bill Hickok wasn't gonna put up with that. So he reached up and took off his hat and let that long brown hair of his fall down around his shoulders, and then he took off them smoked glasses, and one of the other fellas at the table hollered out, 'It's Wild Bill!' Bill looked at the gent who'd been dealin' off the bottom and said in that deep voice of his, 'What are we gonna do about this cheatin' you've been doin', my good man?' That's all he had to say to make everybody around the table dive for cover, because they figured that the air was gonna be full of lead any time about then. Except for the fella Wild Bill was talkin' to, and he was too plumb scared to move."

"What happened then?" another customer asked, eagerness in his voice.

"Well, Bill didn't go for his guns, and neither did the fella who'd been cheatin', so after a minute Bill just reached out and gathered in the pot. Nobody tried to stop him. I got my nerve up, though, and asked him if he'd like a drink on the house."

"Yeah, that took a lot o' nerve, offerin' a man a free drink," somebody in the crowd said, heckling the bartender.

The apron glared. "Listen, if you'd been here and felt the danger in the air that day, you'd damn well know that it *did* take some nerve to speak up. I was half afraid Wild Bill'd be so spooked he'd whirl around and ventilate me, just on general principles." The bartender shrugged and went on. "He took the drink, though, and then he left with the money from the pot."

"What about the other fellas in the game? They didn't do nothin' wrong, but they lost their money anyway."

"That was just too damn bad. I reckon they thought it was a small price to pay for comin' that close to a shoot-out with Wild Bill Hickok involved."

The men who had been hanging on the bartender's story paid no attention to the stranger who was sitting at a table in one corner of the barroom, nursing a beer. He wore a long gray duster and a flat-crowned black hat. Long brown hair touched here and there with gray fell to his shoulders, and he had a close-cropped beard of the same shade. A walnut-handled Colt was holstered on his hip, and a well-used but well-cared-for Henry rifle lay on the table close at hand. He had ridden into Cheyenne late in the afternoon and stabled his horse, then headed for the Gold Room to cut the trail dust in his throat. He had been trying to decide whether he was more interested in getting some supper or a whore.

One of the men at the bar said, "That's a bunch o' bullshit. It didn't happen that way, and you know it."

The bartender stood up straight and glowered. "What are you talkin' about? I seen it with my own eyes. I think I know what I seen with my own eyes."

"The way I heard it," the naysayer responded, "was that Hickok wasn't even in the game, and that when the gent started cheatin', somebody called him on it and he was about to start a ruckus when this policeman Hickok knows came in and tried to arrest the fella. Hickok didn't do anything. He was just there."

The bartender shook his head stubbornly. "You heard it all wrong. It happened the way I said, damn it!"

The wrangling at the bar continued. After a few moments someone said, "I hear Wild Bill's up in Deadwood now. He'll tame that camp, you just wait and see."

"He went there to look for gold, not to be a lawman. I was here the night him and Charley Utter started talkin' about it."

"Utter's settin' up a freight line betwixt here and Deadwood, I hear," another man put in. "Tryin' to start a mail delivery service, too."

"Deadwood's gonna be more than a boomtown, you just wait and see. The place is really growin'."

One of the men shook his head and declared, "No, if the gold runs out, so will Deadwood's boom. It'll dry up and be a ghost town in no time. Mark my words, gents . . . in a hundred years, nobody will have ever heard of Deadwood."

"You're plumb loco. Deadwood's here to stay. Before you know it, there'll be schools and churches up there. They already got a preacher."

"How do you know so much about it?" the other man challenged with a sneer.

"I just come from up there. You never saw such a busy place. All the hotels and roomin' houses were full. I wouldn't have had a place to stay if Preacher Smith hadn't been so generous and offered to share his room with me."

In the corner, the stranger's head slowly lifted. His mind

had registered the mention of a preacher in Deadwood a moment earlier, but he hadn't shown any sign that he noticed. Now that he had heard the sky pilot's name, though, he could no longer conceal his interest.

"If Deadwood's such a great place, how come you're down here in Cheyenne and not up there?"

"Ran outta money," the man who had been boosting Deadwood said with a shrug. "Thought I'd work for a while and then go back with a better stake. And next time I'll find gold, you can bet your balls on that."

One of the men laughed. "I don't bet my balls on anything! They're too valuable to me to risk losin' 'em."

"Don't know why they're valuable, you don't use 'em for anything. You don't even fuck any whores!"

"I'm savin' my money so *I* can go to Deadwood, Goddamn it! When I strike gold and make a fortune, I won't even need to pay for whores. Fine ladies'll be gettin' in line, fightin' over which one of 'em gets to lay down and spread for me first."

"You're a Goddamn lunatic. Fine ladies don't act like that, 'specially not around an ugly son of a bitch like you."

"They do if you got enough money. Let's face it, boys, ain't nothin' makes any woman wet between the legs faster'n a fella with lots of money, no matter what he looks like."

There were nods of solemn agreement from several of the men.

The stranger just sipped his beer and wished the conversation would get back to Preacher Smith in Deadwood. That was what he wanted to hear about. He didn't want to think about women and what excited them. He didn't care about that anymore. He had been married once, a long time ago. His wife hadn't married him because he had money, though. In fact, she was the one who was rich and lived on a big fancy plantation in Virginia. He had been poor, one of several brothers in a family of farmers, nothing special. But the girl had hated her daddy and figured the best way to get back at him was by marrying somebody he considered white trash. That hadn't worked out too well, of course.

But it was all a long time in the past, more than a decade

gone, and the stranger shoved the memories so far back in his brain he couldn't hear them anymore. He lived for today, not yesterday, and the only thing he really cared about was the hunt. The bounties he collected were nice, of course. They kept him in food and ammunition and the occasional soiled dove when the need was too strong to ignore, but it was the hunting he lived for.

Hunting men.

The talk at the bar had drifted to another topic, though it still had to do with Deadwood. "You hear about the race?" one man asked.

"What race?" Any sort of competition always drew quick interest on the frontier.

"Colorado Charley's got him some competition for the mail service. Some other fella's tryin' to set up a Pony Express line, too, so there's gonna be a race between Fort Laramie and Deadwood to see which bunch is the fastest. From what I hear, Dick Seymour's ridin' for Charley Utter."

"Ol' Bloody Dick, the Englishman?"

"One and the same."

"He's a pretty good fella. Knowed him when he was huntin' buffalo a few years ago. Say, didn't I hear somethin' about him marryin' some squaw?"

"I wouldn't know about that. All I know is that he works for Colorado Charley now."

"Well, for old times' sake I reckon I hope he wins."

Another man said, "I sure as hell wouldn't want to be carryin' the mail like that. After what they did to Custer, I'd be afraid the Goddamn Sioux would jump me and lift my hair."

Again heads bobbed in solemn nods of agreement.

Only a few weeks had passed since the terrible massacre of the Seventh Cavalry on a ridge overlooking the stream known as the Little Bighorn. Colonel George Armstrong Custer, the commander of the Seventh and a man considered by many to be invincible, had died along with more than two hundred of his troopers. The stranger in the corner remembered one of his brothers talking about how Custer had been a commander in the Union cavalry during the war and how he'd always won the battles in which he had been engaged.

Some people thought he was a genius, while others considered him just lucky.

The stranger supposed that question had finally been settled. A genius didn't take two hundred men into battle against several thousand bloodthirsty savages. Custer had been lucky all along—and luck was a funny thing. It had a habit of running out at the worst possible time.

"Yeah, I hear the Sioux are mad as hell about Deadwood and all those other minin' camps bein' up there in the Black Hills to start with. They say we broke our treaty with 'em, and that the Black Hills are sacred to them."

"No, they ain't," said the man who had been arguing one of the earlier topics of discussion. "They just don't like white folks. The Black Hills bein' sacred or not ain't got nothin' to do with it."

"Well, that ain't the way I heard it. The Injuns call them hills the Papa Papa, or somethin' like that, and it means sacred ground."

"It's Paha Sapa, and it don't mean nothin' of the sort."

"Well, then, what does it mean, if you're so damn smart?"

"I don't rightly know, but I'm damn sure it don't mean sacred ground!"

Navel of the world, thought the manhunter. That was what Paha Sapa meant in the Sioux tongue. He wasn't sure how come he knew that. Just one of those useless bits of information that a man picks up and discovers later has lodged in his brain for no apparent reason.

"Whatever it means, the Sioux don't want those gold-seekers up there. I've heard that they've ambushed and killed white men within a mile or two of the camp."

"That's right. Killed 'em and lifted their hair."

"Hell of a way to die."

"Ain't no good way, is there?"

The manhunter wasn't so sure about that. He wasn't one to dwell on such things, but he had wondered a time or two how death would finally come to him. He had cheated the old bastard plenty of times in the past, but one of these days it would catch up to him. Might not be so bad if a fella could go down while dealing out death to his enemies, a gun in each hand bucking and thundering as he slammed lead into the sons of bitches who had been foolish enough to get in his way. . . .

Enough of this shit. He drained the last of the beer in the mug, thumped the empty on the table, and stood up. He had places to go and things to do, and he was tired of waiting for the conversation at the bar to meander its way back to where he wanted it to go.

He walked over to the bar, his low-heeled boots thumping on the plank floor. As he came up to the man who had spoken earlier, he said, "You know Preacher Smith up in Deadwood?"

The man looked over at him in surprise and said, "What?" Then he stiffened some as he saw the manhunter's cold gray eyes. "Yeah," he admitted. "I know Preacher Smith."

"What's he look like?"

"The preacher? Well, he's tall and sort of skinny . . . got black hair, really black, almost like an Indian's, and a beard. And he wears a black suit and a white shirt all the time, like you'd expect a preacher to wear."

The manhunter nodded but didn't say "Thanks" or "Much obliged." He wasn't the sort of man to express gratitude.

As the manhunter started to turn away, the man he'd questioned summoned up his courage and said, "You know Preacher Smith, friend?"

The manhunter paused. "Never met the man. But I've got business with him."

Then he walked out of the Gold Room without looking back.

"Lord have mercy," muttered the man at the bar. "I wouldn't want that fella havin' any business with *me*. Did you see his eyes? Coldest damned things I ever saw. Looked at me like I was a bug and he'd just as soon step on me as not."

"Aw, you're just imaginin' things," one of the other men said. "Have a drink. Hell, I'll even buy it."

"I never say no to a free drink."

But as he turned to the bar, the man spared one last thought for the cold-eyed stranger. He hoped that by the time he got back up to Deadwood, that son of a bitch had been there and gone.

Chapter One

RICHARD Seymour had once trod the boards as an actor on the London stage. He'd had a promising career and had hobnobbed with quite a few of the country's wealthy aristocrats. The world had been his for the taking.

Then he had taken something he shouldn't have—the wrong woman—and been banished to America to live out his days far from the finer things of life. That explained how a man who had once sipped the finest champagne from exquisite crystal now guzzled home-brewed Who-hit-John from filthy glasses and how beautiful, tastefully decorated drawing rooms had been exchanged for squalid frontier hotel rooms. Once he had slept in canopied four-poster beds instead of narrow bunks with lumpy mattresses stuffed with bug-infested straw. And there had been a time—oh, yes, there had—when some of the loveliest, most genteel women in all of England had cried out in passion beneath him and clutched at him as he made love to them . . . rather than the doughy prostitute who now said in a bored voice, "You done yet, honey? I got other customers waitin' to fuck me, you know."

How could he forget? This had been a mistake, he thought as he grunted and lunged one final time and spent in her. Quickly he pulled out and rolled off her, standing up on unsteady legs next to the bunk. In the glow of the single candle stuck on the tiny table, he looked down at her and felt like crying. A bitter sense of loss filled him.

But it wasn't the life he had led in England that he mourned. It was the one he had found here in America, on the Kansas plains of all places, with the woman called Carries Water.

The woman who was now dead, murdered along with her children by the Sioux war chief Talking Bear.

"Thanks, sugar pie," the whore said, breaking into Dick's thoughts before he could descend fully into the morass of memory and grief. "You done paid already, so you can pull up your trousers and run along now."

The past few minutes had meant nothing to her, he saw now. Of course not. Why should they, when they would be repeated countless times in the course of an evening, with a variety of partners filling the role he had just performed? He couldn't expect her to give him a second thought. With a sigh, he pulled up the bottoms of the long underwear and the denim trousers. When he had buttoned his trousers and buckled his belt, he picked up his hat from the floor. Then, holding the hat in his hand as if it bore a fine plume instead of dirt and sweat stains, he swept low in a bow and said, "I bid you a very heartfelt adieu, mademoiselle."

That got her attention. She giggled and said, "Ain't you the silliest motherfucker I ever seen?"

Dick straightened and clapped the hat on his head. "Indeed I am, *ma cherie*."

Then he clicked the heels of his boots together, turned sharply, and marched out of the crib.

It was one of a row of such shacks in an alley off Deadwood's Main Street, opposite the point where Sherman Street diverged from Main. Some people referred to the alley as the Badlands, while others used that name for the entire district east of Wall Street, where most of the town's saloons, gambling dens, and brothels were located. This alley was the lowest of the low—well, except for Chinatown, of course, which was located a bit farther east—and Dick wasn't sure what had led him to come here tonight. He had no business debauching himself, not with the all-important race against August Clippinger's Frontier Pony Express coming up in a few days. Dick was going to be riding against Clippinger's man Jed Powell, and he needed to be in his best shape in order to insure a victory. He didn't really care who carried the mail between Fort Laramie and Deadwood, but he had signed on with Charley Utter and honor and loyalty still had to mean something. Without them, a man was truly nothing.

Dick turned west along the street, intending to stop at the No. 10 Saloon or the Bella Union. Perhaps Bill Hickok would be in one of those places. It always made Dick feel better to talk to Hickok. The man had a way of looking at things clearly that had nothing to do with his fading eyesight. He always offered good advice.

Lately, though, Dick recalled, Hickok had been rather moody and distant himself. Most of the people in Deadwood were enthusiastic souls, eager to make their fortunes. But everywhere, one could always find a few dreamers, lost souls such as himself and lately Hickok, who had known too much of disappointment in their lives, those who sensed the passage of time and the inevitable loss, the knowledge that pleasure was fleeting but pain lasted forever, the undeniable awareness that no, things had not worked out as they had hoped and never would. The best one could do was to grasp the moments that weren't so bad and hang onto them for as long as possible.

Lost in self-pity, Dick tripped over something as he passed a wagon and almost went to his knees in the filthy muck of the street. He caught himself on one of the wagon wheels and looked down to see what he had tripped on.

It was a human leg, clad in buckskin and protruding from under the wagon.

Dick could have gone on and assumed that whoever was underneath the wagon was just drunk, but it was possible the fellow had been set upon by thieves and injured. The man might even be dead. It was a rare night when no one was murdered in Deadwood.

He kicked the leg and said, "Hello? Are you all right under there? Hello?"

There was no response. Telling himself that he was a fool to get involved in something that was none of his business, he reached down and grasped the leg. As he hauled up on it, he had the horrible thought that maybe the leg wasn't even attached to a body. He might pull it out of there only to find that it was all that was left of some unfortunate bastard.

The leg *was* attached, however, and he discovered that quickly as the rest of the buckskin-clad shape slid out from under the wagon and began thrashing around.

"What the hell! Leggo me, you sumbitch, 'fore I blow your motherfuckin' head off!"

Dick recognized the harsh voice and dropped the leg. As he stepped back, he said, "Take it easy, Calam. It's just me, Bloody Dick."

"I'll make you think your dick's bloody! I'll carve it off with my bowie knife, you goddamn cocksuckin' bastard— Oh. Oh, hell, it's just you. The Englisher." Miss Martha Jane Cannary rolled onto hands and knees and awkwardly took hold of the wagon wheel in an attempt to pull herself onto her feet. She kept slipping in the muck, though, so she finally said, "Gimme a hand, Dick."

Her buckskins had shit smeared on them from wallowing in the street, so he grasped her arm gingerly and steadied her until finally she was able to stand upright. She kept a tight grip on the wheel, though, and said, "Whoa, things are sure spinnin' around funny. I must've had a mite too much to drink."

Dick would have said that was a reasonable assumption, since the smell of rotgut whiskey that wafted from her was even more pungent than the waste from the street. He had drunk too much tonight himself, but he suspected that his consumption was far, far behind that of the woman known far and wide as Calamity Jane.

"Are you all right, Calam?" he asked. "Maybe you should

go somewhere and sit down. Perhaps even have a cup of coffee."

She let go of the wagon wheel with one hand and wiped the back of it across her nose. "Aw, who'd let me in, stinkin' as bad as I do? Sure as hell can't march into the dinin' room o' the Grand Central Hotel like this. That nigger woman who runs the place'd take a broom after me. Or a shotgun."

Dick knew that Calamity referred to Lucretia Marchbanks, the cook at the Grand Central who was also known as Aunt Lou. She was certainly not the owner of the hotel—it belonged to a man named Charles Wagner—but it was her cooking that brought people from all over the Dakota Territory and it was widely suspected that her word carried more weight than that of Wagner himself. Quite an accomplishment for a woman who had begun her life as a slave.

"What about the Bella Union?" Dick suggested.

"Billy Nuttall threw me out earlier this evenin'. Told me to stay outta the Number Ten until I sobered up some, too. He said he'd given orders to Harry Sam Young not to sell me any more hooch tonight. That son of a bitch. Where's he get off, decidin' when somebody's had too much to drink? Hell, it's his business to sell the goddamn stuff, ain't it?"

"It does seem to be a bit of a contradiction."

Calamity hiccupped. "Damn right it is."

"There's always the Gem."

"Nope," Calamity said with a shake of her head. "I been banned from there. Al Swearengen's got it in for me. He thinks I helped the White-Eyed Kid steal that Silky Jen whore away from him." She chuckled. "Course, I did."

Dick knew a little about that misadventure, but wasn't interested in hearing the details. Without being sure why he was doing it, he said, "Come along with me. You can sit down in my tent, and I'll bring you some coffee."

"You'd do that for me?" Calamity sounded astounded. "Why in God's name are you bein' nice to me?"

"I don't like to see a lady who's distraught."

"Neither would I, if I knew what the hell that meant, and if there was a lady around here."

"Come along, Calam," he said patiently, tightening his grip on her arm.

He shared a tent with the Street brothers, Dick and Brant, who also rode for Colorado Charley Utter and the Pioneer Pony Express. They were out somewhere and probably wouldn't be back for quite some time. Dick intended to have Calamity sobered up somewhat and sent on her way by the time they returned. It wasn't that he was particularly worried about being seen with her—he had long since stopped worrying about his reputation—but more that he didn't want to complicate his life any more than it already was. Simplicity, that was what he strove for these days. Life was less painful that way.

Calamity staggered some, but he got her into the tent and sat her down on an empty keg that served as a stool. "Just sit there and rest," he told her. "I'll be back shortly with that coffee."

She caught at his sleeve. "Thanks, Dick. You're sure bein' good to—"

She didn't get any farther. She doubled over and vomited at his feet. He stepped back hurriedly and gritted his teeth at the stench that filled the tent. The Street brothers were not going to be happy with him when they got back. Why couldn't she have done that while she was outside?

But what had he expected, after all? he asked himself. Calamity followed her. It had even given her her name.

HE got a cup of coffee at the No. 10 and promised Harry Sam Young that he would return the cup later. Bill Hickok was there as Dick had thought he might be, playing cards with several men. As usual, Hickok's chair was turned so that his back was against the wall of the narrow little saloon. He caught Dick's eye and nodded a greeting. Dick would have liked to go over and talk to Hickok, but Calamity Jane was waiting in his tent so he had to just wave briefly instead as he went out.

Calam was still sitting on the keg, hands dangling between her knees, head tipped forward. She was half-asleep and jerked awake as Dick came in. He pressed the cup of coffee into her hands and said, "Drink that. I'll be right back."

"Where you goin'?"

"I won't be gone long," he said without really answering her question.

When he came back, he had a bucket full of dirt that he had gotten from one of the many piles of earth that dotted Main Street. When gold-seekers had first flooded into Deadwood Gulch, in the very earliest days of the camp—all of four or five months previous—they had dug everywhere looking for the precious yellow metal, including the area that had become Main Street. Some of the holes had been filled back in, but not all of them. Dick spread the dirt from the bucket over the puddle of vomit, and almost immediately it smelled better inside the tent.

Calamity Jane sipped at the steaming coffee and said, "I don't know what I done to deserve such a friend as you, Dick."

"One doesn't have to deserve friendship. It has to be freely bestowed."

She sighed. "Damn, you talk pretty. Ever' time I run into an Englisher, I feel like pullin' my drawers down and lettin' him have a poke. How's about you, Dick? You wanna poke me?"

How in heaven's name was he supposed to answer a question like that? Even a . . . a creature such as Calamity Jane was capable of being offended, and he didn't want to give offense to her. In all honesty, though, she was even more repulsive than the whore he had been with earlier.

And that was his answer, he realized. With a sad smile on his face, he said, "I'm sorry, Calam, I had just been in the Badlands before I encountered you. I'm afraid I wouldn't be able to perform suitably right now."

"Yeah, menfolks is mighty frail, all right. Can't come but once or twice an hour, if they's lucky."

"It'll take longer than that for me to recuperate," he said quickly.

She waved a hand. "Oh, hell, don't worry none about it.

Tell you the truth, I'm still a mite too dizzy to fuck right now, anyway." She took another sip of the coffee. "I'd rather just sit right here and talk, if that's all right with you."

She wanted to *talk* to him? He had supposed they would spent the time in silence for the most part. But if conversation was what she wanted, he thought he could manage. He sat down on his bunk and said, "What is it you want to talk about?"

To his surprise and horror, tears began to well from her eyes and roll down her cheeks, leaving trails in the thick coating of grime on her face. "Wild Bill don't love me no more!" she wailed.

Dick was nonplussed. He happened to know that Bill Hickok had never even met Calamity Jane until a few weeks earlier, when she had joined the wagon train headed for Deadwood at Fort Laramie. Hickok had certainly never been in love with the woman.

"He's so pretty," Calamity went on, her shoulders shaking from her sobs, "with that long brown hair and them soulful eyes o' his and them big hands. You know what they say about a man with big hands . . . he's got a big talleywhacker, too. No, wait a minute. That's what they say about an hombre with big feet. What *do* they say about a man with big hands?"

"I have no earthly idea," Dick answered honestly.

"Anyway, Bill's just about the handsomest man I ever did see in all my borned days, and I been smitten with him ever since I laid eyes on him down yonder at Fort Laramie. I thought he was startin' to feel the same way about me, too."

Dick knew that to be incorrect. Bill Hickok might have felt sorry for Calamity Jane. He might have even felt a bit of rough affection for her. But that had been the extent of it, and as a matter of fact, Hickok had gone out of his way to avoid Calamity at times, knowing how she felt about him. There had never been any sort of romance between them, except perhaps in Calamity's mind.

She sniffled and swiped at her nose. "I got to thinkin' that Bill and me ought to get married."

"He couldn't do that," Dick pointed out. "He's already married, to Mrs. Agnes Thatcher."

"It could've been a secret, just 'tween him and me and the preacher. I wouldn't even care if 'n it was legal in the eyes o' the law. Just so's we could be together like man and wife."

That never would have happened, Dick knew. But he felt too much sympathy for Calamity to state it so bluntly. He remembered all the times he had wallowed in sorrow and self-pity over the past few years. Everybody had to give in to that at one time or another. Tonight was one of Calamity's times, he supposed. And he could give her a sympathetic ear while she was going through it.

"Perhaps if things had been different . . ." he began.

"Or if we'd had more time. But Wild Bill's time is runnin' out."

Dick frowned. "What do you mean by that?"

"He's got the Injun sign on him. He ain't long for this world. I can see it in his eyes. And he knows it, too. I've heard him say as much to California Joe and some others."

"You don't mean to say that he's ill? He seems to be the picture of health."

Calamity snorted and shook her head. "A man like Wild Bill Hickok don't get sick and die in his bed. When the Grim Reaper comes for him, he'll come bearin' a six-gun."

"You can't know that."

"I do know it." Calamity tapped a fist against her mostly flat chest. "I know it in here, just like Bill does." Her voice was hollow as she declared, "He won't never leave Deadwood alive."

Chapter Two

"**C**AN I buy you a drink, Wild Bill?"

"Save your money, my young friend. I'll get this."

Bill Hickok laid a coin on the bar in the No. 10 Saloon. Harry Sam Young scooped it up deftly and drew two mugs of beer that he placed in front of Hickok and Leander Richardson. The young, fresh-faced Richardson had drifted into Deadwood a few days earlier and immediately attached himself to Hickok. It would have been a simple matter for the Prince of Pistoleers to shoo the youngster away, but he found himself liking Richardson. In his eagerness and naïveté, the lad reminded Hickok of a big friendly puppy, always tagging along clumsily at his master's heels.

Not that Bill Hickok thought of himself as any man's master. Once, perhaps, but no longer. The years and his own mistakes had taught him something of humility—although he wasn't likely to display that quality in public, at least not too often. Self-confidence—and a bold display of the same—was one thing that helped keep a gunman alive.

The poker game in which Hickok had been taking part earlier in the evening had broken up. Hickok had done fairly well with the pasteboards, coming out far enough ahead that he felt generous, if not overly flush with funds. Comfortably, he turned and hooked the heel of his right boot over the brass rail along the bottom of the bar. His left hand held the beer mug. His right elbow was propped on the bar so that his hand hung near the butt of the revolver holstered on his right hip. He was at ease.

The door of the No. 10 opened and a large man in buckskins came in. A floppy-brimmed hat was crammed down on a rumpled thatch of black hair, and a tangled beard of the same shade jutted from his strong jaw. Dark eyes over an ax blade of a nose swept the room and spotted Hickok, who lifted the mug in a combination of greeting and salute. "California Joe," Hickok said to his old friend. "Come and have a drink with young Richardson and me."

California Joe, who had been born Moses Milner long before he embarked on an adventurous career as a frontiersman and scout, came over to the bar and said, "I'd sure like to, Bill, but I ain't got time. I'm leavin' tonight."

"Leaving?" Hickok repeated with a frown. "What about your gold claim? Are you giving it up?"

"No, sir, not hardly. I've found a mite of color up the gulch, enough to keep me interested. But before he headed down to Fort Laramie, ol' Colorado Charley asked me to put together a bunch o' fellas and go huntin' for Injun ponies. He says if we can round some up, he'll buy a goodly number of 'em for his Pony Express, and we can sell the others and make a damn nice profit." California Joe jerked his shaggy head toward the door of the saloon. "Why don't you come with us, Bill? I'd feel a heap better about venturin' into Sioux territory if you was along."

Hickok turned and set the mug on the bar, then stood there for a long, silent moment before he said, "I don't think so, Joe. Richardson here might be interested, though."

"Aw, why the hell not? We're liable to get in a Injun fight. Be a hell of a lot o' fun." Joe asked again, "Will you go?"

Slowly, Hickok shook his head. "Not a damned foot. There are some gents in this camp who have it in mind to kill me, and they'll either do it or they won't. But until they make their play, I'm not stirring from Deadwood. Not unless I'm carried out."

California Joe slammed a hand down on the bar. "Damn it, Bill, this ain't the first time you've handed me that shit! You might not be so full o' doom and gloom if you'd get outta these saloons once in a while. Get some fresh air and let the sun beat down on you. Hell, there ain't nothin' more invigoratin' in the world than hearin' the war whoops o' savages bent on liftin' your hair and breathin' in the smell o' gun smoke."

Hickok just shook his head.

With a sigh, California Joe turned to Leander Richardson. "How about you, kid? Want to come huntin' Injun ponies with me and some other fellas?"

"Thanks, Joe, but I reckon I'll stay here in Deadwood, too."

California Joe grunted. "Your loss." He held out a hand to Hickok. "I'll see you when I get back, Bill."

Hickok didn't say anything, just smiled sadly as he shook hands with his friend. Shaking his head and muttering curses into his beard, California Joe left the No. 10.

"I'm surprised you didn't want to go, Mr. Hickok," Richardson said when Joe was gone. "It sounds like quite an adventure."

"I've had my adventures, son. More than my share, really." Hickok picked up the mug and sipped from the beer that was left in it. "I'm content to stay here and enjoy a game of cards, a pleasant conversation with friends—"

The door of the saloon slammed open, and a man yelled, "There you are, Foster, you motherfuckin' son of a bitch!" He stepped farther into the room, raising a big revolver in his hand as he advanced on a table where a man had been sitting and having a drink.

This second man leaped to his feet, shouted, "Larson, you shit-eatin' bastard!" and clawed the gun on his hip from its holster.

Larson got a shot off first, and the explosion was deafening in the narrow confines of the No. 10. The bullet slammed into the table where Foster had been sitting. Foster fired a second later, the gun in his fist thundering. All around the room, men yelled angrily and scurried to get out of the line of fire. That was difficult to do, however, because as the two combatants continued pulling the triggers of their guns, their aim deteriorated even farther. Slugs sprayed wildly around the saloon. Clouds of powder smoke choked the air.

And all through the chaos of the gunfight, Wild Bill Hickok stood calmly at the bar, never moving except to lift the mug of beer to his mouth and then tipping his head back to drain the last of the foamy brew. He didn't even turn to look at the two men shooting at each other. When he was finished with the beer, he slowly lowered the mug and set it on the hardwood in front of him.

Leander Richardson crouched at his feet, eyes wide with fear, pressing himself against the front of the bar to present as small a target as possible for the screaming bullets.

The silence that fell was abrupt and almost as deafening in its way as the explosions. Foster and Larson both still stood there, some ten feet apart, facing each other with their revolvers in hand. Gray tendrils of smoke still curled from the barrels of the weapons.

Larson squinted at Foster and asked suspiciously, "You hit?"

"Fuck, no! You?"

Larson looked down at himself and gently patted his shirtfront with his free hand. "Don't seem to be. I'm outta bullets."

"So'm I. You want to reload?"

Larson thought about it for a second and then shook his head. "Not unless you're gonna. I'd just as soon not fight no more, though."

"Yeah, same here." Foster slowly holstered his empty gun. "We callin' a truce?"

"Yeah, why the hell not? I wish I'd blown your damn guts out, but for some reason I just don't feel like killin' you no more."

Foster rubbed his bearded jaw. "Yeah, I reckon that's about how I feel, too. You want a drink?"

Larson waved a hand in front of his face. "Yeah, but not in here. It's too goddamn smoky."

Harry Sam Young rose up from his hiding place behind the bar with a shotgun clutched in his hands. "Both o' you damn lunatics get the hell outta here 'fore I dust your hides with buckshot just on general principles! What's wrong with you, shootin' up the place like that? What am I supposed to tell Billy Nuttall when he sees all the bullet holes?"

Now both of the gunfighters looked sheepish. They came over to the bar, and after some fumbling around in their pockets, they produced coins. "We're sorry, Harry," Larson said. "Maybe this'll help pay for the damages."

"Yeah, here you go," Foster added.

Harry Sam Young took one hand off the shotgun and swept the coins into the cash box. "All right, that's better. Now get out and don't come back in when you're dead set on killin' each other!"

The two men left, and they had about them now the unmistakable air of cronies. That would last until some other slight or insult, real or imagined, set them off again.

Men stood up from behind overturned tables and slunk out of corners. Richardson slowly got to his feet and leaned both hands on the bar to support himself as he took a couple of deep breaths. "I thought we were goners for sure," he said to Hickok. Then his eyes widened even more and he went on. "But you didn't even move, Bill! God Almighty, when those sons o' bitches started shootin', you just stood there with the bullets flyin' around your head and didn't even twitch! I never saw anything so brave!"

A faint smile touched Hickok's lips under the flowing mustache. "Bravery has little or nothing to do with it. No man can outrun fate, so it would be foolish to try." He chuckled. "Besides, I've seen those two shoot before. They have the worst aim you could ever imagine. I knew they weren't likely to hit anything, even by accident."

Harry Sam Young had put the scattergun away. He gestured toward the empty mug and asked, "You want another, Mr. Hickok?"

"No, I believe that'll do it for me. Believe I'll go back to the wagon and turn in." Hickok had taken to sleeping in a wagon that belonged to Charley Utter, since he had given his hotel room to White-Eye Jack Anderson and his paramour, Silky Jen. He nodded toward Leander Richardson and added, "Draw another for my young friend, though, on me."

"Really, Wild Bill?" Richardson said. "Thanks!"

Hickok lifted his left hand in a casual wave of farewell and walked out of the saloon. He waited until he was well out of sight before he paused on the dark street, took off his hat, ran his fingers through his long hair, and blew out a breath.

It was all well and good to prattle about how a man couldn't outrun fate, in order to impress a hero-worshipping youngster. And as a matter of fact, Hickok largely believed what he had told Leander Richardson. Otherwise he could have gone with California Joe on that horse-hunting expedition. It had pained him to refuse his old friend's request.

But he had always been a proud, stubborn man, and every instinct in his body told him that he had enemies here in Deadwood, enemies who wanted him dead.

If they wanted him, they knew where to find him. That was the way Bill Hickok had always lived his life. And he was too old to change now.

IT had been a bad few days for Al Swearengen. First, that bastard with the one white eyebrow had stolen one of his whores from him. Swearengen would have gotten her back, too, and the White-Eyed Kid would be dead now, if that goddamn Hickok hadn't butted in. The chunky, dark-faced owner of the Gem Theater sat at the desk in his office and sipped from a glass of whiskey—the good stuff, not the panther piss he sold to the Gem's customers.

Then, if losing Silky Jen and making an enemy of Hickok wasn't enough, he'd had to partner up with Laurette Parkhurst. God, he hated that woman! He'd hated her ever since she'd come to Deadwood and opened Miss Laurette's Academy for Young Ladies. Academy for fuckin' whores, that was more like it, because it sure as hell wasn't no real academy. It was a whorehouse, plain and simple, and no fancy name could change that.

Of course, the Gem wasn't really a theater, either, not the way Jack Langrishe's place down Main Street was. Swearengen hired performers to put on a show every now and then, but men came to the Gem for booze and cards and pussy, not to see some asshole play the fiddle or listen to some bastard recite Shakespeare. But Swearengen didn't think about that. He was too busy hating the White-Eyed Kid and Silky Jen and Wild Bill Hickok and that redheaded Parkhurst harpy and damned near everybody else he could call to mind. They were all out to get him. Their goal was to make his life miserable, and they were doing a damned good job of it.

He tossed back the rest of the whiskey. Not much longer, he told himself. He had made the deal with the Parkhurst woman because he wanted to get rid of Hickok before the famous gunman had a chance to pin on a marshal's badge and try to clean up Deadwood. Swearengen didn't want Deadwood cleaned up. He made his money from folks being dirty, and he wanted to keep it that way.

Parkhurst wanted Hickok dead, too, although she seemed equally interested in getting rid of Preacher Smith. The preacher was a damned nuisance, all right. Swearengen couldn't argue with that. Smith had a habit of setting a box down in the street in front of one of the saloons or whorehouses and standing on it to preach about how folks hadn't ought to fornicate and gamble and indulge in spiritous liquors. He was bad for business, just like Hickok. In his own way, he might be even worse than Wild Bill, because he preyed on people's guilty consciences.

Swearengen was glad he had been born without one of those pesky things. It would have made his life even more difficult than it had been.

So he'd made the deal with Laurette Parkhurst, and with the gambler Johnny Varnes, whose idea it had been in the first place to get rid of Hickok and Smith. He had gone over to the Academy and fucked one of her whores, that little China doll, in order to seal the arrangement. He had even gone with Parkhurst to the funeral of her son Fletch, who had been gunned down by the woman's pet shootist, that Bridges kid. Swearengen still wasn't exactly sure how that had happened. The woman didn't seem too upset about her son getting killed. Swearengen supposed that the life she'd led as a whore and a madam had sort of eroded any maternal instincts she'd once had.

So the deal was set. Bellamy Bridges was going to kill Wild Bill Hickok, or at least try to. When you went up against Hickok, you never knew what was going to happen. Swearengen had seen the kid slap leather, though. He was fast, and he had that natural ability to put the bullets where he wanted them. You couldn't teach that. A fella had to be born with it, and Bellamy Bridges had been. He'd just never discovered the talent until he came to Deadwood.

Of course, it might have been better to bushwhack Hickok from a dark alley some night, but Bridges wouldn't do that. He'd insist on making a fair fight of it. If he survived . . . if he killed Hickok . . . then somebody would have to have a talk with him about the preacher. He wouldn't be able to goad Smith into a gunfight. That would have to be a bushwhacking.

And then, once Hickok was dead and the preacher had joined him, Swearengen wouldn't need Laurette Parkhurst anymore. He would be free to double-cross her. He picked up the bottle on his desk and tipped more whiskey into the glass, knowing good and well that when the time came, *she* would be just as quick to try to double-cross *him*. He'd just have to see to it that she never got the opportunity.

Fuck you before you have the chance to fuck me. That was Al Swearengen's motto. He tossed back the second drink and yelled, "Johnny!"

Johnny Burnes poked his head in the door of the office. He was a tall, spare, bearded man, and his forehead still showed the fading bruise where Silky Jen had busted a chamber pot over his skull the first time she'd tried to escape from her captivity on the second floor of the Gem. Burnes was in charge of the whores, and spent most of his time up here making sure they carried out their job properly.

"What is it, Al?" he asked with just the right amount of deference and fear. He was a tough man, especially with the whores, but he respected his boss. Actually, Al Swearengen scared the shit out of him. Swearengen knew that and thought it was only proper.

"Who's not busy?" Swearengen asked.

Burnes frowned in thought. "Uh, lemme see . . . Lucy ain't got a customer right now, and neither has Tit Bit or Maizie or that big Scandahoovian gal, what's her name . . . Elsa, that's it. I ain't sure about the others, but I can go check—"

"Just send Lucy in here."

"You got it, Al," Burnes said, his head bobbing in a nod.

"Not yet I ain't," Swearengen snapped. "That's why I told you to go get her."

"Yes, sir!"

Burnes was back a few moments later with one of the whores, a skinny girl with red hair and freckles and a young but already decent body under her shift. She wasn't real pretty, but she would do.

"Here she is, Mr. Swearengen," Burnes said. He gave the girl a little push and then stepped back out into the hall, shutting the door behind him.

Swearengen sat behind the desk, turning back and forth a little in the swivel chair. Lucy stood just inside the door, staring self-consciously at the floor. She knotted her hands together in front of her.

"I don't rightly remember," Swearengen said. "Have I fucked you yet, Lucy?"

"No, sir," she answered without looking up. "Mr. Burnes, he done broke me in, and then Mr. Dority give me a poke, too, but 'cept for them, nobody's poked me but the customers."

Swearengen toyed with the empty glass on the desk. "When you say Johnny broke you in, you ain't meaning to say that you were a virgin before that, are you?"

She nodded and said, "Yes, sir, I was."

Swearengen slapped the desk, and the sharp crack made Lucy jump. "Well, son of a bitch!" he said. "You mean to tell me we had us an honest-to-God virgin in here and I didn't get first crack at you? I'll have to have a talk with Mr. Burnes about that."

She looked up at last, fear shining in her eyes. "Don't be mad at him, please, Mr. Swearengen. I don't reckon he knew until it was too late to do anything about it. I didn't tell him I'd never done it before."

"How old are you?"

"S-sixteen."

"How long you been working here?"

"A week."

"Now how the hell did a virgin wind up in Deadwood?" Swearengen sounded almost amused as he asked the question.

"My . . . my daddy brought me. He come to look for gold, and my mama's dead, and we didn't have no other relatives, so he had to bring me with him."

"Let me guess," Swearengen said. "He ran out of money, and he sold you for a grubstake so he could keep looking for gold."

"N-no, sir. He was diggin' a shaft in the side of the gulch and didn't do a good job of shorin' it up. The roof fell on him whilst he was diggin'. Killed him. When I seen he was dead, I knowed I'd have to earn a livin' some way, so I came here. Thought maybe I could work cleanin' up. But Mr. Burnes, he said I could make a whole lot more money fuckin' and . . . and he made me take my dress off . . ." Her chin trembled, and tears shone in her eyes. "And then he bent me over a bench and got behind me and . . . and . . ."

Swearengen lifted a hand. "That's enough," he said curtly. "You like what you're doing here, Lucy?"

"No, sir, not a whole hell of a lot. Reckon it could be worse, though."

Swearengen rubbed his beard-stubbled jaw. "Tell you what. You know that nigger woman who cooks down at the Grand Central Hotel? Name's Aunt Lou Marchbanks."

"I've heard tell of her, sir. I ain't never been in the Grand Central, though. It's a heap too fancy for somebody like me."

"I'm gonna write a note to Aunt Lou and send you down there with it. It ain't like I'm friends with the nigger or anything like that, but she knows who I am. I'm willing to bet that if I ask her to give you a job helping out in the kitchen down there, she'd do it."

Lucy's eyes widened. "You'd do that for me, Mr. Swearengen? You really would?"

"Sure," he said with a nod. "I been in the saloon business a long time, Lucy. I know when a gal's cut out to be a whore and when she ain't."

She came a couple of steps closer to the desk, hands clasped together in front of her. "Thank you, Mr. Swearengen," she said. "I . . . I didn't want to make no fuss, but I purely do think that I'd be happier helpin' out in the hotel kitchen."

"Well, then, that's what we'll do," Swearengen said. "I'll write that note to Aunt Lou." He turned his chair even more, so that he could stretch his legs out to the side of the desk. His hands dropped to his crotch and started unbuttoning his trousers. "Just as soon as you come around here and suck my cock for me."

Lucy frowned. "Mr. Swearengen . . . ?"

He lifted his hands. "What, you think I'm gonna do a favor for you without you doing something for me in return? Life don't work that way, little sis." He pointed at his groin. "Now come on. Get your skinny ass around here and start sucking."

A moment later, as she knelt between his thighs and leaned toward his erection, he said, "Wait a minute. You ever do this for anybody before?"

"N-no, sir. With Mr. Burnes and Mr. Dority and all my customers, it's just been straight fuckin'."

Swearengen nodded in satisfaction. "Well, then, it's sort of like you're still a virgin, at least like this, right?"

Then he leaned back in the chair and closed his eyes in pleasure as he felt her warm mouth on him. For somebody who'd never sucked a cock before, Lucy wasn't bad. It was sort of a shame he'd promised to send her to Aunt Lou Marchbanks. He wouldn't have minded keeping her around to do this for him every so often.

But a deal was a deal.

Until it wasn't anymore, he added to himself, thinking of Laurette Parkhurst.

Chapter Three

GRAY dawn light snuck into the room around the edges of the dirty shade pulled down over the single window. Bellamy Bridges squinted against it and rolled over in the narrow bunk so that the light wouldn't strike his eyes. Only he wasn't alone, and when he rolled over, somebody said, "Oof."

Bellamy's eyes flew open. He was lying half on top of a pretty Chinese girl. As he pushed himself back, he said, "Sorry, Ling. I reckon I forgot you were here." He was doing good to remember anything, even where he was, the way his head was pounding. He'd guzzled down too much whiskey the night before.

But it hadn't helped. He still remembered. . . .

The hallway is thick with shadows, and the light that spills out from Laurette's office is so starkly bright that it hurts his eyes. He'd heard her shouting angrily, almost screaming, and when he steps out into the hall to see what's wrong, at first all he's able to make out is the man standing there in the doorway pointing a gun at her.

Then, to his shock, he recognizes the man—Fletch

Parkhurst. His friend. But something is horribly wrong. It looks like Fletch is about to shoot Laurette, his own mother. Bellamy hears his voice echo from the walls of the narrow corridor as he cries, "Fletch!"

The tall, black-clad figure spinning toward him . . . the gun blossoming flame . . . the wind-rip of the bullet as it slices past his head and smacks into the wall behind him . . . Then instinct takes over and his fingers close around the walnut grips of the gun on his hip. The Colt seems to weigh little or nothing, the way it comes out of the holster so smoothly. Once, twice, three times it roars and bucks against his palm. He is barely aware of firing the gun because it's all instinct, you see. Someone shot at him, and he's returning the fire. That's all it is. He's not really killing his friend. That's impossible. Not Fletch. He wouldn't kill Fletch.

But it is Fletch who's driven back against the doorjamb by the impact of the bullets, Fletch who drops his gun so that it thuds hollowly on the floor, Fletch who looks down at the blood welling from the holes in his chest and staining his white shirt. Fletch who lifts his eyes to look at Bellamy staring at him open-mouthed, and then turns his head toward Laurette and says in the eerie silence following the shots, "Mother . . ."

Fletch who slides down the wall and dies like a dog, curled on the dirty floor of a whorehouse hallway, killed by someone he considered a friend.

In the dawn light, Bellamy began to cry, his shoulders shaking. He scooted as far away from Ling as he could without falling off the bunk, but she came after him, putting her arms around him, murmuring, "It's all right, Bellamy, it's all right."

He shook his head, knowing it would never be all right again. Not as long as the memories lurked in his brain, as vivid as if that horrible moment had just happened.

But that wasn't the worst of it. No, not hardly.

He doesn't go to the funeral. That would be too painful. And Laurette doesn't ask him to go. She attends with Al Swearengen instead. The two of them are partners of a sort now, and Bellamy knows why. They want Wild Bill Hickok dead. They want him to kill Hickok.

Well, why not? Somebody who'll gun down his best friend will do just about anything, won't he? There's nothing too low for a snake like that.

So when she gets back to the Academy, he tells her as much. Tells her, bold as brass, that Hickok will be dead within the week. For a moment it seems like she's going to think better of the idea and try to talk him out of it, but in the end she doesn't. All that really matters is that Hickok dies.

It doesn't really surprise him all that much when Laurette summons him to her room that night, late, after all the customers have stumbled back to their rented rooms or their mining claims. She wears a green gown, thin and gauzy enough so that he can see her body through it. Her breasts have begun to sag, but she's still an attractive woman. She gives him a drink, stands close to him, raises a hand to brush her fingertips over his cheek.

"Why are you doing this?" he asks. "You don't have to." They both know already that he's going to do what she wants. She doesn't have to let him fuck her first.

"Because I want to," she says, and she comes up on her toes to kiss him.

Naturally, she has the best bed in the place, and she doesn't even use it for business. They wind up in it, their clothes gone, and she's as eager as a young girl, her hands and mouth touching him all over, exploring, clutching, imploring him to move over her and take her, and he can't get it out of his head that she's making love to the man who killed her son. But he can't stop, either, he's weak, just a slave to his lust, and when he enters her and she cries out, "Oh, yes, son, yes!" he can't stop, all he can do is keep fucking hard into her, but far in the back of his brain a tiny part of him prays fervently that she won't call him Fletch, please don't her call him Fletch, and even though he knows he has no right to pray, fornicator and murderer that he is, still the tiny voice pleads, Don't call me Fletch, don't call me Fletch. . . .

Thinking only to comfort him, knowing that it had worked

in the past, Ling reached down to his crotch. With an anguished cry, he pulled sharply away from her and tumbled from the bunk, landing sprawled on the floor of his room. Only a few hours had passed since he had stumbled back here from Laurette's bed. He remembered now that Ling hadn't been there when exhaustion had claimed him and he had fallen asleep. She must have crawled into his bunk later.

She leaned out and extended a hand toward him. "Bellamy . . ."

He rolled over and slid backward on the floor. "Stay away!" he cried. "Don't touch me! I . . . I'm too dirty!"

"Bellamy—"

"Get out of here, Ling! Get out!"

His gaze fell on the holstered Colt and the shell belt coiled and placed on a chair near the bunk. It was within reach, and before he could think about what he was doing, his hand shot out and closed over the butt of the gun. He jerked it free from the holster, not quite sure what he was going to do with it. For a second he thought about jamming the muzzle against his temple and pulling the trigger. Then he thought it might be better to kill Ling instead and save her from the life she was leading. He could kill all the girls, he thought. He could go from room to room and give each of them the gift of a bullet. But he would save the last one for Laurette, who needed that gift the most of them all. Well, except maybe for him. The very last bullet would be for him.

"Bellamy, put the gun down," Ling whispered.

Something about what she had just said finally penetrated his brain. He had never heard her speak in anything except Chinese and broken English. "You want fuckee Ling?" she always asked her customers. But now she sounded much more articulate, as if she had no trouble at all speaking English.

"What did you just say?" he asked as he stared at her. The gun was still clutched in his fist.

"Please, Bellamy, put the gun down. You don't want to shoot anybody."

"You're wrong about that. I'm going to shoot Wild Bill Hickok." He laughed. "The Prince of Pistoleers."

Suddenly, the very idea that he could face a man like Hickok and survive was hilarious to him. Wild Bill would kill him. But that was all right, because he deserved to die, and at least he could go out somewhat honorably, facing his foe. Facing a better man.

Ling was aghast. "Bellamy, what are you talking about?"

"What are *you* talking about?" he said as he finally lowered the gun and let it point toward the floor. "How come you can talk English all of a sudden, when before you couldn't?"

She sighed, seeming to relax a little since it appeared that Bellamy wasn't going to either commit suicide or embark on some sort of killing spree.

"I can speak English pretty good most of the time," she admitted. "I knew some before I came here. My father worked on the Central Pacific Railroad, and my mother did laundry in the construction camps. I was around men who spoke English, so I learned some just by hearing it." A bitter edge crept into her voice. "It was in the railroad camps where I first became a whore."

"I . . . I'm sorry."

She shook her head. "Nothing to be sorry about. One China girl more or less makes no difference. Then when I came here, Fletch became my friend. He taught me more of how to speak your tongue."

"When he wasn't fucking you, you mean."

Solemnly, she said, "Fletch never did that. He never laid a hand on me that way."

"Well, wasn't he a fine gentleman?" Bellamy said with a sneer of contempt.

"Yes. Yes, he was," Ling replied quietly.

Bellamy could only look at her. His head still hurt like blazes, and he was starting to feel sick to his stomach, too. Thinking about what he had done the night before with Laurette didn't help matters. He'd been raised in a God-fearing home. How had he sunk so low in this morass of violence and perversion in such a short time? A month earlier, he had still been on his way to Deadwood in a wagon train with a bunch of other would-be prospectors, gold-seekers who were heading to the Black Hills to find their fortune. How had that gone so wrong?

He should have listened to Dan Ryan, he realized. He should have continued working the claim instead of allowing his lust for Carla Wilkes to take him over and drag him down. Every time he had been confronted with a decision, a fork in the road, he had taken the wrong turn. Every damned time.

Now it was too late to turn back. He couldn't retrace his steps, couldn't reclaim what he had once been, such a short time in the past. Now he was a gunman, a drunk, a killer. An animal who hadn't grieved over Carla's death more than a day or two before he was fucking first Ling and then Laurette. He hefted the gun in his hand, thinking once again that he might be better off—the whole Goddamn *world* might be better off—if he wasn't around anymore.

But not yet. There were things he still had to do, promises he had made that he intended to keep. Even if he was doomed and damned as it seemed, he could still keep his word, by God!

And he laughed again as he thought how inappropriate it was for him to swear by God, even to himself. Surely, God turned His eyes away from a sinner like Bellamy Bridges.

"Bellamy," Ling said, "what was that you said about . . . about shooting Mr. Hickok . . . ?"

"What? I didn't say anything about Wild Bill."

"But you did," Ling insisted. "I heard you."

He shook his head stubbornly. "You must have imagined it. That's crazy talk. How could I shoot Wild Bill Hickok? He's a lot faster with a gun than me."

But was he, really? Bellamy asked himself. Or was Hickok just getting by on his reputation, when in reality his gun-handling skills had deteriorated to the point where Bellamy could beat him to the draw and ventilate him? He was still determined to go through with it, but Ling didn't have to know that. She was liable to pester him constantly about it unless he could deflect her worry.

"I thought—" she began.

"One of us is crazy," he said. "Either you for hearing what I didn't say or me for saying what I didn't mean. But you've got to know I ain't such a damned fool as to go up against Wild Bill Hickok!"

She didn't say anything for a moment, but then she nodded. "Of course. I . . . I must have been confused."

"Damn right you were."

"You want . . . fuckee Ling . . . for old times' sake?"

Old times . . . God, he hadn't even been in Deadwood for a month, and yet in some ways it seemed as if he had been here forever. Ling was right. In a place like this, even the passage of a few days could constitute old times. That was because life was different in Deadwood. Folks here lived it at a different pace, with higher highs and lower lows and an intensity to everything that was just downright exhausting. A man could pack a lifetime's worth of adventure into a few weeks in Deadwood.

But that still didn't mean he wanted to fuck Ling. Everything was crowding in on him—Carla's death, followed by the gunfight with Fletch, and then the sordid night with Laurette. . . .

"Later," Bellamy said. "I . . . I don't feel too good right now."

As if to prove it, his stomach lurched, and he got quickly to his feet and hurried out of the room, hoping he could make it to the privy in time, or at least to the back door so he could get outside before all that whiskey in his belly came up.

He left the gun lying on the floor in his room. Ling stared at it for a long moment after he was gone, and then she stood up and walked over to it and picked it up. She had handled guns before, but she didn't like them. Just touching one made a shiver go through her.

She knew Bellamy had been lying about Mr. Hickok. She knew that Miss Laurette and that man Swearengen wanted Bellamy to kill Wild Bill. She had heard them plotting together. That was why she had gone to Fletch and asked him to stop it somehow. *She* was to blame for Fletch being dead now.

She couldn't allow Bellamy to die, too. She had to *do* something. . . .

But what?

DAN Ryan squatted at the edge of Deadwood Creek and sloshed a mixture of sand, gravel, and water back and forth in the iron pan he held in his hands. He tipped the pan so that a little of the water slopped over the side, taking some of the sand with it. The fine gravel, being heavier, had sunk to the bottom, so it was just a matter of washing away all the sand. Once that was done, Dan would poke through the gravel that was left, watchful for the telltale sparkle that would reveal the presence of gold flecks. Sometimes there would be only one or two bits of gold dust to be found in the pan, and sometimes there was nothing at all but worthless gravel. Panning for gold was a long, tedious, back-breaking process.

But the rewards, when they came, could be good. From time to time, the prospectors who panned for gold in Deadwood Creek found an actual nugget that was worth some real money.

It was better in the long run, though, to sink a shaft in the hillside and search for a vein of gold that way. Anyone lucky enough to find one usually became a rich man in a hurry, because most of the time those veins ran for a good distance before petering out.

Dan knew that digging for gold was more efficient than panning for it. He had dug several shafts on his claim, officially designated as Number Eight Above Discovery. He didn't have another name for the claim. He wasn't sentimental about it, so he didn't call it the Lucky Lady or the Bonanza or anything like that. It was just a piece of ground, three hundred yards from one end to the other, stretching to the rimrock on both sides of the creek. He hoped to find his fortune here, but that was all.

He thought of himself as a man who wasn't sentimental about much of anything. His years in the Army had seen to that, years of hardship and Indian fighting. He had been a sergeant, and a good one, at that. But the day had finally come when he decided it was time to do something for himself, and so he had resigned and headed here to the Black Hills to look for gold, along with hundreds, maybe even thousands, of other men who were equally ambitious.

Dan had spent most of his life outdoors, so sometimes it got to be too much for him, crouching in a dark tunnel and swinging a pickax by the dim light of a single candle. When that happened, he went out and panned for gold in the creek, more interested in the fresh air and sunlight than he was in any color he might find. Of course, it was nice to get a bit of dust out of the pan, too.

Despite the fact that it was summer—August 1st, 1876, he thought, although it was a little difficult to keep up with the date out here—the creek water had a chill to it. That was because the stream was fed not only by underground springs but also by snowmelt from the peaks to the west. A man could freeze his balls off if he hunkered in the creek all day. Dan didn't intend to do that. After a while, he told himself, he would take up his pickax again and get back to the digging.

It would have been easier if he'd had somebody to help him . . . if Bellamy had still been here.

That thought brought a frown to Dan's rugged, deeply tanned face. He hadn't known Bellamy before they started up here to the Black Hills as members of the same wagon train. They had become friends along the way, especially during an attack by the Sioux that had found both of them under the same wagon, fighting side by side. Something like that created a bond between men, as Dan knew well from his time in the military.

Such a bond wasn't unbreakable, though. Bellamy had proven that by turning his back on the claim he and Dan had worked together at first. He had gone to Deadwood to live in a whorehouse and wear a fancy buckskin jacket with fringe on it and strut around like he was something to behold just because it so happened he could draw and fire a gun faster and more accurately than most men. Well, the hell with him, Dan thought with an angry snort. The hell with him and the mules that had pulled the wagon that he'd ridden into Deadwood on.

Kid'd had a run of bad luck, though, Dan told himself as he sloshed the last of the water out of the pan and started poking a blunt finger into the wet gravel. Sure, that Carla girl had been a whore, but Bellamy had fallen for her anyway, fallen hard. He had convinced himself that he loved her, so no matter what she was, it had to hurt him when she was killed. Dan had been there for the funeral, but he'd kept his distance, watching from a hillside rather than going down to join the other mourners. He knew that Bellamy blamed him for the shoot-out that had accidentally taken Carla's life, and he didn't want to make things any worse for the boy. Since then, Dan had continued to avoid running into Bellamy, but he did his best to keep up with how things were going for him. Bellamy had been involved in a couple of gunfights and killed two men, one of them Fletch Parkhurst. That had shocked the hell out of Dan when he heard about it. He'd thought that Bellamy and Fletch were friends. Reckon not, considering what had happened.

Bellamy was still at the whorehouse, still under the thumb of that Parkhurst woman. Dan wished he could sit down and jaw with the kid for a while, maybe talk some sense into his head. The anger he had felt toward Bellamy a moment earlier was gone now, vanished in the genuine concern Dan felt for the young man. Bellamy probably couldn't see that he would be better off away from that place. Dan was no hypocrite; he had been to his share of whorehouses and gone off on his share of benders. Nor was he a psalm-singer like Preacher Smith. He just knew that some people weren't cut out for the sort of life Bellamy was leading—and Bellamy was one of them.

Something sparkled in the pan and made him catch his breath. He leaned his head closer to look at it. Where the hell had it gone? He stirred his finger through the gravel. "Damn it!" he said aloud. The color had been there, and then it wasn't.

Suddenly he caught sight of it again and had to laugh when he saw where it was. The tiny fleck of gold, wet from being washed in the creek water, had stuck to his fingertip. He'd been looking for the color in the pan, and he already had it. Fact of the matter was, there was another one, and another. . . .

Five minutes later, he had six of the little flecks picked out of the pan. He stowed them in the jar that he carried under his shirt as he felt excitement galloping through him. Six bits of color from one pan was pretty damned good. When he had made sure there weren't any more, he cast the gravel aside and dipped up another panful of water and sand and more gravel and started swishing it around. He might have hit something good here.

And if he had . . . if he found a good deal of color to add to his poke . . . he determined then and there that he was going to Deadwood to celebrate. He wasn't going to try to avoid Bellamy, either. In fact, he would take it as an omen if he were to run into the youngster. Whether Bellamy agreed or not, Dan was going to sit him down and reason with him. He had to make the kid see the light.

If Bellamy stayed in Deadwood, sooner or later he was going to do something that would get him killed . . . or worse.

Chapter Four

JOHNNY Varnes laid down a hand of solitaire on the table in front of him. Cards were his livelihood. More than that, they were his friends . . . sometimes he thought they were his *only* friends. So he could never stay away from them for long. Something inside him compelled him to seek out a game, and when there was no game to be had, such as now, he played solitaire. Anything to have a reason to take out the cards, shuffle them, feel them moving so smoothly and surely in his fingers.

There were games going on in the Gem at the moment, of course. It was rare that at least one of the poker tables wasn't occupied. But those were small games, penny-ante, not the sort in which a man like Johnny Varnes wished to participate. He was a professional, and top-notch at his business. He played for bigger stakes, or he didn't play at all.

At the moment, he reflected, he was playing for rather large stakes. Life and death, in fact. He was the mastermind behind the plan to kill Wild Bill Hickok.

He was sure Al Swearengen and the Parkhurst woman thought *they* were the prime movers in the plot, but Varnes knew better. He was the one who had first approached both of them with the idea that those who earned their livings in Deadwood's Badlands ought to band together to eliminate the most deadly threat to them—law and order. Nowhere in Deadwood was there a more potent symbol of law and order than Wild Bill Hickok, the fighting marshal who had cleaned up Hays City and Abilene. True, since arriving in Deadwood Hickok had shown no inclination to pin on a lawman's star, but it could happen. It *would* happen, if the town's more respectable element had its way. They would offer the job to Hickok sooner or later.

So Varnes had come up with the idea of getting rid of Hickok before that could happen. No one else in town posed as formidable a threat as Hickok.

Varnes was a tall, lean man with a gaunt face, a narrow mustache, and a pointed goatee. He knew very well that he looked like the popular image of Satan and didn't mind at all. He even cultivated a deep, sinister chuckle to add to the impression. Vanity, of course, was a largely useless quality. He liked it anyway, liked the way he sometimes caught Preacher Smith looking at him, as if the man recognized the presence of his greatest enemy.

Smith was another one who needed to be gotten rid of. All in good time, Varnes told himself, all in good time.

A footstep beside him made Varnes tense. He had enemies of his own—no man could play poker for a living without making enemies—and there was no way of knowing when one of them might try to settle a score with him. He turned his right arm slightly, bringing it into position so that a twitch of his wrist would send the spring-loaded derringer sliding out from the sleeve of his coat.

The man who had come up to the table wasn't a threat, however. He wore a ragged coat and trousers and nervously twisted a battered, shapeless Keevil hat in his hands. His curly hair was tangled, and several days' worth of beard stubble sprouted on his jaw. He shuffled his feet and said, "Mornin', Mr. Varnes."

"Jack," Varnes said noncommittally. "What can I do for you?"

The man sniffed and wiped the back of a hand across his nose. "I figured maybe there was somethin' I could do for you. Some odd job, maybe. Whatever you want done."

Jack was a pathetic specimen. Varnes didn't know his history or even his last name, but assumed that the man had come to the Black Hills to look for gold, like nearly everyone else in this part of the country. And again like most, he had failed in that quest. He probably didn't have enough money to go back home, wherever that was, so he had become a hanger-on, drifting from saloon to saloon, cadging drinks and food, working at odd jobs when he had to. Varnes had seen him playing poker a few times in various saloons, on those rare occasions when Jack had enough money to take part in a game. In fact, he had seen him the day before in the No. 10, playing cards with Wild Bill Hickok, of all people. Jack was no match for Hickok, who had cleaned him out quickly and then given him back a coin so he wouldn't have to leave the table broke. Varnes supposed it was easy to make a condescending gesture like that when one was the famous Wild Bill Hickok.

Slowly, the gambler shook his head. "No, Jack, I'm sorry, I can't think of a thing I need done today. Unless . . ."

He stopped himself. He had been about to say, *Unless you want to go shoot Wild Bill Hickok for me.* He and Swearengen and Laurette Parkhurst already had Bellamy Bridges for that job.

"Unless what, Mr. Varnes?" Jack asked eagerly.

Varnes waved a slender-fingered hand. "Nothing," he said. "I can't help you, Jack."

"Oh." Jack blinked rheumy eyes and said again, "Oh. Well, all right, Mr. Varnes. But if you think of anything later, I'm your man."

"I'll keep you in mind," Varnes said dryly, knowing full well that he would forget Jack as soon as the man shuffled away to go bother someone else.

And that was exactly what happened.

As a rule, Laurette Parkhurst slept until well after noon every day. She never got to bed until after midnight, and sometimes it was nearly dawn before she turned in. That was a whore's life, and she knew it well. She ought to, she had lived it long enough.

Of course, she wasn't really a whore anymore. She couldn't remember the last time a man had paid to fuck her. She was a madam now. The whores worked for her. In her day, though, she had been a soiled dove, and a good one, too. Always made plenty of money for whatever house she worked in. It wasn't much to be proud of, but hell, you took pride wherever you could find it.

Today she had been awakened early by somebody slamming out the back door of the place. She didn't know who it was—maybe one of the girls on her way to the outhouse. She thought she heard retching. Damn, that meant one of them was probably pregnant. That was an occupational hazard, she supposed.

For some reason, she hadn't been able to get back to sleep after that, so she got up, wrapped a silk robe around her, and went from her bedroom to the office. Might as well use this time to go over the books, she told herself. In any business, it was important to keep up with the numbers. Way back when she was just a girl, one of her steady customers at a house in St. Louis had taught her how to cipher, and it was a skill that had come in mighty handy over the years.

When she sat down behind the desk, she winced a little from the discomfort she felt. It had been a long time since she'd been with a man, and Bellamy had worked her over pretty good the night before. She was liable to be sore for a while.

Bellamy, she thought. What in the hell had gotten into her? Why had she taken Bellamy to her bed? She hadn't needed to in order to get him to cooperate with her plans. He would have done that anyway.

Maybe she had needed comforting. After all, she had lost her son, hadn't she?

Laurette laughed softly. No, that wasn't it. She hadn't really mourned Fletch's death. He had gotten what he deserved for being weak.

Maybe she'd just had an itch that needed to be scratched.

Hell, it wasn't good to think too much about such things. She put it out of her mind and concentrated on the ledger that she opened in front of her. Business was good, but it could be better. It *would* be better, once Hickok and that damned preacher were both dead . . . and so was Al Swearengen.

That would be a job for Bellamy, too. Sometime when Swearengen wasn't expecting it, and as soon as possible after Hickok and Smith were out of the way. She would have to figure out a way for Bellamy to get rid of the body so that it would never be found. When Swearengen disappeared, suspicion would fall on her, of course, but nobody would be able to prove anything. Dan Dority and Johnny Burnes, who worked for Swearengen, might give a little trouble, but they would come around quickly enough once Laurette made it clear to them what their options really were.

Go along, or die. Simple as that.

Once she controlled the Gem, she could turn her attention to Billy Nuttall and Carl Mann. They owned the Bella Union and the No. 10. If she could somehow get her hands on those places, too, then she would be far and away the most important person in the Badlands. The future was unlimited.

Damn, this was a great country!

A noise in the hall made her glance up from the ledger. The office door was partially open. She saw Ling walking by, dressed to go out in a plain gray skirt and blue shirt. In those clothes, and without her face painted up, she looked younger than she really was and almost innocent, which Laurette happened to know she wasn't, by a long shot.

"Where are you goin', Ling?" she asked sharply.

Ling stopped short, and Laurette was convinced that the expression that went quickly across the girl's face was a guilty one. Ling was up to something.

"Go walk around for while, Missy Laurette," she said as she plucked nervously at the waistband of her skirt.

"Why do you want to go out? Goin' over to Chinktown to see some of your relatives?" Laurette happened to know that Ling didn't have any relatives in Deadwood. If the girl claimed otherwise now, she was lying.

"No, Ling just want . . ." She made a sweeping gesture,

as if she was indicating the whole sky above her. "Fresh air."

Laurette stood up and walked out from behind the desk. As she came up to Ling, she smiled and said, "Don't lie to me, girl."

Ling shook her head. "Oh, no, missy, Ling not lie—"

Laurette caught hold of Ling's right wrist with her left hand and used her right hand to grasp Ling's chin. She pushed Ling's head back, her fingers tightening cruelly. "I said don't lie to me," she hissed. "You reckon I don't know when a whore's lyin'? Hell, tellin' somebody what they want to hear is as much your stock in trade as your pussy. I ain't interested in that, but I do want the truth!"

"B-Bellamy," Ling said.

Laurette frowned. "What about him?"

"Ling look for . . . Bellamy."

The older woman's frown deepened. "Where's he gone?"

"Not know . . . Bellamy angry . . . sad . . . look for trouble."

Maybe he had gone to have that showdown with Hickok, Laurette thought. She caught herself listening for the sound of gunshots in the distance, but she didn't hear any.

"And you wanted to go save him from himself, is that it?" She let go of Ling's chin, but not before giving her a little shove that sent the girl stumbling back a step. Laurette laughed. "Lord have mercy, is there anything dumber in this world than a whore? You've gone sweet on him, haven't you?"

Ling started to shake her head.

"The hell you haven't," Laurette said, not believing the girl's denial for a second. "I sent you to fuck him to make him feel better. I never said you needed to go and fall in love with him!"

"Not in love," Ling muttered stubbornly. She reached up to rub the flesh around and just below her chin, where Laurette's fingers had dug in painfully.

"Then get on back to your room," Laurette ordered. "Bellamy can take care of himself. He don't need you wet-nursin' him."

"Missy—"

"I said go!"

Sullenly, Ling turned and started back along the hall toward her room. She looked over her shoulder at Laurette as she went, and the expression on her face was one of anger, maybe even hatred.

She would have to keep an eye on that one, Laurette warned herself. You couldn't trust a Chink. They were all lying, thieving varmints, and they'd as soon stab you or take one of those meat cleavers after you as look at you.

Well, if Ling gave her too much trouble, she'd just kick the bitch out. Nothing said Ling had to keep working at the Academy.

Laurette's thoughts turned to Bellamy. She wondered where he had gone and what he planned to do. It sure would have made things simpler if he had been willing to take a shotgun and cut Hickok down from the mouth of a dark alley some night. That wasn't Bellamy's way, though. Sure, he had changed a lot since he'd first come here and fallen under Carla's spell, but there was only so far that somebody could fall. Then something in their nature stopped them, and it took a while before they could talk themselves into descending further. Bellamy was still at the stage where he had a little honor left. He wouldn't dry-gulch somebody.

With any luck, he'd be over that by the time she needed him to dispose of Al Swearengen.

In the meantime, Laurette went to her room and began to dress. Maybe she would take a walk around town herself and see if she could find Bellamy. He should have told her what he was up to before he left. After all, he still worked for her, didn't he?

She had to admit that she didn't know that for sure. You couldn't ever tell what a kid would do. He might take it into his head to up and quit on her. Who knows what was going on in his brain, especially after what had happened the night before?

He had better not quit, she thought as she began to paint her face. Nobody ran out on her. She was always the one who did the leaving, just as she had when Fletch was a baby. She couldn't wait to get away from the mewling little bastard and the big bastard who was his father. Life had been calling to her, and she sure as hell couldn't answer while she was tied down. So she had taken off as soon as she got the chance, but she was damned if she would let anybody run out on her.

Just let Bellamy try that. Then he would find out what it was like to have a real enemy.

Chapter Five

DAN hadn't been to Deadwood since the day of Carla Wilkes's funeral. That had been less than a week, so a fella wouldn't think that much could have changed in that time. Deadwood was such a volatile place, though, that wasn't always the case. New businesses were always going in, and as Dan walked along Main Street the sounds of hammering and sawing filled the air. The raw pine skeletons of buildings rose here and there on both sides of the street, filling in the empty spaces where previously tents had stood.

Some tents were still in evidence, such as the big one at the southwest corner of Main and Wall Streets. A hastily painted sign had been driven into the ground in front of the tent. It read STAR & BULLOCK HARDWARE AND GEN'L MERCHANDISE. The flaps were tied back so that Dan could look inside and see shelves crudely constructed from crates and planks. A few miners milled around, looking at the goods offered for sale, which consisted of frying pans, ropes, picks and shovels, axes, and numerous other items prospectors might need while they were looking for gold.

A slightly built man with thinning sandy hair, rolled-up

sleeves, and a bow tie stepped out of the tent while Dan was standing there and said, "Good day to you, sir. Step inside and have a look around. We're just getting set up, but we'll be glad to help you in any way we can." He held out a hand. "I'm Solomon Star."

He had a faint accent that told Dan he was a foreigner, but that didn't bother him. He had served in the Army with men from nations all over the world who had found themselves in the United States. As far as Dan was concerned, where a fella came from mattered a whole lot less than where he was going.

"Dan Ryan," he said, introducing himself as he shook hands with the merchant. "Don't reckon I need to do any shoppin' right at the moment, but I'll keep you in mind—"

"If you're not in a hurry, hang around for a few minutes," Star broke in. "What's about to happen ought to be pretty entertaining."

That got Dan's interest. Entertainment was always scarce on the frontier. Hardship and danger could be had in plenty, but they were just about the only common commodities.

A man came around the corner of Wall Street leading a team of mules hitched to a wagon. The back of the vehicle was piled high with crates. The man brought the mules to a halt and climbed into the wagon bed. He was tall and slender except for broad, muscular shoulders, and had dark hair and a thick mustache that drooped over his mouth. His eyebrows were bushy and grew so close together in the center, they almost looked like one continuous eyebrow. He was dressed in a black suit and a white shirt and had a broad-brimmed black hat cocked back on his head. A holstered revolver was on his right hip. He was sweating in the August heat as he raised his arms and called loudly, "Friends, gather round! I've got the best deal here for you that you'll find in the whole Dakota Territory!"

Solomon Star nudged Dan with an elbow. "My partner," he said proudly. "Seth Bullock."

"Reminds me a mite of the preacher they've got hereabouts," Dan said. "What's he selling, snake oil?"

Star grinned. "No potions or purgatives for us, my friend.

What Seth is selling is just what you need *after* you've in-
dulged in one of those concoctions."

As miners came out of the tent and others paused as they
passed by on the street, Seth Bullock reached down and took
the lid off one of the crates. It had already been pried loose
and was just sitting there. He thrust his hand into the crate,
brought out a wad of wood shavings that had been stuffed in
as packing material, and set it aside. Then he reached in
again and lifted into view an object that shone brightly in the
sun. One of the men in the gathering crowd guffawed.

"Yes, sir, you've guessed right," Bullock called to him.
"This is a chamber pot, sure enough. And the very *best* chamber pot you'll find between St. Louis and San Francisco."

"I didn't know I was lookin' for one!" said one of the
prospectors. That brought more laughter.

Bullock smiled, but his eyes looked more like he wanted
to pull the gun on his hip and pistol-whip the heckler. "Yes,
it's funny," he said, "but it wouldn't be so humorous if you
needed one of these items and didn't have one, now would
it? What you would do then, sir?"

The bearded miner sniffed and thought about it, then said,
"Oh, I dunno. Shit in the woods?"

More guffaws came from the crowd. Solomon Star muttered to Dan, "This isn't going as well as I'd hoped. We got
stuck with a whole shipment of the damned things, and Seth
swore he could get rid of them."

Bullock's smile wavered slightly, but then he said, "Sure,
you could do that. So can a bear! What is it, exactly, that distinguishes man from the lower animals? Some people say
it's our intelligence." He tapped the side of his forehead.
"Other, more practical thinkers say that it's our thumbs
which set us apart!" He set the chamber pot down, held up
both thumbs, and wiggled them. "But I say it's something
even more fundamental than that, boys! I say the thing that
distinguishes mankind—which was created in God's own
image, I remind you—from the lower animals is that we
don't shit and piss right out in the open like they do!"

As if on cue, one of the mules in the team raised its tail
and began depositing a large, steaming pile of dung in the

street. Dan had to grin. Howls of laughter came from the on-lookers.

Bullock didn't mind the laughter now. He must have sensed that he had his listeners right where he wanted them, because he smiled and snatched up the chamber pot he had set aside. Brandishing it, he said, "A mule's got no use for one of these, now does he, boys? Of course not! He's just a dumb animal!" Bullock thrust the chamber pot at the heck-ler. "How about you, friend? Do you need one . . . or are you just a dumb animal, too?"

The prospector frowned and grumbled and rubbed his bearded jaw, and finally he said grudgingly, "Well, I reckon it wouldn't hurt anything to have one o' them thunder mugs. A fella never knows when he might have visitors."

"That's right," Bullock agreed. "And we're all civilized folks here, aren't we? We don't want to offend anybody."

Another man called out, "How much you sellin' them for, mister?"

"Two dollars American, in cash, coin, or gold!"

"Two dollars is kinda steep, ain't it?"

"Not for a product of this quality that'll last you for years. Why, you could probably pass it down to your children or grandchildren if you wanted to."

"That'd be one hell of a thing to inherit, now wouldn't it!"

Bullock waited for the laughter to die down again and then said, "Tell you what, since my partner, Mr. Sol Star, and I just got into Deadwood yesterday, we'll offer a special deal on these items. One dollar each, but that price is good today only and until supplies run out! When we have to have more of them freighted in later, don't expect the price to be so in-expensive."

Dan leaned closer to Sol Star and asked quietly, "What'd they cost you, two bits each?"

"A good businessman never reveals his secrets," Star replied with a smile.

"All right, for a buck I reckon it might be worth it," one of the miners called out. "Gimme one o' the damned things."

Bullock leaned down from the wagon and handed over

the chamber pot he held in return for the coin the man offered him. "There you are, sir," he said as he straightened. "Now, who's next?"

The rest of the miners crowded around the wagon as Dan exchanged a grin with Sol Star, shook his head in admiration of Bullock's salesmanship, and started to stroll on down the street.

He stopped when he heard his name called in a woman's voice. Looking around, he didn't spot whoever it was until she called him again. Then he saw Lucretia Marchbanks standing on the other side of the street, a basket of laundry tucked under her arm.

The sight made Dan's mind go back to several weeks earlier, the first time he had ever set eyes on the woman most folks in Deadwood called Aunt Lou. She wasn't old enough to be an aunt to most of them, but that was how people referred to unmarried, adult black women. That other time, she had been on her way back to the Grand Central Hotel with some washing she had picked up from one of the laundries in Deadwood's Chinese district, when a couple of drunks had bumped into her, knocked the clean sheets into the mud, and then been disrespectful to her. Dan had witnessed the incident and stepped in to set the drunks straight. That had led to a brawl, of course, from which Dan was confident he would have emerged victorious if it hadn't been broken up. He'd also had to take a tongue-lashing from the woman, who was proud enough that she didn't want anybody fighting her battles for her. That had been his introduction to Lou Marchbanks.

He had seen her quite a few times since, had even danced with her on one occasion, although not in public. She had visited his camp. But whatever feelings might have grown up between them, had they been given a chance, had been squelched. It was Lou's decision. The fact that he was white and she had been born a slave was more than she wanted to wrestle with. He supposed he couldn't blame her for that.

But he could still be her friend, if nothing more than that, so he smiled, raised a hand in greeting, and started across the street toward her. That was a tricky undertaking, since

Deadwood's Main Street was the repository for a great deal of waste from those lower animals Seth Bullock had been talking about. And contrary to Bullock's comments, many of Deadwood's human inhabitants had been known to take a piss or a shit in the street, too, especially after the sun went down.

So Dan crossed the road carefully, stepping around the worst of the puddles and piles, until he came up to Lou and tugged on the brim of his hat. "Miss Marchbanks," he said. "It's mighty nice to see you again."

"And it's nice to see you, too, Sergeant," she said. She was a little below medium height but seemed taller, probably because she stood so straight and dignified. The brown skin of her face was smooth and unlined, and her black hair was pulled back into a severe bun. Dan found himself wishing, not for the first time, that he could see what she looked like with her hair loose. She went on. "I haven't seen you in Deadwood lately."

"Oh, I've just been workin' my claim." He reached out for the wicker basket. "Let me carry that down to the hotel for you."

"That's not necessary." She turned a little so that he couldn't take the basket from her. "I can handle it just fine. If you want to walk with me, though, that would be all right."

"You're sure? About me not carrying the basket, I mean?"

"Of course." She smiled. "Come on."

He fell in step beside her. He had been planning to stroll past Miss Laurette's Academy for Young Ladies, in hopes of maybe running into Bellamy, but he supposed that could wait. Anyway, it was possible that Lou had seen the youngster recently and could tell him how Bellamy was doing these days. Nearly everybody in town passed through the dining room of the Grand Central Hotel sooner or later.

"So, how have you been?" he asked.

"Middlin'. The hotel's been busier than ever, and it's sure gettin' to be a hot ol' summertime up here. I didn't think it got so hot this far north. It ain't like we're in Mississippi or Louisiana."

Dan chuckled. "No, ma'am, but it still gets hot. I recollect when I was on that scout through these parts with General Custer a couple of years ago. It was so hot that year the boys jumped in every creek we came to, even when they got in trouble for doing it."

"Burnin' hot in the summer, freezin' cold in the winter . . . country full of wild animals and bloodthirsty savages . . . why would anybody want to live up here, anyway?"

"I reckon we both know the answer to that. Gold."

She nodded and said, "Yes, sir, that makes men forget just about ever'thing else, don't it?"

"It does," Dan agreed. "I guess I'm as guilty as any of the rest of them, too. I'm here, aren't I?"

She didn't say anything for a moment, and then quietly she replied, "You ain't like the rest of 'em, Dan. It wasn't just the lure o' gold that brought you here."

"It wasn't?" He was genuinely surprised. "Because I sure as shootin' thought that's what it was."

Lou shook her head. "Nope. The gold's just part of it with you. You tramped around all them years with the Army until the day finally came when you decided you needed to stop somewhere and put down some roots. Someplace where you could help build somethin' that might last."

He looked around. "In *Deadwood*?" He laughed. "This is just a mining camp, Lou. It'll only last as long as the gold does."

"You think so? You look closer. You don't see near as many tents as they was a month ago, do you? What do you see now?" She didn't wait for him to answer. "You see buildin's. Good stout buildin's that'll last a while. I saw you down there listenin' to that Mr. Bullock. Him and his partner been over to the hotel talkin' to Mr. Wagner and Mr. Merrick and the General. They gonna put up a fine hardware store, the finest in the Black Hills. Sure, they just got a tent now, but they only been in town a day or so and they already sold a heap o' goods. Give 'em a month and they ain't no tellin' how good they'll be doin'. Same with all the other business folks that're comin' in. It ain't that Deadwood's *gonna* be a real town one of these days. It already *is*."

Dan couldn't argue with her. Even Main Street, as treacherous as it was, had been improved some since he'd arrived. Many of the holes had been filled in, and quite a few of the tree stumps that had remained after the campsite was cleared originally had been pulled up by teams of mules. Main Street and Sherman Street were lined with businesses, and the side streets were beginning to fill up, too. Cabins had begun to dot the hills that overlooked the settlement. These weren't temporary dwellings like the miners' tents had been; they were permanent residences.

"You see it, don't you?" Lou said. "A lot of folks come here to try to find a fortune. You came here to find a home, Dan."

He nodded slowly. Maybe she was right.

"Here we are," Lou went on, and Dan saw that they had reached the hotel. And with all the talking they had done, he had forgotten to ask her about Bellamy. He couldn't keep her standing on the hotel porch with that basket of laundry, so he opened the door and held it for her.

"I enjoyed our walk," he told her.

"So did I," she said with a smile, but the words and her expression were just friendly. They didn't hold any promise of anything else. That was the way it had to be.

A couple of men were about to leave the hotel. They stepped back to let Lou come in first, tipping their hats to her as they did so. "We'll be back for supper, Aunt Lou," one of them said to her.

She laughed. "Never crossed my mind that you wouldn't, General!"

The men stepped out onto the porch and nodded to Dan. Both were dressed in suits and wore expensive hats. One was short and stocky, with a distinguished sandy beard, while the other was taller, mustachioed, and equally beefy. The shorter one greeted Dan by saying, "Hello, Sergeant."

"Howdy, General." Dan felt like he ought to salute, but he didn't. He wasn't in the Army anymore, and the General was retired.

General A.R.Z. Dawson was the federal revenue agent in

Deadwood. While the settlement had begun life as an outlaw camp—and still was—in defiance of the treaty that had given the Black Hills to the Sioux, that didn't mean the government in Washington was going to ignore it as a potential source of revenue. The unofficial policy adopted by the government was a combination of hands off—the Army no longer tried to prevent prospectors from entering the Black Hills, but it didn't provide any protection from the Indians for them, either—and hands out, because taxes were levied on any activity deemed taxable. General Dawson was in charge of collecting those taxes. So far the politicians had restrained themselves from declaring that eating, drinking, and breathing fell into the category of taxable endeavors, but it was probably just a matter of time until that came about. Meanwhile, despite his job, the General was one of the best-known and best-liked men in Deadwood. He had helped Dan locate a claim to buy when Dan first arrived in the camp.

Dawson's companion was Mr. A.W. Merrick, the editor and publisher of the *Black Hills Pioneer,* one of several newspapers that had been established already in Deadwood. The *Pioneer* was the most popular, and Merrick, like General Dawson, was considered one of the town's leading citizens. Dan shook hands with both men.

"What brings you to town, Sergeant?" the General asked. "Not planning to sell out and leave our fair settlement, are you?"

"No, sir, not by a long shot," Dan answered without hesitation. "Fact of the matter is, I've had pretty good luck finding color lately, and I thought I deserved a little time off." He nodded toward the hotel. "Maybe have me a good dinner in the Grand Central's dining room."

"We'll be there later," Merrick said. "Why don't you join us?"

"Much obliged. I'll try to do that." Dan wasn't quite sure how to work the conversation around to where he wanted to go, and subtlety had never been his strong suit, anyway. So he asked bluntly, "Have either of you fellas seen Bellamy Bridges lately?"

Merrick frowned. "You mean the young man who came to Deadwood the same time you did?"

Before Dan could answer, the General said, "Yes, he's one and the same. In fact, he was a partner in your claim for a while, wasn't he, Dan?"

"Legally, I reckon he still is," Dan said. "He hasn't been out there working it with me lately, though."

"No, he's been busy elsewhere." The General's voice held a trace of sadness. He looked over Dan's shoulder and went on. "In fact, here he comes now."

Chapter Six

D**AN** turned to look along the street in the same direction as the General. He saw Bellamy coming toward them, head down, not really seeming to pay much attention to where he was going. The youngster wore a fringed buckskin jacket, tight brown whipcord trousers, high-topped boots, and a creamy, broad-brimmed Stetson. A double-hung gun rig was strapped around his waist. It was the sort of gaudy getup that Wild Bill Hickok had sported in earlier times. Lately, the famous shootist had taken to dressing more conservatively. His friend Charley Utter was the one who was usually gotten up like a dude these days.

Bellamy's outfit would have been more impressive had the clothes not been stained and wrinkled, as if he had slept in them several times. There was nothing less than pristine about the guns, though. Those he kept in tip-top shape.

Dan glanced back at the General and Merrick and said, "I'll see you gents later."

As he started to intercept Bellamy, he heard the General say quietly, "Be careful, Sergeant. That young man only resembles the one you remember."

Dan didn't believe that. Despite the flashy clothes and the long debauch on which Bellamy had embarked, deep down he was the same good, honest farm kid from Illinois, the one who had grown up listening to his father read from the Bible every night by firelight. Bellamy just had more than his share of wild oats to sow. Dan let himself hope that most of them were out of his young friend's system by now.

As he watched Bellamy approach, Dan looked for any signs that he was drunk. He didn't seem to be. His steps were steady and sure, and he wasn't weaving any. But he didn't look up until Dan was right in front of him, and when he finally raised his eyes from the street, Dan caught his breath at what he saw there.

During his years in the Army, Dan had seen plenty of dead men, seen the way their eyes seemed to turn to cold, unfeeling glass when life departed. Bellamy's eyes looked almost that bad. Dan had heard it said that the eyes were the window to the soul. But there was nothing like that behind Bellamy's eyes. It was like gazing through into emptiness.

"Bellamy," he said quickly. "Bellamy, how are you?"

Bellamy didn't respond. He just veered to the side, as if he intended to step around Dan and go on down the street. Dan moved, too, sliding to block Bellamy's path.

That finally brought Bellamy to a halt. He said, "Get out of my way, Dan."

"Come on, kid, stop and talk to me for a while. Wherever you're going, it can wait, can't it?"

"No. It can't."

Again Bellamy tried to go around. Dan put out a hand to stop him, laid it on Bellamy's arm.

Bellamy jerked back, grimacing, and for an awful second Dan thought his hands were going to dip to the butts of those Colts on his hips. In that instant, Dan felt like he was staring right into the face of death.

Then Bellamy relaxed slightly, and he dragged in a deep breath. "Better not grab me again, Dan," he said. "That's a good way to get hurt. Sometimes I do things without meaning to." A humorless smiled played across his lips. "Like that time in Abilene when Wild Bill Hickok killed his own deputy. Remember hearing about that, Dan?"

"Yeah." Dan's pulse was still racing from the close call he'd had. "Yeah, I remember. I wouldn't say anything to Hickok about it, though, if you happen to run into him. I imagine he's a mite touchy about it."

"I plan to find out. I'm going to look him up and ask him how it felt to gun down one of his best friends."

Dan shook his head. "Kid, that's crazy—"

"Not really. It's something that Hickok and I have in common, after all."

He was talking about Fletch Parkhurst, Dan realized. So there *was* something wrong about that whole deal. He wished they could sit down somewhere and talk about it, but right now he had a more pressing problem. He had to convince Bellamy to abandon the idea of goading Hickok about that tragic incident back in Abilene.

"Still, you don't want to bring up the subject with him," Dan said. "You don't know how he'd react."

"I know how he'll react when I tell him he's a killer and a no-good bastard."

Bellamy's voice was level and emotionless. He might as well have been talking about going down the street and buying a chamber pot from Seth Bullock. It meant that little to him.

My God, Dan thought, he *wants* to push Hickok into a gunfight.

Dan had no idea whether Bellamy could beat Hickok to the draw. From what he'd heard, Bellamy was fast and accurate with his guns. But Hickok was a legend.

A legend who hadn't actually done anything to merit his reputation for several years now, Dan reminded himself. In fact, he couldn't remember the last time Hickok had traded shots with anybody. It might have been that night in Abilene, when he'd downed the gambler Phil Coe and then shot his own deputy, Mike Williams, who'd come running up out of the shadows at the wrong time. There were also the rumors that Hickok couldn't see as well as he used to. As hard as it was to believe, Bellamy might actually stand a chance against him in a showdown.

But winning a gunfight with Wild Bill Hickok might be almost as bad as losing, Dan told himself. The word would travel fast, and overnight, Bellamy would be famous. Sooner or later—probably sooner—someone would come after him, determined to become known as the man who killed the man who killed the Prince of Pistoleers. If Bellamy survived that fight, there would just be another . . . and another . . .

Those thoughts went through Dan's brain in the blink of an eye, and he knew that somehow he had to stop Bellamy. He couldn't let the youngster anywhere near Wild Bill Hickok.

"Listen, why don't you come have a drink with me?" he asked, his voice low and urgent. "For old times' sake? What do you say?"

"Not now," Bellamy replied with a curt shake of his head. "Maybe later." The droll inflection he gave the words made it clear that he didn't really expect there to be a "later."

Dan suddenly wondered if this was Bellamy's way of killing himself. Likely he would have been raised to believe that it was a sin to commit suicide . . . but getting killed in a gunfight, well, that wasn't quite the same thing, was it? Only it really was the same under some circumstances. But maybe Bellamy could live with that . . . or die with it, rather . . . and still have a clear conscience.

"Now, damn it, Bellamy, is that any way to act? We don't see each other for all this time, and you won't even have a drink with me?"

Bellamy smiled thinly. "It hasn't been all that long, Dan."

"Well, long enough, I reckon." Dan's mind cast around desperately for some other way to stop him. "Long enough for me to fill up a pretty good-sized poke with gold dust. Half of it belongs to you, you know."

That made Bellamy pause and frown. "I gave you my half of the claim."

"Yeah, but I told you I wouldn't take it until I could pay you for it."

"I'm in no hurry for the money, especially not now," Bellamy said with a negligent wave of his hand.

"Maybe not, but we got to do things proper-like," Dan said stubbornly. He poked a finger against Bellamy's chest, figuring he could get away with that. "Listen here, we've got to settle this." He lowered his voice and leaned closer so that no one passing by on the street could hear. "It just so happens I've got that poke with me. I say we go in the Bella Union—"

No, Hickok might be there, he reminded himself. The sight of the famous gunfighter would just set Bellamy off on his chosen course of self-destruction. The No. 10 was out, too, since that was also one of Hickok's favorite hangouts in Deadwood. And Dan didn't want to go into the Gem Theater. He didn't trust anything about Swearengen's place.

The Grand Central was close, though. He hurried on. "Let's go in the hotel dining room, maybe get a cup of coffee, and I'll give you your share of the gold. Then, if you want, we'll call it quits, you and me." He gave a decisive nod. "I won't pester you no more."

Bellamy sighed. "You sure about that, Dan?"

"If that's the way you want it, I'm sure." He didn't let any doubt or hesitation enter his voice.

"Well, then, if we have to, let's get this over with."

WHY did he have to have the bad luck to run into Dan Ryan on today of all days? Bellamy couldn't answer that. But maybe this wouldn't take long, and then he could get on about his real business.

The idea had crystallized in his mind while he was hunched over behind the Academy, throwing up. There was no point in waiting; today was as good a day as any. When he was finally finished emptying out his guts, he stumbled back inside and pulled on the rest of his clothes, ignoring Ling's questions about where he was going and what he planned to do. It was none of her business, after all. True, he had grown fond of her since Carla's death, but he wasn't in love with her or anything like that. He didn't love anybody. He wasn't sure anymore that he knew how.

He sure didn't love Laurette Parkhurst. Despite its empty state, his stomach clenched painfully when he thought about her. He had proven to himself that a man could always sink lower than he believed possible. Human depravity *had* no limits.

He took out his guns, made sure they were clean, in good working order, and loaded. He even slipped a cartridge into the empty chamber in each one. He didn't expect to need the extra bullets, but you never could tell. From what he'd heard, strange things sometimes happened during gun-fights.

Ling caught his arm as he started to leave the room. "Bellamy, please don't go—" she began.

The iron-edged control he was trying to exert over himself slipped for a second, and he put a hand on her shoulder and shoved her hard, making her fall back on the bunk. "Stay out of this," he grated at her. "It's none of your business."

With that, he had stalked out of the Academy without stopping by Laurette's room to tell her what he planned to do. He didn't think he could stand to see her again, and anyway, she would hear about it soon enough, no matter how things turned out.

Then, as he was walking down the street, looking for Hickok, he'd encountered Dan Ryan. Dan didn't know what he was getting into, but Bellamy couldn't bring himself to hurt Dan. They had been good friends once, not all that long ago, really. It was just that Deadwood had a habit of changing people, and not necessarily for the better.

Curbing his impatience, he allowed Dan to steer him into the dining room of the Grand Central Hotel. The place wasn't very busy in the middle of the afternoon like this. A couple of tables were occupied, but that was all. The hotel lobby, on the other side of the arched doorway leading into the dining room, was empty except for Charles Wagner, the owner, who was at the registration desk.

"Sit down, sit down," Dan babbled as they came up to one of the empty tables. He looked over at the counter where a waiter girl in a white apron stood and asked, "Could we get some coffee over here?"

The girl, a hefty blond Scandinavian from Minnesota, said, "Yah, Sergeant Ryan, just one minute."

Bellamy lowered himself into a chair, took off his hat, and ran his fingers through his sweaty blond hair. "Let's get this over with," he said tonelessly as he replaced his hat.

"Now, kid, you can't rush business—"

"I can."

Dan shrugged and reached inside his shirt. He brought out a leather pouch that was obviously fairly heavy. As he set it on the table, he said, "I don't know how much this dust is worth. We can take it and have it weighed, get an exact figure so we can divide it properly—"

Again, Bellamy interrupted. "I don't have time for that. In fact, I don't even want any of the damned gold dust."

Dan spread his hands and asked, "Well, then, how else am I gonna pay you your share? I don't have anything else."

"You don't have to pay me. I told you, you can have my share. I don't want anything for it."

"And I told you, I can't do that. Wouldn't be right."

Bellamy struggled to control the anger that threatened to well up inside him. He didn't want to lose his temper. He didn't want to give in to any emotion, ever again.

The waiter girl brought over the cups of coffee and set them in front of the two men. "No charge," she said.

Dan frowned. "What?"

"Aunt Lou, out in the kitchen, tells me no charge for the coffee. I don't know about you, Sergeant, but I don't argue with Aunt Lou."

"No, I reckon not. Tell her thanks."

"There you go," Bellamy said as the girl moved away. "You got me a free cup of coffee. That's payment enough. Now let it go, Dan."

"Maybe I will . . . if you'll drink the coffee first."

Bellamy knew Dan was just stalling, trying to keep him here as long as he could, hoping he would change his mind. But that was never going to happen. It was time for the showdown with Hickok, and nothing could prevent it.

Bellamy reached for the coffee cup as the other customers in the dining room stood up and left. He would take a sip, and that was it. If Dan wanted to be stubborn after that, then whatever happened would be on his head, not Bellamy's.

There was only so much waiting a man could do when he was ready to kill or be killed.

DAN saw the opportunity and acted without thinking about it. He and Bellamy were alone in the dining room at the moment, except for the waiter girl, and nobody was passing by outside the front windows. He reached out, moving fast, and hit the bottom of the cup in Bellamy's hand, upending it so that the steaming-hot coffee splashed right in his lap.

Bellamy let out a startled yelp and started up out of his chair. The cup smashed on the floor as he dropped it. He didn't reach for his guns. He was probably too shocked— and in too much pain from the hot coffee—to even think about drawing.

Dan lunged across the table, putting all the strength he had in his stocky body behind the punch that he aimed at Bellamy's jaw.

All those brawls he'd had over the years paid off. The blow landed cleanly and solidly, jerking Bellamy's head to the side. He went over backward, tumbling over his chair and crashing to the floor. In the second before he'd fallen, Dan had seen his eyes roll up in their sockets.

The boy was out cold, and he would stay that way for a while.

As Dan stood over Bellamy's sprawled body, fists still clenched, he became aware that the waiter girl had let out a surprised little scream. She stood at the counter, watching him with wide blue eyes. Charles Wagner hurried in from the lobby, drawn by the crash of the cup and the general commotion, and Lou came through the door to the kitchen, equally curious about what was going on.

"He hit him!" the waiter girl exclaimed, pointing at Dan. "Dumped coffee on him, and then hit him!"

"Dan!" Lou said. "What in heaven's name has gotten into you?"

He said quickly, "Listen, I had a good reason for doing this. You know me and the kid used to be partners. Well, he plans to do something really stupid, and I have to stop him any way I can." He started to say something about Bellamy wanting to force a showdown with Wild Bill Hickok, but then he thought better of it. If he got into details, they would be all over Deadwood in a short time. He went on. "I'll pay for the cup, Mr. Wagner, and that's all the damage. You can take the gold dust for it outta that poke on the table, and then lock up the rest in your safe, if you would."

Wagner nodded as he came forward. "I reckon I could do that. I don't like folks brawling in my dining room, though, Ryan."

"And I'm mighty sorry about havin' to do it," Dan said sincerely. "Have you got some rope or cord or something I can use to tie him up?"

Wagner picked up the pouch of gold dust and said, "I don't want anything more to do with this."

Lou said, "There's some twine out in the kitchen. Go get it, Hannah. Now!"

The waiter girl scurried to do Lou's bidding. Meanwhile, Lou stared steadily at Wagner as if daring her employer to do anything to stop her from helping Dan. Wagner just shrugged. He wasn't going to challenge the woman whose cooking brought him a significant portion of his business.

"I'd appreciate it if you wouldn't say anything about this to anybody, sir," Dan added.

Wagner nodded curtly. "All right."

Dan figured he would probably take an extra pinch or two of gold dust out of the poke in return for his silence. That was all right. It was well worth the dust.

Hannah came back with the twine and gave it to Lou, who handed it to Dan. Working quickly, he trussed up Bellamy's hands and feet. Bellamy had a bright red bandanna around his neck. Dan took it off and rigged a crude gag out of it.

"What are you gonna do with him?" Lou asked. "I reckon you better get him outta here in a hurry."

"I'll take him out to my claim and try to talk some sense into his head. Don't quite know how I'll get him there, though . . ."

"They's a buckboard belongs to the hotel out back. Put him in it, throw a blanket over him, and won't nobody think twice about it when you drive outta town." Lou paused. "Come to think of it, I'll drive. That way I can bring the wagon back when you're done with it."

Dan looked at her. "You'd do that?"

"I reckon you got to have a good reason for dumpin' hot coffee on folks and cloutin' 'em like that. You ain't never give me no cause not to trust you, Dan Ryan."

He wanted her to hug her, but he knew she'd balk at that. He settled for saying, "Thank you."

"Well, pick him up and let's get goin'." She glanced at the waiter girl. "You ain't gonna say nothin' about this to nobody, right, Hannah?"

"Yah, Aunt Lou. I mean, no, I don't say nothin'."

With a grunt of effort, Dan hauled Bellamy up off the floor, staggered a little under the young man's deadweight, and then managed to sling him over his shoulder. Following Lou, he headed for the rear door of the Grand Central Hotel.

Chapter Seven

LAURETTE was aware of the hostile stares directed her way by the more respectable citizens of Deadwood. Many of the merchants and businessmen of the settlement slipped down to the Badlands at night to indulge in appetites they couldn't satisfy in their own homes, but that didn't matter to them. They were still quick to disapprove whenever one of the denizens of the red-light district dared to show her face west of Wall Street. Laurette had encountered that attitude everywhere she'd ever been, and she had developed a simple philosophy to deal with it.

If they didn't like it, the hell with 'em.

She walked along Main Street with her head held high—but not so high that she couldn't watch where she was going. She kept an eye out for Bellamy, too. He was the reason she was here. She had checked in all the saloons at the other end of town, even going so far as to set foot in the Gem and ask Dan Dority behind the bar if he had seen Bellamy. Dority had just shaken his head.

The damned kid seemed to have disappeared. How was

that even possible? Deadwood had grown rapidly during the few months of its existence, but it wasn't so big that Bellamy should be able to hide from her like this.

And that was just it—he shouldn't be hiding. If he had gone off to force a showdown with Hickok, as Laurette expected, then he should have been out in the open somewhere, either looking for Hickok or mouthing off about him in an attempt to draw the famous gunman to him.

"Good day to you, Mrs. Parkhurst."

The friendly greeting took Laurette so much by surprise that for a second she couldn't comprehend that someone had spoken to her. Then she looked around and saw the tall, skinny, black-clad figure of Preacher Smith. He smiled at her as he clasped his Bible in front of him.

"Did you say something to me?"

"I said good day." Beaming, he looked up at the swath of blue sky visible between the looming, pine-covered hills. "And isn't it a beautiful one?"

"Yeah, I reckon. I ain't much on sky and clouds and shit like that, though. The wonders of nature. I'm more of an indoor gal."

"The glories of the Lord can be found anywhere and everywhere," Smith said.

Laurette reined in the irritation she felt. The preacher could get under her skin without even trying, just by being himself. But he was always around and knew as much about what was going on in Deadwood as anybody.

"I ain't lookin' for the glories of the Lord right now. I'm lookin' for Bellamy Bridges. You seen him lately, Preacher?"

Smith's smile disappeared momentarily as he frowned in thought. "I believe so. . . ." Then his expression cleared abruptly. "Yes, of course. He was going into the Grand Central Hotel."

"Was anybody with him?"

"I don't recall. I had stopped to speak with General Dawson and Mr. Merrick, and I just caught a glimpse of young Mr. Bridges as he went inside the hotel."

Laurette had almost reached the Grand Central. If she'd

just kept going instead of stopping to talk to the preacher, she might have found Bellamy by now. She said curtly, "Much obliged," and started to turn away.

"Mrs. Parkhurst?"

With an effort, she curbed her impatience and asked, "Yeah? What is it, Preacher?"

"You know that God loves you, despite your sins?"

"And I reckon I'd appreciate that, if I had more time, and if I believed in Him, which I don't."

A stricken look came over Smith's gaunt face. "Oh, Mrs. Parkhurst, don't say that! You can't mean that!"

"Preacher, I always mean what I say. Every damn word of it."

With that, she headed for the Grand Central, and she didn't let the damned sky pilot distract her again.

It would be his turn soon enough, she told herself, and the thought pleased her. Soon enough, he would never annoy her or anybody else, ever again.

THE buckboard was about a quarter of a mile out of Deadwood, headed up the gulch toward the claim, when Dan heard someone call out behind them. He turned around on the seat as Lou continued to handle the reins, and he was shocked to see a girl hurrying to catch up to the buckboard. Her long black hair had come loose and streamed out behind her as she ran.

"Hold on a minute," he said to Lou. "Here comes somebody."

Lou hauled back on the reins and brought the two mules to a halt. She turned around on the seat, too, and said, "Who in the world is that?"

Now that the girl was closer, Dan thought he recognized her. She worked at the Academy for Young Ladies. Her name was . . .

"Ling," he said abruptly. He hadn't recognized her at first because she wasn't dressed in silk and flashy finery and all the other gaudy trappings of a soiled dove. Her hair was down and her face wasn't painted. She looked younger and was just different somehow.

As she came up to the back of the buckboard, she slowed to a halt and grasped the boards of the wagon bed to support herself as she tried to catch her breath. Bellamy lay there motionless, covered with a blanket, with some crates stacked around him as if the buckboard was loaded with supplies. Dan hoped he looked like a couple of bags of flour or something like that. Bellamy seemed to still be out cold. When Lou had pulled away from the back of the Grand Central, she'd followed the alley to the edge of town, rather than venturing out onto Main Street. As far as Dan had been able to tell, no one had paid any attention to them as they left the settlement.

Obviously, he had been wrong in the case of at least one person. Ling had seen them and had chosen for some reason to follow them.

"Ling," he said, "what're you doin' here?"

"I . . . I was looking for . . ." She was still out of breath from running. ". . . looking for Bellamy."

Dan started to shake his head. "Haven't seen him—"

Before he could finish, Ling reached out and grasped the blanket, pulling it back so that one of Bellamy's booted feet was revealed. At the same time, the shape under the blanket began to stir with returning consciousness.

Dan had mixed emotions at that moment. He was relieved to see that Bellamy was still alive. The kid had been so still, Dan had started to worry that he might have hit him too hard, or that Bellamy could have suffocated under that blanket. At the same time, he didn't want Ling to interfere with his impromptu plan. If she went back to Deadwood and told Laurette Parkhurst that Dan was taking Bellamy to the claim, Laurette might hire some toughs to come out there and haul him back to the settlement.

"Listen, Ling," he said sharply. "You don't understand—"

"Yes, Sergeant Ryan, I do, more than you know."

Dan frowned as it occurred to him that Ling was talking a lot better English all of a sudden. He'd never heard her speak that much, but from the little he had been around her, he'd assumed she couldn't speak anything except Chinese and a little crude English, mostly having to do with her work at the Academy. Whorehouse talk, in other words.

"I saw you bring Bellamy out the back door of the hotel," she went on. "He was tied up, so I know you're abducting him."

"Now, I wouldn't go so far as to call it abducting!"

She shook her head so emphatically that the long black hair flew out around her shoulders. "Now it is you who do not understand. I think this is a good thing. Bellamy needs to be abducted."

Dan's frown deepened. This girl was full of surprises. "You know what he was fixin' to do?" he asked suspiciously.

"I am not sure, but I believe he intended to have a gunfight with Mr. Wild Bill Hickok."

"Good Lord!" Lou said. "Is that what's goin' on here?"

Dan nodded, his expression grim. "Yeah, that's about the size of it. I'm not sure if he thought he could actually win a showdown with Wild Bill . . . or if he was tryin' to get himself killed."

Ling said, "I fear it may have been more of the second than the first."

That was the impression Dan had gotten, too. He said, "You can see, then, why I had to stop him any way I could, even if it meant knockin' him out and haulin' him off to my claim."

Ling nodded solemnly. "This is a good thing."

Under the blanket, Bellamy began to make angry, muffled noises. Dan reached down and flicked the blanket back to uncover his face, which was flushed with rage. "Take it easy," he advised the youngster. "This is for your own good."

He was glad he had tied Bellamy tightly and taken his guns. At that moment, judging from the look in Bellamy's eyes, he would have gladly filled Dan with lead, friend or not.

Ling reached out and rested a hand on Bellamy's shoulder. He squirmed and tried to jerk away from her. Ling looked up at Dan and said, "Take me with you."

Bellamy wrenched his head from side to side and made more angry noises. They were louder now that the blanket wasn't over him.

"I don't know if that's a good idea. . . ." Dan said.

"I can help you with him. You plan to make him see that he is wrong to feel the way he does about . . . about many things, do you not?"

"I figured to talk some sense into his head. Try to, anyway."

Bellamy twisted his head to glare up at Dan.

"It will be very difficult for him," Ling went on. "But I believe we can get through to him if we try. I must believe this."

Dan scratched his jaw and looked over at Lou. "What do you think?"

"Land's sake, leave me out o' this!" she said. "I don't hardly know what's goin' on here. Don't expect me to tell you want to do, Dan Ryan. You're a man full-growed. Make up your own mind."

He sighed. That was about what he had expected her to say. In a way, life had sure been a lot simpler back when he'd been in the Army. Then there had always been officers around to tell him what to do. All he had to do was pass along those orders to the enlisted men.

Of course, being a sergeant meant that from time to time he'd had to improvise, to think on his feet. You couldn't expect some wet-behind-the-ears shavetail to know everything. Occasionally, a good sergeant had to sort of lead his officers around without them being aware that they were being led.

"All right," he said as he came to a decision. "Climb in the back of the buckboard, Ling."

Bellamy tried to yell through the gag and banged his feet on the wagon bed. He shook his head violently.

Ling ignored him and climbed up beside him. She sat down cross-legged, a serene expression on her face now, and said, "I am ready."

"That Parkhurst woman's gonna be mad as hell when she finds out you've run away. With Bellamy gone, too, she's liable to think—"

"I know," Ling said with a nod. "She will think that we have run away together. And in a way that is right, is it not?"

Dan just hoped Laurette wouldn't send any ruffians out to the claim to look for her two wayward lambs. He might have a hard time hiding both of them.

"You know what you're lettin' yourself in for?" Lou asked quietly.

"Nope," Dan said. "I ain't got the foggiest notion. I just know I got to do it, and hope it works out."

"Lord have mercy," Lou said as she flapped the reins and got the mules moving again.

BURLY, bearded Dan Dority looked up from swiping at the bar with a dirty rag and frowned at Laurette as she marched into the Gem Theater with a determined expression on her face. She didn't know how much Al Swearengen had told his employees about the new alliance between the two of them. Swearengen was a man who played his cards pretty close to the vest. Dority and the others who worked in the Gem might think that she was still their boss's mortal enemy.

And of course, she was, but Swearengen didn't know that. Or maybe he did. It would be just like him to play both ends against the middle and wait for a chance to double-cross her.

At the moment, though, they were allies, or at least it was in their best interests to pretend to be. Laurette came up to the bar and asked bluntly, "Where's Swearengen?"

Dority's eyes flicked toward the second floor, but he said, "I don't rightly know where Al is at the moment—"

"Oh, stop that bullshit," Laurette said. "He's either in his office figurin' out some new way to swindle his customers or in his room doin' some whore, and it don't matter to me which. I don't mind interruptin' either o' those things." She started for the stairs.

A man got up from one of the nearby tables to intercept her. Her hand was in her bag, clutching a straight razor, and she was about ready to jerk it out and cut the son of a bitch when she realized he was Johnny Varnes, the third member of their little group.

"What's wrong?" he asked in a low voice.

"Plenty," Laurette snapped. "I got to talk to Swearengen. You can come along, too, if you want to."

Dority had stepped out from behind the bar, evidently planning to stop Laurette from going upstairs. Varnes motioned him back and made a gesture as if to say that he would take care of things. Dority frowned, no doubt wondering what gave a tinhorn gambler like Varnes the right to take such responsibility on himself. But he shrugged and moved back behind the bar, willing to let things work themselves out.

Laurette didn't care about any of that. She just wanted to let Swearengen know that their plan was screwed.

She went up the stairs quickly, ignoring Varnes's nervous questions as he hurried along beside her. She didn't want to have to tell the story twice. When she reached the second floor, she went along the balcony to the door that she knew led into Swearengen's office. She had paid men to scout the Gem and knew its layout fairly well. That had been in case she ever decided to hire a gang to raid the place and clean it out with lead and flame.

Without knocking, Laurette opened the door and walked into Swearengen's office. He was at his desk, and he looked up angrily as she strode in. He had a bottle of whiskey in front of him, as well as a glass with a couple of inches of liquor in it. He had been adding something to the whiskey, something that he poured from a small brown bottle clutched in his hand.

"Is your brain clear enough to think straight?" she asked. "Or are you too muddled from laudanum?"

His face dark with barely controlled fury, Swearengen replaced the cork stopper in the small bottle. "What are you doing here?" he demanded. His gaze flicked over to the gambler. "Varnes, was this your idea?"

Varnes held up his hands and shook his head. "I don't know what has the fair lady so upset, Al. I came along to find out."

"Bellamy's gone," Laurette said.

Swearengen stood up quickly. "What do you mean, gone?"

"What do you think I mean? He's disappeared!"

"He's got to be somewhere," Varnes put in.

Laurette turned toward him. "Well, you go find him, then, tinhorn. I've looked all over Deadwood, from the shittiest crib in the Badlands to the Grand fuckin' Central Hotel! The only hombre who'll admit havin' seen him today is that damned preacher. He claims he saw Bellamy go into the Grand Central, but Charles Wagner says Bellamy hasn't been there."

"Wagner must be lying," Swearengen said without hesitation. "Smith may be a threat to our business and the most annoying bastard on the face of the earth, but I don't see him lyin' about a thing like that. Or anything else, for that matter."

Varnes muttered, "Thou shalt not lie." When both Laurette and Swearengen turned to glare at him, he shrugged. "That's what the preacher goes by. I didn't say it applied to anybody else."

"Anyway, whether he was in the Grand Central or not, he ain't there now," Laurette went on.

"How do you know?" Swearengen asked. "I'm sure you didn't check every room."

"No, but I raised enough of a ruckus so that Wagner showed me his registration book just to get rid of me. The hotel's plumb full up. All the rooms are rented, and none of 'em to Bellamy Bridges."

"He could be staying with somebody else," Swearengen suggested.

"He doesn't *know* anybody else in Deadwood. He hasn't hardly set foot outside the Academy lately except on business for me."

Swearengen grimaced. "Likely he's just holed up somewhere else with a whore or a bottle of booze, or both."

Laurette shook her head. "He could get both of those things at my place. Anyway, he already got stinkin' drunk last night. I don't think he's ready to go on a bender again so soon."

She didn't say anything about the fact that Bellamy had gotten himself a whore the previous night, too. An older one, and one who hadn't taken part in that aspect of the business for a while, but still definitely a whore.

Swearengen picked up the glass and threw back the whiskey in it. Laurette didn't know if he had already laced it with laudanum or had been just about to. Either way, he didn't offer her or Varnes a drink, which was just fine. She didn't want any of Swearengen's rotgut.

He thumped the empty glass onto the desk. "The little yellow bastard's run off. That's all there is to it. He got scared of Hickok and wanted to back out of the deal, but he was too ashamed to tell you so he ran off."

"Or somebody got him and did something with him."

Swearengen made a rude sound with his lips. "Who'd want to do that?"

"Hell, Al, people disappear here in Deadwood all the time. Somebody could've killed him and hid his body just because they wanted that goddamn fancy jacket he wears!"

Swearengen frowned in thought. There was something to what Laurette suggested. Murder wasn't an uncommon occurrence in Deadwood, and it didn't require much of a motive, either. Most of the victims were discovered fairly quickly, but nobody in this room doubted that there were plenty of unmarked graves up and down the gulches where Deadwood Creek and Whitewood Creek ran.

"Well, the most important thing isn't what happened to him," Swearengen finally said.

"No, I reckon not," Laurette agreed, "although I'd sure as hell like to know for sure. This ain't like Bellamy. It just ain't like him at all. I thought that kid would do anything I wanted him to, no questions asked."

"Well, I'll ask a question, if no one else will," Varnes said, a hard edge of worry in his voice. The other two looked at him, and he went on. "With the kid gone, who are we gonna get to kill Wild Bill Hickok for us *now*?"

Chapter Eight

BELLAMY had settled down by the time the buckboard reached the claim known as Number Eight Above Discovery, but he wasn't any less angry. He was just too worn out from thrashing around and trying to yell curses through the gag in his mouth. He had attempted to roll off the back of the buckboard, too, but the crates piled around him blocked his escape. So did Ling, who took hold of him with surprising strength when he tried to throw himself to the side.

"You might as well just take it easy, Bellamy," Dan told him as the buckboard rocked to a stop near the tent. "You're gonna be here for a while, until you get this foolish notion of facing down Wild Bill out of your head."

Dan didn't know what he was talking about, Bellamy thought. He just didn't. There was nothing foolish about it. Dan couldn't understand that Bellamy had to go through with it. Not for Laurette's sake—he no longer cared about her—but for his own. He had to end the pain he was in, and a showdown with Hickok was the fastest way to do that.

It had taken Bellamy totally by surprise when Dan dumped

that cup of coffee on him and walloped him. It had been a good punch; he had to give Dan credit for that much. Bellamy didn't even remember hitting the floor after Dan clouted him. He'd been out cold when he went down. Even now his jaw throbbed and his head hurt like blazes.

But he wasn't in such bad shape that he couldn't get away if Dan would give him just half a chance. That was all he wanted.

It looked like he wasn't going to get even that. Dan was very careful as he pulled Bellamy off the buckboard and carried him into the tent. He didn't loosen the bonds around Bellamy's wrists and ankles and didn't let his guard down.

Sooner or later, though, he would. Bellamy was counting on that.

Ling came into the tent and helped Dan lower him onto the bedroll. When they had done that, Dan put a hand on Ling's shoulder for a second and said, "I'll leave you here to keep an eye on him while I go talk to Lou."

Bellamy wasn't surprised that Dan had somehow gotten Lou Marchbanks to help him. He knew that Dan was sweet on her. And she returned the feeling, too; she just wouldn't let either of them do anything about it because they weren't the same color. That was just stupid. Ling wasn't white, either, but Bellamy hadn't ever given one second's thought to that while he was fucking her.

She dropped to her knees beside the blankets and rested a hand on either side of Bellamy's face. He wanted to pull away from her, but he didn't have the strength. At least, that's what he told himself. He had to admit, though, that her hands were awful cool and smooth and felt mighty good as she touched him.

"Bellamy, darling Bellamy," she said softly. "You're in such pain. If you could just let go of all your sadness, you would feel so much better."

Let go of his sadness? Release himself from the pain he felt? Didn't she understand? That was exactly what he'd been planning to do! Only death could bring him relief, and that was what the showdown with Hickok would have accomplished. Either now, or soon . . .

Outside the tent, Dan stood awkwardly next to the buck-board, searching for the right words to say to Lou. Finally, he settled for "Thank you."

"Maybe you better not thank me," she said. "I ain't sure I done you any favors by helpin' you bring that boy out here, Dan. From the looks of him, you might as well be tryin' to talk sense to a mountain lion. It ain't gonna happen, and as soon as that lion gets a chance, he'll jump you."

"I can handle Bellamy."

"I hope you're right. You just be careful." She lifted the reins. "So long, Dan."

"Bye, Lou."

She slapped the reins against the bony backs of the mules and got them moving. The buckboard rolled away, heading back down the gulch toward Deadwood.

Dan went back into the tent and stood there looking at Bellamy and Ling. Bellamy glared up at him, eyes still full of anger. Dan said, "I don't want to keep you tied up all the time, Bellamy, but I'll sure do it if I have to. I don't reckon we got to keep that gag in your mouth now, though. No-body'll hear you if you holler." He bent to untie the gag.

As Dan leaned over, Bellamy drew his legs up and lashed out with them, aiming the kick at Dan's midsection. Dan twisted aside, lost his balance, and bit back a curse as he sat down hard on the ground. Bellamy kicked at him again, but missed. Then Ling threw herself across Bellamy's legs, pin-ning them down.

"Stop it!" she cried. "Stop it, Bellamy! Dan's just trying to help you!"

Bellamy mouthed something incomprehensible around the gag.

Dan scooted back and stood up, brushing himself off. "Ling, why don't you take off the gag?" he suggested. "I don't think he'll try to hurt you."

"Of course he won't." Nimbly, she untied the knot in the bandanna and pulled it away from Bellamy's mouth. He spat and shook his head, trying to get rid of the taste of it.

After he had worked his mouth for a moment, he said in a

hoarse voice, "Goddamn it, Dan, I'll never forgive you for this as long as I live."

"Yeah, well, if I'd let you go up against Hickok, that wouldn't have been very long, now would it?"

"You had no right to interfere!"

"I'm your friend. I reckon that gives me the right."

Bellamy shook his head. "No. No, you've ruined everything." His tone grew hollow as he went on. "We'd have all been better off if you'd left me alone."

Some of the fight seemed to have gone out of him. Dan took a chance on getting within kicking distance again and knelt beside the young man. "Do you *want* to die, Bellamy?" he asked. "Is that what this is all about?"

Bellamy turned his head to the side and wouldn't look at him. "Leave me alone," he said, and his voice seemed to contain all the weariness in the world. "If you won't let me go, just leave me alone. There's nothing you can say that will help."

Ling said, "There must be something—"

"No." The word came out flat, hard, like a stone washed clean by the waters of Deadwood Creek.

Dan shook his head slowly, wishing that he knew what to do, what to say, that would get through the barrier Bellamy had put up around himself. Finally, he said, "Maybe you'll feel better later, after you've had time to think about things."

Humorlessly, Bellamy laughed. "You still don't understand. Thinking about things won't do any good. I've already done too much thinking."

Maybe that was right, Dan told himself. But if thinking wasn't going to help, then he'd just have to come up with something else.

Because the one thing he knew, above all else, was that he wasn't going to give up on Bellamy Bridges.

By that evening, Laurette wasn't any closer to any answers. She still didn't know where Bellamy was, and now she was faced with another disappearance—Ling was gone. That fact gave added weight to Swearengen's theory that Bellamy had gone off somewhere and holed up with a whore. Laurette knew that Ling was sweet on Bellamy, although she would have sworn that Bellamy didn't return the feeling. He had been fucking Ling, sure, but what man wouldn't take pussy when it was offered to him? Fucking didn't have to *mean* anything.

Anyway, Bellamy didn't have to run off just to be with Ling. He could have had her right here at the Academy, any time he wanted. As much as she hated to admit it, it looked like Bellamy had turned yellow. He had run off so that he wouldn't have to go through with his boast that he was going to kill Wild Bill Hickok.

Which left Laurette facing an even more important question, the one that Johnny Varnes had given voice to:

Who were they going to get to kill Hickok?

She left the running of the Academy that evening to a whore who called herself Samantha, who had been around long enough to be able to handle anything short of real trouble. Then she withdrew into her office with a bottle to help her think.

Johnny Varnes showed up not long after dark, insisting that he be allowed to see her. Laurette told Samantha it was all right, and the gambler sauntered into the office, trying to appear casual. Laurette knew from the way his eyes were jumping around that he was anything but.

"Still no sign of young Mr. Bridges?" he said as he lowered himself into the chair in front of Laurette's desk.

"Nope. The boy's taken off for the tall and uncut. That's plain as day." She paused, then added, "One of my whores is gone, too."

"Damn it! Swearengen was right."

Laurette shrugged. "Maybe. Probably. It don't make a damned bit of difference now, though, does it?"

Varnes took out a thin black cigar, snapped a lucifer to life with his thumbnail, and lit the smoke without asking her if it was all right for him to smoke. As he puffed on it, he said, "What are we going to do now? Jim Levy and Charlie Storms have both left town. At least, I haven't seen them around."

"And they both said no already," Laurette pointed out.

Varnes and Swearengen had approached the two notorious gunmen and broached the possibility of paying them to gun down Hickok. Both men had declined in no uncertain terms. "Anyway, I don't think Storms could take Wild Bill. I've seen him shoot. He's fast, but not fast enough."

"Levy could do it."

"Levy's one o' the craziest sons o' bitches west of the Mississippi. He only kills when he wants to. Anyway, if he's gone, it don't matter, does it?"

Varnes chewed on the cigar. "We've got to do *something*."

"Why?"

The question seemed to take him by surprise. He stared across the desk and said, "What do you mean? We're running out of time!"

"How do we know that? Hell, Hickok's been in Deadwood three weeks already. He's not wearing a star, is he? Maybe even if somebody finally gets around to approaching him about the marshal's job, he'll turn it down."

Varnes shook his head. "I don't think so. You saw how he and his friends mixed in to save the White-Eyed Kid from Swearengen. Hickok's just a natural-born meddler. On top of that, he's the most vain man alive. He exists for the adulation of the crowd. It's like meat and drink to him."

"He hasn't been acting much like it while he was here. Most of the time, it seems like he doesn't want anybody makin' any fuss over him. He just wants to play cards and drink and be left alone." Laurette took a deep breath. "I reckon we'd be better off biding our time rather than rushin' into something that might not work out."

Varnes glared at her. "I don't understand. You were just as anxious as Al and me to see Hickok dead. And what about that damned preacher?"

"The preacher's still gonna die, and so is Hickok. I just don't want to get stampeded into anything that could backfire on us."

Varnes leaned forward and poked the cigar at her. "Well, then, here's something that maybe you haven't considered— what if Bridges goes to Hickok and tells him what we've been planning?"

That brought a frown to Laurette's face. Would Bellamy betray her? She didn't think so, especially not after she had taken him to her bed, but she couldn't say for sure that he wouldn't. He'd been raised in a religious family, after all. Maybe his conscience had started eating at him. Maybe he felt so guilty over killing Fletch that he'd decided he couldn't sin anymore.

"Shit," she muttered.

"Ah, you *hadn't* thought of that, had you?" Varnes put the cigar back in his mouth and said around it, "That's why we have to go ahead and do something."

The possibility that Wild Bill Hickok might become the marshal of Deadwood was bad enough. The idea that he might have a personal grudge against them was worse. Laurette closed her eyes and rubbed wearily at her temples. Why couldn't things ever work out?

"Let me think about it," she said. "Deadwood's still about the roughest place in the whole territory. There's got to be somebody around here who'd be willing to gun Hickok for us, if the money was right. If Ord and Clate Galloway hadn't gone and got themselves killed . . ."

But that was sort of what had started the ball rolling, she reminded herself. The gunfight in which the murderous Galloway brothers had been killed was the same one in which a stray bullet had struck down Carla Wilkes. That was also the same day the wagon train with which Hickok had traveled from Cheyenne had arrived in Deadwood. That very afternoon, a chain of events had been set in motion that could wind up proving disastrous for her.

"It's too late to do anything tonight," she said. "We'll come up with something tomorrow."

Varnes nodded. "I think we'd better."

"Until then, lie low. Don't get mixed up in any trouble that might draw attention to you."

"All right. And if you think of anywhere we haven't looked for that Bridges kid—"

"I'll let you know," Laurette promised, although she was convinced that Bellamy was no longer in Deadwood. She believed that she would have found him before now if he was.

Varnes got to his feet. "If any of your girls aren't occupied at the moment . . ."

"Go ahead, fuck any of 'em you want to," Laurette said with a wave of her hand. "Hell, fuck 'em all if you can get it up that often. Tell Samantha I said it was all right."

He smiled thinly. "I'm obliged."

"Don't be. Pussy's somethin' I've got plenty of."

An answer to her problems—*that* was what was lacking.

JOHNNY Varnes paused on Main Street after leaving Miss Laurette's Academy for Young Ladies an hour or so later. He chewed on an unlit cigar this time, rather than lighting it. He had taken Laurette up on her generous offer. Not that he had fucked *all* the whores in the Academy, of course. He was a man of prodigious appetites, but human flesh had its limits. He had settled for two of them, a skinny brunette with large tits and a high yellow gal from New Orleans. Varnes liked nigger pussy; he had gotten plenty of it during his riverboat days. He sighed nostalgically as he remembered a particularly fetching little pickaninny girl from Baton Rouge. . . .

Pleasant though they were, he had to shove those thoughts out of his mind. Even though Laurette had seemed to come around to his way of thinking, he was afraid she still wasn't taking the threat seriously enough. As long as Bellamy Bridges was out there, his whereabouts unknown, he represented a distinct danger to the triumvirate of Varnes, Parkhurst, and Swearengen. They'd had no choice but to let him in on their plans if they were going to use him to kill Hickok, but it had seemed at the time that he was securely under Laurette's thumb. His disappearance made them reconsider everything.

They couldn't afford to wait, Varnes thought as his teeth clenched on the cigar. Hickok had to die as soon as possible.

The No. 10 Saloon was only a few steps away. Varnes moved slowly toward it. He paused in front of the window and peered in through the somewhat grimy glass. The No. 10 was a long, narrow room, with the bar to the right and a few tables scattered along the left-hand side of the room. In the left rear corner, at a round table with three other men, sat Hickok himself, playing cards. His back was to the wall behind him. Occasionally as Varnes watched, Hickok tipped his chair onto its rear legs and rocked it a little. That allowed his back to touch the rough planks of the wall. Was he reassuring himself that it was there? Varnes wondered. Making certain that no one could slip up behind him?

Varnes carried a gun under his coat as well as the derringer in his sleeve. If he walked in there now, could he get close enough to draw one of the guns before Hickok realized what was going on?

A footstep nearby made Varnes glance around. A stocky man with a riverboat man's cap on his head and sweeping walrus mustaches came up to the door of the saloon and gave Varnes a pleasant nod. Varnes recognized him as Captain William Massie, who had captained a steamer on the Mississippi before coming to Deadwood. The two men were vaguely acquainted. Massie gave Varnes a friendly nod, said, "Good evenin', sir," and went on inside the saloon.

Varnes watched Hickok. The legendary gunman's eyes had risen from the table as soon as Massie touched the doorknob. Rumor had it that Hickok couldn't see all that well anymore, but his gaze seemed keen enough as it followed Massie all the way to the table, where one of the other players had just thrown down his cards in disgust and stood up, evidently cleaned out. Massie moved to take the empty seat.

From what he had just seen, Varnes knew that he couldn't hope to kill Hickok himself. He was no shootist, although he could bring the derringer into play quickly if he needed to. But Hickok would be watching him all the way, just as he had Massie. The man was just too damned cautious. Varnes knew that even if he managed to shoot Hickok, there would be time enough for Hickok to return his fire. He would die, too—and he didn't want that. Then Laurette and Swearengen would reap all the benefits, and all he would get was a cold, cold grave.

As Varnes watched, Hickok said something to the man who had just quit the game. The man paused, and Hickok picked up a coin from the stack in front of him and flipped it to the man, who caught it in midair. He jammed the fist hold-ing the coin into his pocket and turned to shamble toward the door.

To Varnes's surprise, he recognized the man as the layabout called Jack. Somebody must have given him a job that earned enough money for him to sit in on the game. Of course, the pathetic bastard had turned around and lost it all again. He stumbled out of the No. 10, muttering something about how once again Hickok had condescendingly given him a coin so he wouldn't be broke.

"Jack," Varnes said quietly.

The man stiffened and jerked his head around. "Who's that?" he said nervously. His hand went under his coat, as if he were reaching for a gun. "Who's there?"

"Take it easy, Jack. It's me, Johnny Varnes."

"Oh." Jack took his hand out from under his coat. "Howdy, Mr. Varnes."

"I see Hickok cleaned you out again."

"Yeah. That damned bastard. I hope he ain't a friend o' yours, Mr. Varnes, 'cause I hate his guts."

"No, Hickok's no friend of mine, Jack. In fact, if you'd like to go somewhere and have a drink with me, we could talk about a job offer I have for you. A good job that'll make you plenty of money."

That certainly got Jack's interest. He perked right up as he said, "Really? That'd be great, Mr. Varnes!"

"Well, come along then, Jack. . . . What *is* your last name, by the way?"

The man rubbed the back of his hand across his mouth as he fell in step beside Varnes. "It's McCall," he said. "Some-times I go by Bill Sutherland, but my real handle is Jack McCall."

Chapter Nine

JACK Anderson, variously known as White-Eye Jack or the White-Eyed Kid because his left eyebrow was stark white instead of brown like the rest of the hair on his head, stirred from sleep and stretched and smiled as he felt soft, warm female flesh shift against him. Jen murmured in her sleep but didn't wake up. Jack lay there for a while, luxuriating in the feel of her, before his bladder grew uncomfortably full and he had to get up and relieve himself in the chamber pot.

He slid the pot back under the bed and stood there looking down at Jen, watching her sleep. Silky Jen, she was called sometimes because of the long, soft brown hair. He didn't use that name for her anymore, though, because that had been her whore name, and she wasn't like that now. He just called her Jen, or sometimes when they were alone, Jenny. He liked the intimacy of it.

At first when they had moved into this room in the Grand Central Hotel, they hadn't shared the bed. Jen was still too spooked for that, after being held prisoner in the Gem Theater and suffering monstrous abuse at the hands of Al Swearengen.

When Jack had brought her here she had been covered with cuts and bruises and her hair had been lank and filthy. With Calamity Jane's help he had cleaned her up, washed her hair, and doctored her hurts as best he could. There wasn't much he could do for the hurts she had suffered inside, though. She needed time to get over those.

And time was already working to heal her. Most of the bruises had faded, and Jen was strong enough and confident enough now to leave the haven of the hotel room and venture downstairs for meals. The night before, she had asked him to sleep in the bed with her instead of in an armchair on the other side of the room. They hadn't done anything but snuggle together, but for now, that was enough. Jack knew that if he was patient, her feelings would eventually get back to normal.

He could afford to wait. She was worth it.

Quietly, he got dressed and slipped out of the room to go downstairs. He wanted some coffee, and maybe he would bring a breakfast tray back up here to the room for him and Jen. Sure, she could come downstairs now, but he liked the idea of just the two of them sharing breakfast up here.

When he reached the dining room, he saw that the place was busy as usual at this time of morning. Aunt Lou Marchbanks's flapjacks were little round pieces of heaven. They drew plenty of customers to the dining room from all over, not just the hotel guests.

Jack spotted Dick Seymour sitting alone at one of the tables and went over to it. "Mind if I join you?" he asked.

Dick just nodded to one of the empty chairs, because his mouth was full. After he swallowed, and as Jack was sitting down, the Englishman said, "Help yourself."

"How're the plans coming along for the race?"

"All right, I guess. Charley ought to be back in town today or tomorrow. From what I hear, they're bringing a hundred copies of the *Daily Leader* from Cheyenne to Fort Laramie. Then they'll give fifty copies to Jed Powell and fifty copies to me, and we'll see who gets back to Deadwood with them first."

"When's this supposed to happen?"

"In about a week," Dick said. "I don't know the exact day we'll start."

"Well, my money's on you," Jack said. He ordered coffee from the plump waiter gal who came up to the table, and asked if he could get a tray with two breakfasts on it. She said she would talk to Aunt Lou and headed for the kitchen.

Bill Hickok came into the dining room and looked around. Catching his eye, Jack lifted a hand and motioned him over. "You don't mind if Bill joins us, do you?" he asked Dick.

"Not at all." Like Jack, Dick Seymour had been friends with Wild Bill for a while.

Several people spoke to Hickok as he crossed the room. He paused at the table where General Dawson sat and exchanged a few words with the General. Mayor E.B. Farnum greeted him as well. Hickok shook hands with a couple of men who were sitting with the mayor.

"Who's that?" Jack asked. "I don't reckon I've seen them around before."

"That's because you've been spending most of your time upstairs. Their names are Bullock and Star. They've got that big tent set up where they're selling hardware and other goods." Dick chuckled. "I reckon Mayor Farnum's stuck between a rock and a hard place. He owns a hardware store, too, so Bullock and Star are his competition, but as the mayor, he feels like he's got to get along with all the businessmen who come to Deadwood, too."

Jack didn't care about Mayor Farnum's dilemma. He just wanted to say hello to Bill before he went back upstairs.

Hickok finally made it to the table and sat down next to Jack, opposite Dick Seymour. "Mornin', boys," he drawled as he thumbed his hat to the back of his head.

"You're as popular as ever, Bill," Dick said.

Hickok shrugged and nodded. "Anonymity has its advantages, my friends."

"That's good, because I'm about as anonymous as it gets," Jack said with a grin. "Nobody's ever gonna remember me."

"Nor me," Dick put in, "but a hundred years from now, the name of Wild Bill will still be legendary."

Hickok grimaced. "Bein' a legend ain't always all it's cracked up to be."

The waiter gal brought Jack's coffee and took Hickok's order. She said to the Kid, "That tray will be out in a few minutes."

"Much obliged, ma'am," he told her.

"I thought Jen was coming downstairs for her meals now," Hickok commented.

Jack nodded. "She is, most of the time. But she was still asleep when I came down, and I just thought she might like to have breakfast in bed."

"A romantic, chivalric notion," Dick said, "worthy of an Englishman."

Jack flushed a little. "I just like to make things easier for her when I can."

Hickok said, "She's getting over . . . everything that happened?"

"Seems to be." Jack took a deep breath. "I ain't sure that I am, though. I think all the time about much I'd like to take a gun and go into the Gem and blow Al Swearengen's damned head off."

Hickok frowned. "First of all, Jack, it's unlikely you'd ever get close enough to Swearengen to take a shot at him, and secondly, even if you did, you'd never get out of there alive. His henchmen would fill you full of lead before you reached the door."

"I know. And most of the time I'm not enough of a god-damn fool to consider it seriously. But there's times, when I look at Jen and think about what she went through. . . ."

"Maybe it would be best not to think about it," Hickok advised.

"Sure," Jack agreed. "Now tell me, Bill, how do you go about not thinkin' about the things that haunt you?"

"I wish I knew, youngster. I surely do wish I knew."

The conversation cast a pall over the table. Hickok stayed only long enough to drink his coffee and then left, claiming that he wasn't hungry. As the waiter gal brought out the tray for Jack, Dick watched Hickok step out onto the street and saunter away.

"Bill sure seems to have a lot on his mind these days," Dick commented. "But then, so do we all, I suppose."

"He'll be all right," Jack said. "Hell, he's Wild Bill Hickok."

"I know, but last night I started into the Number Ten with Tom Dosier, and Bill was standing there in the doorway, leaning a shoulder against the jamb, and he looked like his thoughts were a million miles away. I've never seen him look more distracted. I asked him to come in and have a drink with us, but he wouldn't do it. He said . . ." Dick hesitated. "He said the night was full of death."

Jack frowned. "Damn. You're right, that doesn't sound much like Bill. But what can you do? Everybody gets moody from time to time. Maybe Bill'll snap out of it."

"I hope so. He's too good a man to be mired down like that. He's always been so full of life and vitality, but since he came here to Deadwood, he's been . . . different."

Jack sympathized with his friend's concern for Hickok, but he had other things on his mind, too. He picked up the breakfast tray and said, "I'll try to look him up later, maybe play a little poker with him this afternoon. Take care of yourself, Dick."

With that, he went back upstairs, and for a while, all of his thoughts were on Jen again, and how lucky he was that the two of them were together at last.

DICK was pretty much at loose ends until the day of the race arrived, so he headed down to the corral Colorado Charley Utter had rented for the horses belonging to the Pioneer Pony Express. As a man who loved horses, Dick could always kill some time looking over the fine animals Charley had gathered. At the moment, California Joe and some other men were out on a horse-hunting expedition, in hopes of bring back a herd of swift Indian ponies. Dick looked forward to seeing what they would be able to capture.

The thought of Indian ponies made him remember the impromptu race he had run during his first trip to Fort Laramie with the mail. The stakes then hadn't been as high as which of the competing Pony Expresses would carry the mail. No, all that had been riding on that race was . . . his life.

Only luck and the timely arrival of Jack Bowman and some of his ranch hands had saved Dick that day. Otherwise, the Sioux war chief Talking Bear would have killed him. Talking Bear . . . the man who had led the raid that resulted in the deaths of Dick's wife and children. For all Dick knew, Talking Bear had killed Carries Water and the two young'uns himself.

And the proud, arrogant, bloodthirsty son of a bitch was still out there somewhere, riding around the Black Hills and the bordering prairie in search of more innocents to murder.

Dick knew very well what the White-Eyed Kid was feeling when he talked about wanting to blow Al Swearengen's head off. He felt the same way about Talking Bear.

That was one more reason to win the upcoming race with Clippinger's man. If the Pioneer Pony Express continued carrying the mail between Deadwood and Fort Laramie, then sooner or later Dick would encounter Talking Bear again. He was sure of it. The Sioux was too filled with hate for all white men to allow them to travel back and forth unmolested, especially lone riders like the Pony Expressmen. Dick's hand dropped to the walnut butt of the revolver on his hip. He would put a bullet through the redskinned bastard if he had to.

But it would be more satisfying to kill Talking Bear with his bare hands. . . .

"Hey, Englishman," an unpleasant voice jeered. "Thinkin' about drawin' on me?"

Dick turned to see who had spoken. He recognized Jed Powell, who would be riding in the race on behalf of August Clippinger's Frontier Pony Express. Powell was a little taller and heavier than Dick, and that should have given the Englishman an advantage since his horse would be carrying less weight. But Dick knew that Powell was a good rider, and Clippinger had some fine horses. Any advantage Dick might have would be a slim one.

"I wasn't thinking about you at all, Powell," he said. "I have better things to do."

Powell laughed. He had carrot-colored hair, a drooping mustache, and a rugged face with a nose that had been broken at least once. "Like what?" he challenged. "Bein' scared that you're gonna get your ass whipped when you try to race against me?"

Coolly, Dick said, "We'll see about that. Time will tell the tale."

"It sure will. And I'll be back here to Deadwood with those copies of the Cheyenne paper a long *time* before you are. Haw, haw!"

Dick just shook his head and started to turn away. He had no desire to stand here and trade gibes with a dullard like Jed Powell.

Powell wasn't so ready to end the conversation, though. He reached out and grabbed Dick's shoulder, jerking him around. "Hey! I'm still talkin' to you, you goddamn Englisher!"

"But I'm not listening to you," Dick muttered as he suppressed the urge to smash a fist into the middle of Powell's ugly face. He and several of his friends had gotten into a brawl with Powell and some of his cronies a few days earlier, and that hadn't solved a thing. The hard feelings between them still existed. Dick considered it likely that they always would. The race might decide who provided mail service for Deadwood, but it wouldn't resolve the enmity between the competing factions.

Powell gave him a hard shove that sent him back a step. "I don't give a shit what you want," he said. "This is over when I say it's over. I oughta bust you up, you—"

"Frightened, are we?" Dick cut in with a faint smile.

"Frightened?" Powell frowned in surprise. "Of what?"

"Of losing. You're afraid that I'm going to beat you, so you've decided to pick a fight with me and bust me up, as you say, so that I can't ride against you. Then Charley Utter will have to pick someone else to ride, someone you think you'll stand a better chance of defeating."

"Well, that . . . that's just bullshit! I ain't scared of losin' to you."

Even as Powell made his blustery declaration, though, Dick saw the lack of confidence in the man's eyes and knew that his guess had been correct. Powell had more faith in his fists than he did in his riding ability, so he wanted to defeat Dick with them.

"Sorry, old man. I don't intend to fight you. I have to be in good shape for the race, you know."

Powell's eyes narrowed. "You're sayin' that you're a coward?" His voice rose, so that plenty of people on the street would hear what he was saying. "You're sayin' that you're a lily-livered coward, Seymour? Nothin' but a yellow snake?"

"I'm saying that I'm going to beat you in that race," Dick returned quietly. "And there's not a thing you can do about it."

Desperation showed on Powell's face now. He was getting the idea that he wasn't going to be able to goad Dick into a fight. He clenched his fists, stepped closer, and bellowed, "What'd you call me?"

Instantly, Dick saw his strategy. Powell would strike first and then claim that Dick had called him an insulting name. He hoped to put enough into one punch to break Dick's jaw or put him out of the race some other way, maybe even kill him. That way, Dick would never be able to dispute Powell's claim that he had started the trouble.

Dick tensed, hoping he could duck the blow. It looked like he was going to be forced to fight back, whether he wanted to or not.

But before Powell could throw the punch, the sound of a gun being cocked cut through the air and a harsh voice warned, "Better not, you peckerwood! I'll blow your damn head off, don't think I won't!"

Dick looked past Powell at the squat, buckskin-clad figure and recognized Calamity Jane. She had her Colt pointed at Powell, who had been frozen by the unexpected threat.

Through gritted teeth, he asked Dick, "Is that that crazy woman?"

"It's Calamity Jane," Dick said.

"That's who I'm talkin' about." Powell opened his hands and lifted his arms a few inches. Turning his head, he said over his shoulder, "Take it easy back there. You don't want that hogleg to go off accidentally."

"If it goes off, it won't be no damn accident," Calamity Jane said. "And it's just your bad luck I ain't drunk right now, mister, so there's a good chance I'll hit what I'm aimin' at, which happens to be that goddamn ugly noggin o' yours. You savvy what I'm sayin'?"

"Yeah, yeah," Powell muttered.

"Then get the hell outta here before I lose my patience."

Powell lowered his hands and started to turn away from Dick, but he paused to point a finger at the Englishman. "Like I said, this ain't over."

"No, it won't be until the race is finished. But then . . . it will be."

Powell just glared and stalked off.

The barrel of the gun in Calamity's hand was trembling enough to make Dick nervous. "I think you can uncock your weapon and holster it now," he told her.

"I'd like to uncock that son of a bitch with a dull knife," Calamity said as she carefully lowered the hammer on her Colt and slid the gun back into its holster. She passed a hand over her eyes and went on. "Lord, I'm in a foul mood. I wish the bastard had given me an excuse to shoot him. Might've made me feel a little better."

"What's wrong?" Dick asked as he walked over to her. "I'm obliged for the assistance, by the way."

"Oh, hell, I was glad to pitch in. As for what's wrong, didn't you hear me say I'm sober? That's an appallin' state of affairs. I ain't had any whiskey since last night, and I don't remember the last time I had a good fuck . . . or even a bad one." She leered at Dick. "Why don't you buy me a drink, Dick, and then maybe you can help me out with that other problem, too."

"I'll certainly buy you a drink, Calam, but I'm afraid I can't be of any assistance in the other matter."

"What's the matter, talleywhacker gone lazy on you? I know all sorts o' tricks that'll perk it right up." She linked her arm with his. "Come on, old son. We'll have us a time."

"I don't know . . ." he said uncertainly. "I have that race coming up, and I have to stay in top shape, so I should probably refrain from any amorous activities."

"No, no, you don't want to do that. Ever'thing's better after a good bout o' fuckin'. You'll see."

Desperately, Dick wondered if he would have been better off fighting Powell. Unless he could escape somehow, before she was done with him Calamity Jane might just kill him. . . .

Chapter Ten

❦

HARRY Sam Young was behind the bar, polishing it, when Bill Hickok walked into the No. 10 Saloon a little after noon. Four or five men stood at the bar drinking, but the tables were all empty except for the one at the rear of the room, where three men sat playing poker. Bill knew them all. Captain Massie sat on the side of the table next to the left-hand wall, Carl Mann—Billy Nuttall's partner in the Bella Union and the No. 10—was to Massie's right, and to Massie's left, in the chair against the rear wall that Bill usually occupied, was Charles Rich, a gambler from Cheyenne who had caused a ruckus one night in the Gold Room while Bill was there. The only empty chair was the one on the right, with the end of the bar behind it.

The end of the bar—and the narrow door there that opened onto the alley.

Bill frowned slightly as he studied the setup. Distractedly, he returned the nod that Harry Sam Young gave him. He planned to while away the afternoon playing poker, as he so often did, and he was even wearing his favorite outfit for that pastime, an elegant Prince Albert frock coat that hearkened

back to the days when he'd been a flashy dresser, before de-
ciding to leave that distinction to Colorado Charley. But it
was going to be difficult for him to play without his back to
the wall. He feared it would ruin his concentration. Maybe
Rich wouldn't mind swapping chairs with him.

"Want a drink, Bill?" Harry asked.

"Not just now, thanks."

"That young fella Richardson was in a little while ago,
looking for you."

Bill smiled. He had gotten rather adept at dodging young
Leander Richardson, just as he'd become accomplished at
avoiding Calamity Jane. Of the two, Calamity was the greater
threat. Richardson just wanted to hang around and hero-
worship him. Calam still had her heart set on dragging his
tired old bones into bed.

"I'm sure he'll be back later," Bill said as he moved on
toward the poker table. A hand had just ended. Carl Mann
looked up at him and smiled.

"Howdy, Bill," he said. "Pull up a chair and sit in for a
while."

Bill rested his left hand on the ladder back of the empty
chair. "That's my intention. I was wondering if perhaps
you'd let me have that chair where you're sitting, Charlie.
It's my accustomed seat, you know."

Rich glanced up and grinned, but it wasn't a very friendly
expression. He and Bill had never been friends, despite being acquainted for several years. "I sort of like this chair," he
said. "Maybe it's got a bit of the famous Hickok luck left in
it. Why don't you take that chair? I don't reckon anybody's
gonna sneak up behind you and ambush you in broad daylight."

Bill frowned down at the empty chair. It was wrong, just
plain wrong.

Massie said, "I sort of like the idea. Bill took me for a
considerable amount last evening. Maybe this will even the
odds a mite."

"It's all right, Bill," Carl Mann said. "Harry's got a bung-
starter under the bar. Troublemakers know to steer clear of
here."

All three of the men at the table were smiling. They wouldn't come right out and laugh at him for being superstitious, but that was what they were thinking, Bill decided. They didn't realize that he was just being cautious.

He had never liked the idea of anyone laughing at him. That was one reason he had remained back East for only one season when he was taking part in Bill Cody's stage plays. Even though he was playing himself and his parts were deadly serious, he always harbored the suspicion that some members of the audience were amused by all the strutting and pontificating that the scripts called for him to do. It had been an affront to his dignity.

"All right," he said as he pulled the chair out slightly and moved around it to lower himself onto the hard seat. "Deal me in."

COLORADO Charley Utter was tired. In the past week he had been to Fort Laramie and several ranches on Sage Creek and Hat Creek, between there and Deadwood. He had arranged for Dick Seymour to pick up fresh horses on the Bowman and Hunton spreads. Unfortunately, the ranchers were going to provide a change of mounts for Clippinger's rider, too. That was fair, of course—ultimately, the outcome of the race would come down to the skill and heart of Charley's rider, Dick Seymour, and that was the way it should be.

Charley's brother Steve rode alongside him as they approached Deadwood. Several other men followed them. With the Sioux still lurking about the area, it was wise for anyone who left the settlements to do so only in heavily armed groups. Charley pulled out a colorful bandanna and mopped sweat off his face.

"You nervous, Charley?" Steve asked. "You hadn't ought to be. Dick'll win, you'll see."

"He ought to," Charley agreed. "He's a hell of a rider. But I won't rest easy until it's over and we've put that bastard Clippinger out of business. The gall of the man, coming in to start a Pony Express when we already have one going!"

"Yeah, he's a pushy sort. Them Dutchies usually are."

Steve didn't sound particularly worried, but then, he seldom was. He was a much more stolid sort of hombre than his brother, a plain dresser and hard worker, just the sort of brother that a promoter like Colorado Charley needed. He didn't know what he'd do without Steve.

But even so, he annoyed the hell out of Charley sometimes with his easygoing attitude. There was nothing wrong with being nervous under the right conditions. It kept a man sharp and on his toes.

"Wonder how Bill's doin'," Steve said out of the blue.

Charley snorted. "I hope he ain't mopin' around as much as he was when we left. Damn, I wish he'd have come with us, or gone horse-huntin' with California Joe. Deadwood's done something to him. He ain't the same old Wild Bill that he used to be."

"None of us are the same as we used to be, Charley," Steve pointed out. "We're all gettin' older."

"Yeah, I know." Charley looked around at the dark, tree-covered hills rising on all sides. They seemed to be closing in on him, and he suddenly had an overwhelming urge to get back to Deadwood in a hurry. He wanted to kick his horse into a gallop.

But they'd be there in another hour or so, he told himself. Whatever it was that had him so antsy, he didn't figure an hour more or less would make a hell of a lot of difference.

LUCKILY, the whiskey had taken Calamity Jane's mind off her more carnal urges. Dick didn't really mind drinking with her, even though the aroma that came from her was rather pungent. But then, some folks said that Indians stank, too, and Dick had never found that to be the case. In fact, Carries Water had smelled wonderful to him.

But that was probably because he had been in love with her, he reminded himself.

They were sitting in the Bella Union, at a table with a bottle and glasses in front of them. Between drinks, Calamity was spinning some yarn about how she had saved the life of a cavalry officer while she was scouting for the Army.

"So there we was, tryin' to get back to the fort, with all them goddamn Sioux a-larrupin' along right behind us, just itchin' to lift our hair. Lord knows what them bucks would've done to me once they found out I was a white woman. . . . Well, sir, I looked back over my shoulder, and I seen that Cap'n Egan was hit. He was reelin' in his saddle like he was about to fall off his horse, and I knowed that if he did, that'd be the end o' the trail for him. Them Sioux would've got him, sure as shootin'. . . . So I turned my horse around and galloped right back into the teeth o' them bullets and arrows, and I come up alongside the cap'n just as he's about to tumble out o' his saddle. Just as cool as can be, I ignore them whoopin' savages, who by now are almost close enough to take a piss on, and I grab the cap'n and pull him over on my horse, in front o' my saddle. Then I tell that horse to get all our asses outta there as fast as he can. . . . We outrun the Sioux, and when we got back to the fort, Cap'n Egan, he comes to long enough to say, 'You done saved my life. From now on I'm a-gonna call you Calamity Jane, the Heroine of the Plains.' " She set her empty glass on the table. "So that's how come folks started callin' me Calamity Jane. It's all 'cause o' that handsome young cap'n whose life I saved." She hiccupped and reached for the bottle to fill her glass again.

Dick had a strong suspicion that there wasn't a lick of truth in Calamity's story. He had heard her tell it differently on several occasions, and she never remembered who she had told it to in the past or what version of it they had heard. Dick thought it was more likely Calam had gotten the name because sooner or later trouble usually broke out wherever she went. She was a walking, talking calamity. And yet, he didn't know anyone who didn't like her, although some of the men she set her cap for, such as Bill Hickok, sometimes went to great pains to avoid her so they wouldn't have to reject her advances and hurt her feelings. But again, that was an indication of how they were fond of her.

Calamity took another slug of whiskey and sighed. "Cap'n Egan, he was a handsome devil. I figured once he recuperated some from bein' shot by the Sioux, him and me would get together. Poor sumbitch couldn't get it up no more, though, on account of his wound done somethin' terrible to his innards. That's what he told me, anyway." She drained the glass again and looked over at Dick. "Speakin' o' not bein' able to get it up, I recollect I was gonna try to help you out with that."

Dick tried not to wince. He had been hoping that she had forgotten about that. Obviously, she hadn't. With a leer, she went on. "Let's go back to your tent, Dick, and we'll see what we can do about it. I'm bettin' I'll have you randy as a ol' coon dog, lickity-split." She raised a finger. "Speakin' o' which—"

Dick had never been so glad to see anyone in his life as he was at that moment when he looked up and saw Leander Richardson entering the saloon. He caught the young man's eye and called, "Hello, Richardson."

The youngster hurried over to the table and said, "Howdy, Dick. Howdy, Miss Calamity. Either of you seen Wild Bill?"

Calamity sighed and got a dreamy expression in her eyes at the mention of Wild Bill. Dick was struck by how the look completely transformed her. She was as dirty as ever, and her features were still blunt and rough-hewn, but suddenly, they softened, and for an instant—just an instant, mind you—Calamity Jane was almost pretty. It was a shocking sight, and Dick felt a surge of pity for her. She was a strong, self-reliant woman, no doubt about that, and for all of the wild yarns she spun, she really had led an active, adventurous life on the frontier. Seeing her like this, and realizing that she could be brought low by the power of unrequited love, just like anyone else, was a humbling reminder of his own humanity. He swallowed, cleared his throat, and said, "Ah, no, not since this morning. I'm sure he's around somewhere, though."

"Maybe over in the Number Ten," Richardson said. "I was there earlier, but I'll have another look. I wanna ask him again about the time he shot it out with the McCanles gang."

Calamity started to her feet. "I'll go with you, kid. Wouldn't mind seein' Wild Bill myself."

Dick couldn't think of any way to stop her, short of inviting her to his tent so she could demonstrate her amatory skills on him, and while Bill Hickok was a friend, he wasn't *that* good of a friend.

"I'll go, too," he said as he got to his feet. The three of them started toward the front door of the Bella Union. The No. 10, which had almost become Hickok's home away from home, was just a few steps down Main Street.

DURING the game the night before, Hickok has beaten Captain Massie easily, winning hand after hand from the stout riverboat man. But today was a different story, as it always was when it came to cards. The luck that sat on a man's shoulder one moment would often desert him the next. So it came as no surprise to Bill that he lost more hands than he won, and when he lost, the victor was usually Captain Massie.

Hearing the front door open, Bill glanced over his left shoulder in that direction. He saw a shabbily dressed man enter the saloon. Something was familiar about him, but it was difficult to make out many details about the man, with the afternoon light behind him like that. He swung the door closed, and then Bill could see him better. He recognized the newcomer as a layabout he had played cards with a couple of times in recent days. Sunderland, Sutherland, something like that was his name.

Bill turned his attention back to the table, not giving the man another thought.

"OUGHT to be in Deadwood in another ten or fifteen minutes," Steve Utter said. "She's just around a couple more hills."

"Can't be too soon for me," his brother muttered.

"Yeah, I know what you mean. A saddle gets to be hell to sit on after a while, don't it?" Steve smiled. "There's a gal works at the Grand Central that I'm plumb anxious to see again, too."

That bit of news was a welcome distraction from his worries for Charley. He looked over at Steve and said, "The Grand Central ain't a whorehouse."

"And I never said this gal was a whore, neither, now did I? She's one of the waiter gals there."

"Let me guess. That big blond Scandahoovian girl's the one you're talkin' about, ain't she?"

Steve looked down at the trail and said quietly, "Her name's Hannah."

"Are you blushin'?" Charley let out a laugh. "By God, you are! You're blushin'!"

"Now don't you rag me about this, Charley," Steve said quickly. "I know you're my brother and all, but I'll whale the tar outta you if you start a-raggin' me about Hannah."

Still chuckling, Charley said, "You're the one who brought it up. But I reckon everybody's got a right to get sweet on somebody sometime."

"Yeah, Wild Bill married that Mrs. Thatcher lady, what used to run the circus. Even he ain't immune to the charms of a woman . . . 'less, of course, she's Calamity Jane."

They both laughed about that, but Charley felt his momentary good mood slipping away again. He wondered if it was because Steve had mentioned Wild Bill.

"Come on," he said, clucking to his horse and heeling the animal to a faster pace. "Let's get where we're goin'."

DICK Seymour, Calamity Jane, and Leander Richardson stepped out of the Bella Union just as Jack Anderson and the former Silky Jen passed along the street in front of the saloon. Jack's hand tightened a little on Jen's arm as he saw them. This was the first time Jen had ventured out of the hotel, and he wasn't sure it was a good idea. She had insisted, though, saying she was tired of being cooped up.

He'd been particularly leery of the idea of coming down here to this part of town. The Gem was almost directly across the street, and he would have thought the place would hold too many bad memories for her. Once or twice he had seen her eyes cutting in that direction and had felt her take a deep breath as she walked closely beside him, and he knew she had to be thinking about the things that bastard Swearengen had done to her.

But maybe that was the point. Maybe she figured if she could get through this, nothing else would bother her and she would be all right again.

She stopped short at the sight of Calamity Jane, and so did Jack. Without Calamity's help, she might still be a prisoner over there on the second floor of the Gem. The rugged frontierswoman was yet another vivid reminder for Jen of what had happened to her. After a second, though, Jen managed to smile and say, "Hello, Calam. It's good to see you again."

Dick, Richardson, and Calamity came over to join Jen and Jack. Calamity let out a low whistle. "Lord have mercy, gal," she said, "you're lookin' just fine. Can't hardly tell no more that that damned Swearengen beat the shit outta you."

Jen flinched a little, but she kept the smile in place on her lips. Jack was proud of her bravery. "I am fine," she said, "thanks to you and darling Jack and Mr. Hickok."

Calamity hooted and dug an elbow in Jack's side. "Hear what she called you, White-Eye? 'Darlin' Jack'! I reckon you got yourself a little sweetie-pie!"

"Take it easy, Calam," Jack said, hoping she wouldn't make too big a scene. "Jen knows how I feel about her."

"And I reckon we all know how she feels about you." Calamity moved alongside Jen and slung an arm around her shoulders. "Tell me, gal, when you get all healed up, are you goin' back to whorin'?"

Jen was as imperturbable as ever. She just kept smiling, looked over at Jack, and said, "I reckon those days are over."

That was all it took to make him feel warm inside. Just those words, and the look in her eyes, and the smile on her lips . . .

By God, this was a beautiful day!

A loud popping noise came from inside the No. 10 Saloon, which was close at hand. The men looked around, and Dick Seymour said, "That sounded like a gunshot."

IT was the oddest thing. Time seemed to have stopped. Bill had never known that to happen before. There had been times, true enough, during gunfights when time appeared to slow down around him, so that the other man was moving as if he'd been dipped in molasses while Bill was able to draw and fire at normal speed. It was that quirk of perception, perhaps, that gave him his ability to win those gunfights.

But this was different. Everything was frozen just like it had been an instant earlier. The four men were seated around the poker table, and Harry Sam Young was behind the bar, where he had just returned after bringing Bill some pocket checks because that scoundrel Captain Massie had broken him. In fact, Bill had just said as much. As the hand ended, when the two pair he held proved not to be enough to win, Bill had said without any rancor, while still holding the cards, "The old duffer . . . he broke me on that hand."

Then he had heard, vaguely, the scrape of boot leather on the floor behind him, and a voice he didn't really recognize shouted, "Damn you, take that!" and there was a loud bang.

That was when everything stopped, and somehow in that timeless instant, Bill Hickok knew what had happened. He had known all along it was coming, he just hadn't known how or when, and as the realization went through him he welcomed it with a part of his being, while another part raged at the unfairness of it all.

But then . . . life was unfair, and death was a part of life. Bill blinked, and time unfroze, and the terrible impact drove his head forward as darkness rose up to claim him.

DICK and the others had barely turned toward the No. 10 when several men burst out the door in a state of near-panic. Carl Mann and Harry Sam Young were among them, and a chill went through Dick as Mann shouted, "He went out the back! Somebody stop him! He shot Wild Bill! Wild Bill Hickok is dead!"

Chapter Eleven

DAN Dority had moved out from behind the bar in the Gem and gone to the front door to step onto the porch and get some fresh air. Of course, just how fresh the air was in Deadwood's Main Street was open for debate, considering all the men and horses and mules and the piles of shit in the street. But at least the air was moving a little and wasn't as stale as that inside the Gem.

As soon as he came out onto the porch, Dority looked across the street and spotted the small group of people standing between the Bella Union and the No. 10. His eyes widened as he recognized the girl with the long brown hair and slender figure. Turning swiftly, Dority went back inside.

Just inside the door, he hesitated. Swearengen stood at the bar, nursing a drink. He looked hungover and probably was. Dority had intended to tell him about Jen, but suddenly he wondered if that was such a good idea. Al was easily upset, and if he knew that the gal was parading around Deadwood on the arm of that funny-looking White-Eyed Kid, he might fly off the handle. No telling what he might do. But odds were it wouldn't be good.

Damn, that was brazen of the whore, walking around this part of the settlement like that. Almost like she wanted Swearengen to see her. That was it, Dority decided. She was thumbing her nose at Al. Now he was surer than ever that he shouldn't say anything. Let Jen have her fun. She would go on back to the hotel after a while, and Al wouldn't have to know anything about it just yet. Sure, sooner or later he would hear that she had come out into the open again . . . but he wouldn't hear about it from Dan Dority, who was too smart to be the bearer of bad news. Nonchalantly, Dority started behind the bar again.

That was when somebody across the street started yelling, and the commotion made Swearengen turn and stalk toward the door, muttering, "What the hell's goin' on out there?"

Well, that was it, thought Dority. Al would see Jen when he looked out. The shit was flung.

But at least he hadn't done the flinging.

LAURETTE was in the Academy's parlor when she heard the yelling. She couldn't make out the words, but whoever it was sounded mighty upset.

She was none too happy herself. It had been a bad night, and she hadn't slept well because of all the worrying she had done about the problem of what to do about Wild Bill Hickok. Then to get up this morning and find out that Samantha hadn't run things as well as Laurettte would have hoped— she had let a couple of miners slip out without paying, for God's sake!—had been almost too much. Laurette had Samantha in the parlor, chewing her out good and proper for her laxity. Samantha sat on one of the chairs with her head down, taking the chewing out meekly. Laurette stopped and looked up as she heard the shouting from the street.

"What the hell's that all about?" she muttered as she went to the door. She opened it in time to see several people rush past, heading toward the No. 10. And then she heard clearly the words that sent a shock through her.

"Wild Bill's dead!"

Laurette stiffened and her eyes widened in surprise. She

glanced across the street, and then looked again as she saw Al Swearengen step out onto the porch of the Gem Theater. Swearengen seemed shocked, too, and for a second their eyes locked across the street. Laurette gave a quick shake of her head to indicate that she didn't know what was going on. Swearengen shrugged, and she took that to mean that he was ignorant, too.

But there was no doubt about what she had heard. Several people had taken up the hue and cry, and the message was plain. Hickok was dead, and the killer was getting away. Somehow, she and Swearengen had gotten what they wanted.

But who the hell had done it?

AL Swearengen's first thought was that Johnny Varnes must have done the deed himself. But when he glanced back over his shoulder, he saw the satanic-looking gambler sitting at a table in the Gem, playing poker with a couple of prospectors and a bull-whacker.

"Varnes!" Swearengen called from the front door. "Come here!"

Varnes didn't look happy about having to leave the game, but his cards must not have been too good because he threw in his hand, stood up, and walked over to the front door of the Gem to join Swearengen. "What is it, Al?" he asked. He looked past Swearengen at the commotion across the street. "What's going on over there?"

"According to those assholes who're runnin' around and yellin', Wild Bill Hickok is dead. Somebody shot him." Swearengen looked intently at the gambler. "You happen to know anything about that, Varnes?"

Varnes looked surprised, but only slightly. Even more so, he looked pleased. "I might," he said as he hooked his thumbs in his vest.

Swearengen leaned closer to him and hissed, "You stupid bastard, what have you done?"

Varnes blinked, obviously taken aback by Swearengen's barely contained fury. "But . . . but, Al," he said, "you wanted Hickok dead. Didn't you?"

"Shut the hell up," Swearengen snapped. The yelling was drawing more attention now, and several people inside the Gem were headed for the door to see what was going on. He didn't want them to hear what Varnes was saying. "Just don't say anything to anybody until we've had a chance to talk, you got that?"

"Yeah. Yeah, sure, Al. Whatever you say."

"Go back to your game, while I see what happened." Swearengen left Varnes there and stepped out into the street, intending to cross it.

He stopped short when he saw the girl standing in front of the No. 10. His heart slugged heavily in his chest, and he didn't know if the reaction came from rage or a sense of loss . . . or both.

There she was. *Silky Jen.*

CALAMITY Jane felt like she'd been kicked in the gut by a mule. Bill, her sweet, darlin' Wild Bill . . . dead? That just wasn't possible. As Dick Seymour and the White-Eyed Kid and Leander Richardson ran off after whoever had done the dastardly deed, Calam grabbed Harry Sam Young by the shoulders and shook him. "What happened in there, Harry?" she demanded. "What the hell happened?"

Harry was a pretty salty hombre, but he was so affected by what he had witnessed that he was shaking a little. He passed a hand over his eyes and said, "I . . . I don't hardly know how to tell you, Calamity. This fella came in . . . I don't know his real name, some folks call him Jack and some call him Bill . . . and then he walked up behind Wild Bill and took a gun out of his pocket and *shot* him! Yelled, 'Take that!' and just shot him!"

Calamity shook the bartender again. "That ain't possible! Bill never let nobody come up behind him. He always sat with his back against the wall!"

Harry shook his head and said, "Not today."

Calamity felt like the world had suddenly started spinning the wrong way. For a second she thought she was going to heave her guts up. But she steeled herself and told Harry, "Go on. Are you sure Bill's dead?"

"He sure as hell looked like it. That son of a bitch shot him right in the head. Don't see how he could have lived, shot like that. The bullet knocked him forward, so that he was sort of leanin' over the table for a second, and then he toppled over backward onto the floor. He . . . he was still holdin' his cards, but he dropped 'em when he fell. . . ."

Calam didn't give a goddamn about the cards. She said, "The fella what done it . . . where'd he go?"

"Don't know," Harry said. "He waved his gun at us, and everybody broke for the door." He paused to wipe sweat off his forehead as it dripped into his eyes. "I swear he pulled the trigger twice while he was pointin' that pistol right at me. I thought I was a dead man, Calam, I surely did. But it must've misfired, because he didn't shoot no more."

"Where'd he go?" Calamity asked again through gritted teeth.

"Carl said he ran out the back. That's all I know."

Calamity looked at the door of the No. 10, torn between the desire to rush in there and cradle Bill's bloody head in her lap, and the need to seek vengeance on the killer. She was about to step toward the door and let somebody else track down the murdering bastard—Dick Seymour and some of the others had already gone after him, after all—when Carl Mann stepped up, thrust a key into the lock, and turned it, barring entrance into the saloon.

"What the hell!" Calamity said. "Bill's in there!"

"There's nothing we can do for him now," Mann said. "This is a matter for the law."

"Law! What law? There ain't no law in Deadwood!"

"There'll have to be now. This is no ordinary killing."

That was true, Calamity realized. On this hot afternoon of August 2nd, 1876, a man had died in the No. 10.

But more than that, a legend had been murdered.

DICK Seymour, Jack Anderson, and Leander Richardson reached the corner of the building that housed the No. 10 Saloon just in time to see a running man duck around the rear corner. A horse stood in the alley, moving around skittishly, and the saddle it wore was pulled far over to one side. A glance was enough to tell Dick what had happened. The killer had run out the side door of the saloon, spotted the horse tied in the alley, and jumped on it to make his escape. The horse must have been left there by someone else. If it had belonged to the killer, surely the man would have known that the saddle cinch was loose. The saddle had slewed sideways, dumping the killer and forcing him to flee on foot.

Those thoughts flashed through Dick's mind as he pounded down the alley in hot pursuit. He and Jack outdistanced Richardson and went around the rear corner first. It was only as he made the turn that Dick realized the gunman might be waiting back here in ambush.

That proved not to be the case. The area behind the saloon was deserted. Dick glanced toward the woods, wondering if the fugitive had sought shelter there. A sudden outcry from the street told him differently. The killer must have circled around, maybe hoping to lose himself in the hustle and bustle of Main Street. If that had been his plan, it was a failure, because the shouts told plainly that the citizens of Deadwood were still after him.

Dick and his two companions hurried around the building and joined the chase. "Which way did he go?" Dick called to a wide-eyed miner.

The man pointed a grimy finger. "Down yonder, toward the Senate!"

A crowd had gathered in front of the Senate Saloon. It was unlikely the killer could have gotten through it without someone grabbing him. But people were looking around in puzzlement and confusion, and it occurred to Dick that the killer must have ducked off the street into one of the buildings.

"Let's split up," he suggested to the White-Eyed Kid and Richardson. "Look in every one of the businesses."

This organized search was more likely to bear fruit than the haphazard milling around being done by most of the citizens. They knew something bad had happened, and some of them even knew that Wild Bill Hickok had been killed, but they weren't sure who they were looking for.

Neither was Dick. He hadn't gotten a good look at the man, and if Carl Mann or one of the others who had been inside the saloon had identified the killer, it had been after Dick and his companions took off after him.

A bearded man came up beside Dick and asked, "You know what the hell happened, Seymour?"

Dick looked over at him and recognized Ike Brown, who owned one of Deadwood's grocery stores. The man had a reputation as a hothead, so Dick didn't know if he wanted Brown helping him search or not. But before he could say anything, someone yelled from the door of Shroudy's Butcher Shop, "He's in here! Somebody come get him! He's in here!"

The man seemed pretty sure about that, so Dick took a Sharps rifle off the saddle of a horse that was tied to a post. He could return the weapon later, and he didn't think the owner would mind him borrowing it to help capture the assassin of Wild Bill Hickok.

With Brown at his heels, Dick strode up to the door of the butcher shop. The man who stood there wore a bloodstained apron. He pointed a finger and said, "Yonder in the back!"

"Is there a rear door?" Dick asked.

The butcher shook his head. "Nope, this is the only way in or out."

They had the killer trapped, then. Dick nodded grimly and stepped into the store, alert for any sign of the man. He expected to hear the crack of a shot at any second. Surely the killer wouldn't let himself be taken without a fight.

The shop was dimly lit and stank of blood and guts. An appropriate place for a craven murderer to hide, Dick thought. He heard a rustling somewhere in the shadows at the back of the place and leveled the heavy-caliber weapon.

"I've got a Sharps rifle here, mister!" he called. "It'll blow a hole through you the size of a fist! Better come out while you still can."

He expected to see Colt flame bloom in the shadows, but instead a shaky voice replied, "D-don't shoot! For God's sake, don't shoot!"

Ike Brown had drawn a pistol. He pointed it and said,

"Come on out, then, you son of a bitch!" He leaned closer to Dick and added, "What'd this bastard do? Somebody said he shot Wild Bill Hickok, but that can't be true!"

"I'm afraid it is," Dick replied. He lifted his voice and ordered, "Throw your gun out first!"

A cheap pocket pistol came sliding across the rough planks of the floor, followed a moment later by the shuffling feet of a nondescript man with his hands raised. The man's clothes were ragged and dirty and stained with the blood of butchered beef. His eyes were wide with fear.

"Hell, I know that little bastard!" Brown exclaimed. "A good-for-nothin' little weasel like that couldn't have killed Wild Bill!"

A resentful look appeared on the captive's sullen face. "Did so!" he said. "I done it. You just ask anybody who was in the Number Ten." Then he caught himself and added, "But I had a good reason!"

"Save it for the trial," Dick told him. Keeping the Sharps trained on the killer, he said to Brown, "Pick up his gun."

Brown did so, and Dick motioned with the rifle for the man to come ahead. Several people had crowded around the door of the butcher shop, and the word spread quickly that the fugitive had been captured. Dick heard one man shouting, "Brown got him! Ike Brown caught Wild Bill's killer!"

Dick's mouth quirked. The outcry wasn't exactly true, but on the other hand, Dick didn't really care who got the credit for capturing the assassin. What really mattered was that the man was in custody and would face justice for his cowardly act.

As Dick herded the prisoner out the door, the man looked back over his shoulder at him and asked, "What trial were you talkin' about, mister? There ain't no law in Deadwood."

"I've got a hunch you're about to find out different," Dick told him coldly.

MOST people who knew the killer claimed that his name was Bill Sutherland, but he insisted that he was really Jack McCall. As the word spread that Ike Brown had captured him, people began to suggest that Brown be appointed sheriff and that the prisoner be turned over to him for safekeeping. Brown basked in the attention and marched McCall down Main Street to a sturdy building, partially constructed of logs and partially of planks, with a door on it that could be barred.

Nobody paid much heed to the wiry frontiersman who replaced a Sharps rifle in a sheath on a saddled horse. Dick Seymour's part in McCall's capture had gone largely unnoticed by the crowd, and that was fine with him. Since leaving England, he'd had no interest in notoriety.

A large crowd was still gathered in front of the locked door of the No. 10. Ellis T. "Doc" Peirce, who did more barbering than doctoring, bound up the left wrist of Captain Massie, who had discovered that there was a pistol ball lodged in it. In the confusion earlier, he hadn't noticed the injury right away. Given the way the poker players had been seated at the table, the inescapable conclusion was that the ball had passed through Hickok's skull, traveled on across the table, and then struck Massie's wrist.

A pale-faced Colorado Charley Utter pushed his way through the crowd, followed by his brother Steve. As they came up to the door, Charley spotted White-Eye Jack Anderson and grasped his arm tightly. "Tell me that what I heard ain't true, Kid," he said. "Tell me it ain't true!"

"I'm sorry, Charley," Jack said. "I'm afraid it is." He inclined his head toward the saloon. "Bill's in there, shot through the head."

"Well, goddamn it, let me in there!" Charley bellowed.

He had been Wild Bill's best friend in Deadwood, and no one was going to deny his demand. Carl Mann unlocked the door, and a solemn group filed into the saloon, led by Colorado Charley. Halfway along the bar, Charley paused and said in a despairing voice, "Oh, hell, Bill."

Hickok lay on his side where he had tumbled out of his chair. His knees were drawn up slightly, and there was a pool of dark blood around his head. There was no question that he was dead, and had probably been killed instantly by the shot. The lamps that lit the place still burned, and in their wavering illumination the face of Wild Bill Hickok was so pale and life-less that it might have been carved out of marble.

Calamity Jane came up beside Colorado Charley and rested a rough hand on his shoulder. "He's gone, Charley," she said in a hollow voice. "Wild Bill's gone."

From behind them, the others looked on—Bloody Dick, the White-Eyed Kid, young Leander Richardson with tears running down his cheeks, the beautiful Silky Jen, Steve Utter, Captain Massie holding his wounded wrist, Doc Peirce, General Dawson, newspaperman A.W. Merrick, Carl Mann, Billy Nuttall—who had come running over from the Bella Union, Mayor Farnum, Charles Wagner from the Grand Central, the still-shaken Harry Sam Young, and a dozen more citizens of Deadwood, all come to stare solemnly at the body of the settlement's most famous visitor, the Prince of Pistoleers himself, the one and only Wild Bill.

Colorado Charley shook himself loose from Calamity Jane and went forward slowly to kneel beside the corpse. "He told me he felt the death hug on him," Charley said in a choked voice. "He said he would never leave this camp alive. Damn it, Bill, why'd you have to be right?"

Then he stood up, his shoulders shaking with grief, and kicked aside the cards scattered on the floor, the hand that hadn't been good enough to win.

Dead man's hand.

Chapter Twelve

AL Swearengen stood in front of the bar in the Gem, his hand wrapped tightly around an empty shot glass. He lifted the glass and grunted. Behind the bar, Dan Dority didn't have to ask what his employer meant. He filled the glass from a bottle of Swearengen's private stock. Swearengen downed the shot.

Dority frowned worriedly. Swearengen had been drinking like that ever since he had come back into the saloon after the commotion over Wild Bill's murder. The only reason could be that he had seen Silky Jen with the White-Eyed Kid. Al could say he didn't give a shit about the whore all he wanted to; Dan knew that wasn't completely true. It still bothered him, losing her to the Kid like that.

Deadwood was still abuzz over what had happened earlier in the afternoon. A lot of people were on the street. There was talk of putting together a coroner's jury and then putting Jack McCall on trial for the killing. Nobody in Deadwood had the legal authority to preside over any such trial, but being good frontiersmen, if there was no legal and proper way to do a thing, they'd just do it illegal and improper.

A sudden burst of shouting from the street caught Swearengen's attention. Thinking that a lynch mob might have formed and dragged McCall out of his makeshift prison, Swearengen said, "Go see what that's about, Dan." Despite being upset about Jen, he hadn't forgotten that McCall represented a danger to him. If the grubby little bastard started talking about how Varnes had paid him to kill Hickok, sooner or later the trail might lead back to Swearengen.

Even though he hadn't had a chance yet to discuss the situation with Varnes, Swearengen was sure the gambler had hired McCall for the job. Varnes had been in such a nervous state the day before, after the disappearance of Bellamy Bridges, that he would have grasped at any straw—and Jack McCall was a mighty flimsy one, at that. But bizarrely enough, somehow McCall had managed to kill Hickok. It was almost unbelievable. Swearengen felt sure that ninety-nine times out of a hundred, an attempt by McCall to kill Wild Bill Hickok would have ended with McCall full of the famous gunman's lead.

Dority came back from the front door of the Gem, where he had looked out to discover the cause of the fresh uproar. Quite a few of the saloon's customers had left to see what was going on.

"A greaser just rode into town swingin' the head of an Indian on a rope," Dority reported. "He was ridin' up an' down the street like that, whoopin' and swingin' that head."

Swearengen stared at him. "What the hell?"

"Yeah, it's pretty damned strange. But from what I heard the Mex tellin' folks, the Sioux are raisin' hell over around Crook City. The greaser and some fellas with him shot it out with a war party, and he took the head of a dead Sioux as a souvenir." Dority glanced at the door. "If you don't believe me, here he comes now."

Swearengen looked around and saw a Mexican in sweaty, dust-covered clothes and a big sombrero striding into the Gem. In his left hand he carried a human head, his fingers tangled in the long black hair. Thankfully, the head had already bled out, so it didn't drip gore on the plank floor. With a crowd of men yelling and cussing excitedly around him, the Mexican carried the head over to the bar and lifted it to set it on the hardwood. "A drink, Señor!" he bellowed. "I need a drink!"

"Get that head off my bar, you damn greaser!" Swearengen told him. "Ain't you got any common damn decency?"

Reluctantly, the Mexican removed the head from the bar and propped it on the brass rail beside his feet. Dority put a glass of Who-hit-John in front of him, and the Mexican knocked back the drink. Men crowded around, eager to buy him more whiskey in return for hearing about the Sioux depredations.

Muttering under his breath, Swearengen made his way out of the crowd. He didn't care about the Indians. He was more concerned with the possibility that some of the blame for Hickok's murder might be laid at his feet. He looked around the room for Varnes. The bastard was nowhere to be seen.

He'd better not have run out and left Swearengen here holding the bag. If that was the case, then one of these days Swearengen would catch up to him somehow, he told himself, and then Johnny Varnes would wish he had never been born, the stupid bastard.

HICKOK'S body had been taken to Colorado Charley's tent. Charley had insisted on that, and also it was convenient to the No. 10. Charley never permitted anybody to share his tent with him; he was much too fastidious for that and couldn't abide anyone else around, cluttering things up and maybe even going through his gear. But he had asked that Bill's body be brought to his tent, and would have enforced the decision at gunpoint, if necessary.

He wished it was an exception he had never been forced to make.

Once the body had been laid on a hastily cleared table inside the tent, Charley ordered everybody out except Doc Peirce. "Clean him up, Doc," Charley ordered in a choked voice. "Some of the boys have gone to knock together a coffin, so he needs to be cleaned up."

Peirce nodded. He was a stocky man with thinning dark hair and a mustache. "Don't you worry, Charley," he said. "I'll fix him up right nice." He studied the body. "Won't have to do much, though. I don't reckon I've ever seen a prettier corpse."

Charley swung around and glared at him, and Peirce hastily got to work.

None of the blood had gotten on Hickok's clothes, only in his long brown hair and a little on his face. With a basin of water and a cloth, Peirce washed away the blood, parting the hair to reveal the black-rimmed hole in the back of Hickok's head. It wasn't very large, not even the size of a man's little finger—but large enough to have been deadly.

Peirce plugged the hole with wax, then turned his attention to the wound on Hickok's face where the pistol ball had emerged. It was just under the right cheekbone and formed the shape of a cross once Peirce laid the torn flesh back down in its normal position. No one in Deadwood knew exactly how much medical training "Doc" Peirce really had, but he stitched the exit wound closed quickly and neatly and professionally. Then, falling back on his barber training, he pulled out a comb and ran it through Wild Bill's long hair and mustache. Colorado Charley stood nearby while this was going on, keeping his eyes averted as if he couldn't stand to watch but wanted to be close to Hickok as much as he could before it was time to say good-bye forever.

Jack Anderson stuck his head inside the tent, daring Charley's wrath. "They're here with the coffin," he announced quietly.

Charley jerked his head in a nod. "Tell 'em to bring it in."

The coffin was made out of raw pine boards, but someone had tacked white cloth all over the inside to cover the rough surfaces, and draped black cloth suitable for mourning on the outside. Several of Hickok's friends picked up the body and placed it in the coffin, then lifted the coffin onto the table. They backed off and removed their hats respectfully as Peirce moved in and saw to the arranging of the body. Hickok was already dressed appropriately for burial in his dark suit and white linen shirt. Peirce stretched Hickok's right arm alongside his body so that the hand rested scant inches from the butt of the revolver still holstered on his hip. He lifted Hickok's left arm and placed it across his chest.

"He needs his rifle," Charley said, emotion making his voice harsh. "He told me more than once he wanted to be buried with that old Sharps of his."

"I'll look in the wagon where he's been sleeping," Dick Seymour offered. "Maybe it's there." The Englishman ducked out of the tent.

A few minutes later he was back, carrying the heavy rifle. Charley took it from him and stepped reverently to the coffin. He placed the rifle in the crude box so that it lay along Hickok's right side.

"I reckon that's all we can do for him," Charley said. "Thanks, Doc."

Peirce nodded. "I'd say it was my pleasure, Charley, but truly, it wasn't. I wish I'd never been called on to perform this service for Bill."

Charley clapped him on the shoulder and nodded, unable to speak for a moment. When he recovered his voice, he went on. "Let's leave him in peace for a while."

The other men filed out of the tent. Leander Richardson was the last to go. The young man's eyes still brimmed with tears.

Charley hung back, hesitating briefly in the privacy of the tent. He drew a razor-sharp bowie knife from a sheath on his belt and leaned over the coffin for a second. When he straightened, he had in his hand a lock of Hickok's hair a little more than a foot long. He slipped the knife back in its sheath, wrapped the lock of hair around his left hand, and stepped out of the tent. The crowd had dispersed from the immediate area, except for Richardson, who was sitting on a keg near the tent, staring glumly at the ground and occasionally wiping the back of his hand across his nose as he sniffled.

Charley hesitated, then unwrapped the lock of hair from his hand and carefully parted it into two sections. He held one of them out toward Richardson and said, "I reckon you ought to have this." There were plenty of others in Deadwood who had been closer to Wild Bill, but none who had idolized him more.

Richardson looked up, his eyes widening as he realized what Charley was offering him. "Are . . . are you sure, Mr. Utter?" he asked.

Charley nodded. "I'm sure. You hang on to it, kid. A keepsake, I guess you'd call it. Something to remember Bill by."

With a look of awe on his face, Richardson took the lock of hair. "Thank you," he said in a half whisper. "I don't reckon I need it to remember Wild Bill by, because I'll never forget him, never. But I'll always treasure this, Mr. Utter."

Charley looked off up the gulch, with its dark, looming, pine-covered slopes, and said quietly, "You'd be surprised what we forget in life, kid. People and places and the things we do, they all fade. So hang on to what you can and treasure the memories that last." He took a deep breath. "In the end, they're all we've got."

As expected, before the day was over the leading citizens of Deadwood had put together a coroner's jury, headed by C.H. Sheldon. There wasn't much question about what had happened, so the jury wasted no time in rendering a verdict that stated Hickok had been killed by a shot through the head from a pistol fired by one Jack McCall, also known as Bill Sutherland. The question that remained was whether McCall was guilty of murder, and it would take an actual trial to determine that.

Laurette stayed in the parlor most of the evening, listening to the talk from the men who came into the Academy. Everybody was still interested in the killing of Wild Bill Hickok and the rumors about an impending Indian attack on Crook City. Of course, none of that kept the customers from coming in. No matter what was going on, men still wanted to get laid. But they talked a lot, both among themselves and to the whores, and Laurette wanted to keep track of the situation. She knew quite well that McCall might represent a threat to her, through her involvement with Johnny Varnes.

Not everybody was going on about their usual business. The community leaders took over the McDaniels Theater building and held a meeting for the purpose of organizing a trial for the assassin. Laurette heard all about it from one of the men who had been there. W.L. Kuykendall was elected judge and president of the court. He had been the secretary of the Wyoming Stock Growers' Association before coming to the Black Hills to look for gold, so folks figured he had experience at taking care of details. Ike Brown, still basking in the glory of being the one to capture McCall—even though he really hadn't had much of a hand in it—was elected sheriff. Colonel George May would prosecute the case; a lawyer named Miller was appointed to represent McCall. The trial would take place the next day, probably in the Bella Union, since it was just about the biggest building in town and no doubt plenty of folks would want to be on hand for the proceedings. After all, it wasn't every day a fella got to attend the trial of somebody who had killed a living legend.

Hearing all those details made a chill go through Laurette. Things were moving too quickly. In less than twenty-four hours, McCall might be on the witness stand, testifying in his own defense. What was he going to say?

Johnny Varnes paid me to kill Wild Bill, and he was partners with Miss Laurette Parkhurst and Al Swearengen. They're the ones who are really to blame!

Laurette could see that happening. She told herself that the citizens of Deadwood wouldn't lynch a woman. Surely they wouldn't.

But maybe McCall didn't know about the connection Varnes had with her and Swearengen. What they needed to do was to sit Varnes down and have a long talk with him, find out exactly what he had said to McCall. She wished Bellamy was here. If he had been, she would have sent him to find Varnes.

But then, if Bellamy was still around, then Varnes never would have turned to McCall in the first place. So, in a way, it was all *Bellamy's* fault. . . .

Samantha came up to her and said quietly, "Miss Laurette,

Mr. Swearengen is back in your office. He came up to the back door and said he wanted to talk to you."

Laurette frowned. She suspected this would be more bad news. There didn't seem to be any other kind these days. She nodded and said, "All right. See to it that we're not disturbed."

When she came into the office, Swearengen was already sitting in front of the desk, an unlit cigar clenched in his teeth. "Make yourself right at home," Laurette said coldly.

"Don't get on a high horse with me," Swearengen replied around the cigar. "We're still in this together, whether either of us likes it or not."

Laurette sat down behind the desk and sighed. "I reckon you're right. What do you want? Have you talked to Varnes?"

Swearengen took the cigar out of his mouth and said, "I can't find the bastard. I thought he might be over here."

Laurette shook her head. "I haven't seen him all day. He spends a lot more time at your place than he does here."

"He was there earlier, when Hickok got shot. I stepped out to get a better idea of what had happened, and when I came back, Varnes was gone. I'm pretty sure, though, that he paid McCall to shoot Hickok."

"I was afraid of that. Do you know if McCall knows anything about us?"

"I don't have any idea."

"Well, what *do* you know?"

Swearengen leaned forward in his chair. "I know that if I get my hands on Varnes, he'll talk, and if he's put me in any danger from the law, I'll kill the son of a bitch. Did you know they're gonna have a trial for McCall tomorrow? A real trial! That's the last thing Deadwood needs."

"The last thing you and me need, you mean. Every toehold that the law gets here, the worse it is for us."

Swearengen nodded glumly. "I don't know how we can stop that. So that leaves us back where we started . . . McCall points a finger at Varnes, and then Varnes points a finger at us."

"We don't have any choice," Laurette said. "We've got to find Johnny Varnes . . . and kill him."

THE look on Al Swearengen's face had been enough to convince Varnes that the wisest course of action was for him to lie low. He had slipped out the back door of the Gem while Swearengen was in the street and headed for Deadwood's small but crowded Chinatown. One thing you could say about Chinamen—they loved to gamble. Varnes had made numerous friends among them. He was also a regular patron of one of the whores who had a crib down there. For enough money, she would let him hide out there, and the other Celestials would keep his presence a secret.

Of course, while he was there, and since he was paying her anyway, he had the whore suck his cock. She was busy with that while the mob brought Jack McCall down the street and locked him up less than a hundred yards from the crib where Varnes was hiding. He heard the uproar and told the China girl, "Wait just a moment, my dear." He stood up from the bunk and went over to the door with his erect penis still jutting from his trousers. Opening the door slightly, he peered out and saw McCall being thrust into the log and plank building. The door was closed and barred. Varnes eased the door of the crib shut and went back to the bunk so the whore could resume her task. He closed his eyes and gave himself over to the enjoyment of what she was doing, but a part of his brain was still scheming.

Once it got dark, he thought, he was going to have to find a way to talk to Jack McCall. . . .

Night had fallen, but of course Deadwood was still wide awake, with people in the streets and all the saloons and whorehouses doing a brisk business as usual. If anything, the settlement was busier than usual tonight because people were still all worked up over the killing of Wild Bill Hickok and the possible Indian threat. Varnes waited as long as his patience would let him, then slipped out of the crib. Instead of his usual sartorial elegance, he wore work clothes that the China girl had taken off the body of a prospector whose heart

had given out from excitement while he was humping her.
Varnes hoped that no one would recognize him in a ragged
jacket and battered old hat.

He had read murder in Al Swearengen's eyes. Ruthless-
ness was second nature to the man. Swearengen must have
figured that now with Hickok dead, he and Laurette Parkhurst
didn't need the third member of their trio anymore. They
would cover their trail and obscure their own involvement in
Hickok's death by getting rid of Varnes.

He wasn't going to let that happen. He would tell McCall
exactly what to say at his trial, and then he would leave town.
Despite the lucrative opportunities to be found in Deadwood,
it was no longer safe for Johnny Varnes to stay here. Regret-
table but true. He had thought to make Deadwood a safer
place by removing Hickok, but instead the plan had backfired
on him.

That was what a fellow got for involving himself with
cold-blooded bastards like Al Swearengen, Varnes supposed.

Ike Brown was no longer standing guard over the
makeshift jail, Varnes saw as he approached, head down, his
eyes darting every which way under the sagging brim of the
old hat. But a local character known as Thimblerig Johnny,
who ran a portable shell game in front of various saloons,
was sitting on a stool near the door, a shotgun across his
knees. Varnes would have let McCall out of jail if he could,
but that wasn't going to be possible with a guard sitting
there.

For a second, Varnes toyed with the idea of killing the
thimblerigger, then discarded it. He was not a murderer himself; that was why he'd been forced to employ Jack McCall's
dubious services. He turned off the street, his gait deliberately a bit unsteady as if he were drunk, and began circling
toward the rear of the jail. He couldn't remember if there
was a window back there or not.

Lady Luck was with him, as she had been so often over
the years. The jail did have a window in its rear wall. It was
small, and had had planks tacked over it so that McCall
couldn't crawl out that way, but several small gaps had been

left between the boards. Varnes made his way carefully to the window and when he got there, he put his mouth to one of the gaps and said quietly, "McCall! Come here! McCall, do you hear me?"

For a moment, Varnes was afraid that the man wouldn't respond. Then, from the other side of the window, a nervous voice asked, "Who's out there, damn it?"

"It's me, Johnny Varnes."

Not much light penetrated back here in the alley, but Varnes was able to get a glimpse of the desperate face pressed to the narrow opening between planks. "Mr. Varnes!" McCall said. "You gotta get me outta there! They're gonna hang me for shootin' Wild Bill!"

"Nonsense," Varnes said. "And keep your voice down. There's a guard out front, and you don't want him to hear you talking to anybody."

"Oh. All right." That note of panic entered McCall's voice again as he went on. "They say they're gonna put me on trial tomorrow mornin'!"

"They have to, but it's more to put on a show than anything else," Varnes assured him. He had thought long and hard about what he was going to tell Varnes, and he had come up with a plan that he thought had at least a reasonable chance of working. "If you'll just listen to me and do exactly as I tell you, nothing will happen to you."

"A-all right, Mr. Varnes. What do you want me to do?"

"When you're called on to testify at the trial—"

"I should tell 'em I didn't shoot Wild Bill?" McCall interrupted.

"No, that won't do," Varnes said, struggling to maintain his patience. "Too many people saw you do the deed. No, what you tell the jury is that you killed Hickok because he killed your brother down in Kansas."

A few seconds of silence ticked by before McCall said dubiously, "But I ain't got a brother in Kansas. Nor anywhere else, for that matter, leastways as far as I know."

Varnes sighed. "That doesn't matter. Just say that Hickok killed your brother and threatened to kill you, so when you encountered him here in Deadwood, you felt that you had to shoot him before he could shoot you. That makes it self-defense."

It was a flimsy story based on a lie, but Varnes had been on the frontier long enough to know how fragile justice could be out here. The doctrine of self-defense was widely embraced. A jury would seize on any excuse to find a killer not guilty. It might work in McCall's case—or it might not. Varnes didn't really care one way or the other. He just wanted to give McCall a good story to tell.

"You really think they'll believe that?" McCall asked.

"Of course they will! For all they know, it's absolutely true, and in a case like this, a man has to be proven guilty beyond a shadow of a doubt! Just don't—whatever you do—just don't say anything about me. Pretend that we never even met."

"You reckon that's best?"

"I know it is," Varnes said firmly. "Will you promise me that, Jack?"

"Well . . . well, I reckon I do. What you said sounds like it might work, and I know you're a whole heap smarter than me, Mr. Varnes. . . ."

"Of course it will work. You'll be a free man before the sun goes down tomorrow, Jack. You have my word on it. As long as you don't mention my name, that is. If you do, it'll make you look so bad that they're liable to string you up."

"All right," McCall said. "You've done right by me, Mr. Varnes, and I'll do as you say. Maybe we can get together after the trial and have a drink."

"Of course," Varnes agreed, although he planned to be long gone from Deadwood by then. "I have to go now, Jack, but you remember everything I told you."

"I will. So long, Mr. Varnes. See you tomorrow."

Varnes just grunted noncommittally as he slipped away from the window. He made his way back along the side of the building until he reached the street and headed for the corral where he kept his horse. By morning, he would have already put some distance between himself and the settlement. He had no idea where he would go next, but they would be greener pastures than these. Johnny Varnes knew how to make the best of a bad situation.

He hoped he never saw Al Swearengen or Laurette Parkhurst again. That alliance hadn't worked out nearly as well as he had hoped. But if their involvement with Hickok's killing was ever exposed, they would have to deal with that problem themselves. He would be far away by then, perhaps in Denver, or even San Francisco. . . .

An arm came out of the darkness, looped itself around his neck, and jerked him back into deeper shadows. His head was forced up so that the skin of his throat was stretched taut. Cold steel touched it, stilling any struggle Varnes might have made.

"There you are, Johnny," Al Swearengen said quietly into his ear. "I been lookin' for you the whole damned day."

Chapter Thirteen

⁊⁊⁊

CALAMITY Jane's sleep was haunted by nightmares. She had tried to drink enough the night before to make sure she passed out in an insensible stupor, but she reckoned there wasn't enough booze in the world to blot out the pain that filled her. Bill was dead, and now she would never know what it was like to feel his lovin' hands on her.

She stumbled bleary-eyed into the Bella Union the next morning. Tacked to the wall just inside the door was one of the funeral notices Colorado Charley had had printed up late the previous afternoon by A.W. Merrick:

FUNERAL NOTICE
Died, in Deadwood, Black Hills, August 2, 1876, from the effects of a pistol shot, J.B. Hickok (Wild Bill), formerly of Cheyenne, Wyoming.

Funeral services will be held at Charles Utter's camp, on Thursday afternoon, August 3, 1876, at 3 o'clock P.M.

All are respectfully invited to attend.

Calamity had to avert her eyes. She couldn't bear to look at the piece of paper. To think that a man's tragic death could be boiled down to a few lines of ink like that. It just wasn't right.

And first, before the funeral, they had a trial to get through. A trial . . . and a hangin'.

Despite the early hour, the Bella Union was already crowded because word had spread during the night that this was where Jack McCall's trial would be held. Some of the men who were in the saloon now hadn't even gone to bed the night before.

Calamity spotted Jack Anderson, Dick Seymour, and Leander Richardson sitting at one of the tables drinking coffee. She went over to join the three young men, pulling out a chair and asking, "Mind if I sit down, boys?"

Dick gestured toward the empty chair and said with typical British politeness, "Please do, Calam." When she had settled gratefully in the chair, he went on. "You look a mite under the weather this morning."

"Bad night." She shook her head. "Mighty bad night, fellas. I couldn't stop dreamin' about poor ol' Wild Bill."

"McCall will get what's comin' to him, the murderin' bastard," Richardson said. "He'll be strung up before the day's over."

Calamity looked across the table at Jack Anderson. "Where's Jen, White-Eye?"

Jack shook his head and said, "She stayed at the hotel. She's upset and doesn't feel well. She knows that if Bill hadn't come along when he did, we wouldn't have been able to keep Swearengen from grabbing her again."

"You reckon it's safe to leave her there?" Calamity asked with a frown. "That bastard might try to get his hands on her again."

"Not even Al Swearengen would kidnap a woman out of a respectable hotel in broad daylight," Jack said, but he didn't sound totally convinced.

"Ain't much tellin' what that son of a bitch might do."

Jack shoved his chair back. "You're right. I'd better go back over there, just in case. It won't matter whether I'm here for the trial or not."

He went out hurriedly. Calamity thought about going with him, just to make sure Jen was all right, but Judge Kuykendall and the other officers of the court were filing in. The trial was about to get under way.

Billy Nuttall announced that the bar was closed until the conclusion of the proceedings. A groan went up from the crowd, but there was nothing that could be done about it. Continuing to sell drinks during a trial would have been too much even for an outlaw town like Deadwood.

Poker tables and chairs were cleared away to make an open space, and a longer table was brought in to serve as Judge Kuykendall's bench. Other tables were set up for the prosecution and the defense. Two rows of six chairs each were placed to one side for the jury.

Jack McCall was brought in with an armed guard on each side of him. Calamity started to get up from her chair as Mc-Call was escorted to the defense table, but Dick Seymour stopped her by laying a hand on her arm and shaking his head. Reluctantly, Calam settled back down in her chair.

Kuykendall gaveled the proceedings to order, using a carpenter's mallet as a gavel, and asked McCall how he pled to the charge of murder. McCall stayed in his chair, his arms crossed and a sullen expression on his face, as Miller, his lawyer, stood up and declared, "My client pleads not guilty, Your Honor."

Kuykendall glared at McCall, but accepted the plea with a nod. "Let's get on with it, then," he said.

Choosing the members of the jury was the next order of business. Earlier, the judge had sent messengers up and down the gulches around Deadwood, looking for men who were willing to serve. They had a hatful of names of volunteers written on slips of paper, and twelve of them were drawn at random. Each time, Kuykendall asked the man whose name had been drawn if he was still willing and able to serve, and there were no dissenters. One by one, they went over to the chairs and sat down until all twelve seats were filled.

Calamity leaned over to Dick and asked in a whisper, "You know those fellas who are on the jury?"

"Some of them," he replied.

"Square shooters, are they?"

Dick shrugged. "They're a rather motley bunch, in my opinion. A bit too fond of drinking and gambling, maybe."

"That shouldn't matter," Calamity said. "As long as they ain't crooked, there ain't no doubt they'll find that bastard guilty."

With the defendant's plea entered and the jury seated, the actual trial got under way. Colonel May, the prosecutor, first called Charlie Rich to the witness stand, which was just a chair at the end of the judge's table. Rich testified that he had seen the defendant come up behind Hickok, take a pistol from his pocket, and shoot Hickok in the head after crying out, "Take that, damn you!" The story prompted quite a bit of angry muttering from the crowd. It was one thing to have heard all the rumors; it was quite another to hear what had happened all laid out in blunt, plain-spoken words.

Rich said nothing about how it had been his refusal to switch seats that left Wild Bill sitting without his back against the wall.

Harry Sam Young took the stand next and agreed with Rich's testimony regarding the shooting, and he was followed by Carl Mann, who said pretty much the same thing. They had all seen what happened. Captain Massie followed them to the stand and provided the trial's first real drama when he lifted his bandaged left wrist.

"The ball that killed Wild Bill is lodged here in my arm," he said. "That's the only conclusion that can be reached, because the ball that killed him wasn't found anywhere on the floor or in the table or the wall. The doctor tells me it would be better to leave the ball where it is rather than try to remove it, so, gents, I'll carry around the ball that killed Wild Bill Hickok for the rest of my life."

That drew amazed exclamations from the members of the crowd who hadn't already heard about the riverboat man's wound.

The prosecution rested following Massie's testimony. Lawyer Miller rose to his feet and proceeded to call as witnesses a Deadwood businessman for whom McCall had done

odd jobs, along with several of the assassin's cronies. All of
them testified that McCall was normally a peaceful man who
had never caused any trouble in the settlement. That was true
as far as it went, and the implication was obvious—McCall
must have had a compelling reason to snap as he had done
and gun down Wild Bill. The defense made no claim that Mc-
Call hadn't done the shooting. Considering the number of
witnesses, that would have been a waste of time.

Dick leaned over to Calamity and said quietly, "They're
not disputing the fact, so the crux of their defense has to lie
in McCall's motivation. They plan to show that while Mc-
Call killed Bill, he didn't actually commit murder."

"Well, that's just a bald-faced, motherfuckin' lie." Calam
said. She glowered at the back of McCall's head and fin-
gered the handle of the knife sheathed at her waist. Scalpin'
would be too good for that son of a bitch. She wondered if
the judge could be talked into sentencing him to be staked
out in the sun on an anthill. That'd be a good start on what
McCall had comin' to him, Calamity decided.

Finally, the time came for McCall to testify in his own behalf. His demeanor was almost jaunty as he stepped up to the
witness chair. He was sworn in and sat down, and as he did
so, he thrust his right hand into his shirt and scratched at his
chest as if he didn't have a worry in the world.

Miller said, "Mr. McCall, tell us why you did what you
did."

Right to the point, Dick thought.

McCall looked calmly around the packed saloon before
he responded. He began, "Well, men, I have but a few words
to say. Wild Bill killed my brother for no good reason, and
I killed him."

Calamity started to lunge to her feet, but Dick snagged
her buckskin shirt and held her down in her chair. "You can't
interrupt," he told her.

"But that's a damn lie," Calamity said between clenched
teeth. "Bill never killed nobody that didn't have it comin'.
Well, there was that one time . . . but that don't matter!"

"Wild Bill threatened to kill me if I ever crossed his

path," McCall was saying. "I am not sorry for what I have done. I would do the same thing over again." He gave a curt nod and without any prompting from his lawyer, stood up and walked stiffly back to his chair at the defense table.

The testimony sounded rehearsed to Dick, as if McCall had spent a long time saying it over and over to himself. Of course, that didn't mean it wasn't true. Bill Hickok had killed quite a few men. There was no way of knowing at this late date if one of them had been Jack McCall's brother.

Instinctively, though, Dick doubted the story. It was too pat, too calculated to create doubts on the part of the jury members. Dick's gut told him it was a lie.

But it might be an effective one. That was exactly the sort of story that might work to save McCall's hide, and Dick doubted that the killer was smart enough to have come up with it himself. Someone had coached him, probably his lawyer.

Miller got to his feet and said, "The defense rests, Your Honor."

Kuykendall looked worried as he said, "Both sides will sum up now. Colonel, you're first."

Colonel May got to his feet and launched into a stirring oration about Wild Bill Hickok's illustrious career as a lawman. It was good speechifying, but it didn't address the point McCall's testimony had raised. When Miller stood and said simply that his client had acted to avenge his brother's death and to preserve his own life from a deadly threat, a couple of members of the jury nodded. Dick's heart sank. As unlikely as an acquittal had seemed when this trial began, suddenly it was a distinct possibility. If McCall was found not guilty, it would be a travesty of justice.

More importantly, would Bill's friends stand for it, or would they take the law into their own hands?

The jury retired to a back room to deliberate, and Judge Kuykendall adjourned the court, saying, "When the jury has reached a verdict, we'll reconvene in the Number Ten, where the crime took place. Seems fitting that the decision ought to be announced there."

Billy Nuttall asked, "Does that mean the bar's open again, Judge?"

Kuykendall brought the mallet down on the table. "Bar's open!" he said.

ALL morning, men had been coming into Colorado Charley's tent so that they could file solemnly past the coffin and pay their last respects to Bill Hickok. Most of them hadn't known him at all, and if they had, it had been for only the short time Hickok had been here in Deadwood. But it was fair to say that there were almost as many people around Charley's tent as there were up the street at the Bella Union, where Jack McCall's trial was taking place.

Charley sat beside the coffin on a three-legged stool, his hat in his hands and his head down. He raised it from time to time when one of the men touched him on the shoulder and spoke to him. He shook hands with some of them as they offered their condolences. They treated Charley as if he had just lost a brother, and in truth, that was the way he had felt. He couldn't have been any more devastated if it had been Steve lying there. That realization made Charley feel a mite disloyal to his own flesh and blood, but it was the truth.

Around the middle of the day, Dick Seymour and Calamity Jane came into the tent. Charley's shoulders jerked when he saw them. He knew they had attended McCall's trial. A part of him had wanted to be there, too, but he had decided to stay here with Bill.

Besides, he wasn't sure if he could be in the same room as McCall without pulling his guns and ventilating the goddamn polecat.

"What happened?" he asked harshly. "Have they strung the bastard up yet?"

Dick shook his head. "The jury's deliberating."

"Deliberatin'?" Charley repeated dumbfoundedly. "What's there to deliberate about? The bastard killed Bill! Half-a-dozen people saw him do it!"

"He ain't denyin' that," Calamity said. "But you oughta hear the load o' shit he's tryin' to peddle, Charley."

"Tell me," Charley grated out.

"He claims that sometime in the past, Bill killed his brother and threatened to kill him, meaning McCall, as well," Dick explained.

Charley frowned. "Well, that's just crazy. Bill never killed nobody named McCall, leastways not that I can recollect."

"Perhaps the man wasn't going by that name."

"I still don't believe it," Charley said stubbornly.

"To tell you the truth, neither do I. But I'm afraid the jury may have found the story believable."

Charley came quickly to his feet and clapped his broad-brimmed hat on his head. His hands went to the butts of the guns at his hips. "You don't mean to say they might let him go!"

Dick nodded and said, "I think we have to be prepared for that possibility, yes."

Charley started for the entrance flap of the tent. "By God, I'm goin' down to the Bella Union. I got to see this for myself."

Dick caught his arm. "Charley, I know how upset you are, but if the jury delivers a verdict of not guilty, you can't take the law into your own hands."

Charley jerked free of the Englishman's grip and stalked out of the tent. Calamity Jane started after him, but paused long enough to look back over her shoulder and say, "We'll just see about that." Then she called, "Wait up, Charley! The judge said they was comin' back to the Number Ten, not the Bella Union!"

THE jury deliberated for an hour and a half, and nobody knew what to make of that. Some said it meant they were going to find McCall guilty, while others claimed that they must be going to say he was not guilty; otherwise the jury would have been back before now.

But it was safe to say that none of the men—and Calamity

Jane—crowded into the narrow confines of the No. 10 Saloon really knew what was going to happen.

Sheriff Ike Brown had placed armed guards around the place to keep the peace and quell any disturbances. There were guards inside the saloon, too, flanking Jack McCall, who was brought from his jail and made to sit down in a chair. McCall's earlier bravado had deserted him. He trembled so badly that his feet drummed on the rough plank floor, and his face was washed out from terror. He even let out a little moan as the jury was brought in.

"Has the jury reached a verdict?" Judge Kuykendall asked sternly.

One of the men nodded. "We have, Your Honor." He stepped forward to hand the judge a folded piece of paper.

Kuykendall glared at McCall. "The defendant will stand while I read the verdict."

McCall got unsteadily to his feet. He might have sagged back into the chair if one of his guards hadn't grasped his arm.

Kuykendall took a deep breath, unfolded the paper, and read, "Deadwood City, August 3rd, 1876. We, the jury, find Mr. John McCall not guilty."

A roar of mingled disbelief and outrage exploded from the crowd, but there were a few cheers mixed in, too. Not everybody in Deadwood had been friendly to Wild Bill, or even admired him. The noise drowned out Kuykendall as he went on to read the names of the jury foreman and the other jurors. Finally, the judge folded the paper on which the verdict was written and slipped it into his pocket.

McCall's face had lit up at the words "not guilty," and now he looked ecstatic. From barely able to stand one second, he now seemed energetic enough to dance. Ike Brown came up to Kuykendall and asked, "Is he free to go?" The judge jerked his head in a nod, and Brown turned to his deputies to say, "Get him the hell outta here!" They hustled McCall through the side door of the No. 10 to the alley.

Dick Seymour stood with an ashen-faced Colorado Charley. Calamity Jane was beside them, and she looked like she wanted to cry. Her rawhide-tough exterior had been shattered by what had just happened here. But both Charley and Calam were calm, and they weren't going after McCall and trying to murder him. Dick supposed they all had that to be thankful for.

Finally, Charley nodded slowly and said in a hollow voice, "Reckon we'd best get on back to the tent. We've still got a buryin' to take care of."

Chapter Fourteen

A T the western end of Sherman Street, near the spot
where Deadwood Creek and Whitewood Creek flowed
together, a small, wooded hill rose. It was one of the prettiest
spots in the gulch, and from the top of that hill, which was
called Ingleside, you could look down and see all of Deadwood laid out before you. Higher hills rose all around, creating an effect something like that of an amphitheater. Not
surprisingly, considering the beauty of the scenery and the
hill's proximity to the settlement, someone had established a
graveyard there under the pines. That was where they carried Wild Bill Hickok later that afternoon, to be laid to rest.

Six men bore the closed coffin: Charlie Rich, the gambler
who had been at the table to Hickok's right when he was
killed; Tom Dosier; Bill Hillman; Charles Young; Jerry Lewis,
a business associate of Billy Nuttall and Charles Mann; and
John Oyster. Charley and Steve Utter trailed behind, along
with Calamity Jane, Dick Seymour, the Street brothers, Leander Richardson, White-Eye Jack and his Jen, and a large
number of Deadwood's citizens, both the respectable ones
and the not-so-respectable. A.W. Merrick took furtive notes,

not wanting to be too callous about doing his job as a news-paperman.

In front of the coffin, solemnly leading the way, strode Preacher Smith, his old black Bible clutched tightly in his hand.

They reached the freshly dug grave, a raw wound in the earth with a tall pine looming over it. The sun was hot and bright and made people squint against its glare as the six men carefully lowered the coffin into the grave. They stepped back and respectfully took off their hats, as did the others in the crowd, as Preacher Smith began to pray.

"Lord, we commend to Your mercy the soul of James Butler Hickok, known to all as Wild Bill."

Calamity bit back a sob. Dick put a hand on her shoulder and squeezed, trying to give her the strength to get through this. She wasn't the only one who had grown misty-eyed. Colorado Charley knuckled away tears, and Jen dabbed at her eyes with a silk handkerchief Jack had given her. Several of the men in the crowd sniffed from time to time and blinked rapidly. Some of the people were there because they thought this was a historic occasion, the laying to rest of a man who had truly been a legend in his own time. Many had come to mourn a friend, though, and an inescapable feeling of sorrow and tragedy filled the air.

The preacher's eulogy was brief; he hadn't known Wild Bill all that well. But Smith's words were heartfelt. If there was anyone in Deadwood who truly loved all mankind, it was Preacher Smith. He spoke of God's mercy and the place prepared in heaven for those who believe. He spoke of the healing power of love and goodness. And then he prayed again, and the service was over.

Steve Utter had carried something up the hill that had a cloth draped over it. Now he moved to the head of the grave and unwrapped the object, which was revealed to be a wooden headstone cut from a single thick slab of pine. It must have been quite heavy, but Steve had carried it with no complaint. He set it up and held it in place while several men with shovels piled dirt and rocks around the base of it.

Earlier in the day, his brother Charley had painted an epi-taph on it:

WILD BILL
J.B. Hickok
killed by the assassin
Jack McCall
in
Deadwood, Black Hills
August 2, 1876
Pard we will
meet again
in the happy
Hunting ground
to part no more.
Good bye
Colorado Charlie
C.H. Utter

Steve stood beside the marker, resting one hand on it, while Charley moved up and knelt on the other side of the grave to stare down one last time at the coffin containing the body of his best friend. A few feet away, off to one side, a photographer had set up a large, bulky camera with a black cloth draped over it and himself as he bent to peer through the lens. Charley didn't pay any attention to the photographer. In fact, he seemed to be lost in his own thoughts, paying no heed to any of the large crowd gathered just below the grave site.

Finally, he sighed and rose to his feet. "So long, Bill," he said as he put his hat on. He walked around the head of the grave and started down the hill toward the settlement. The crowd parted to let him through, and then the others began to follow him. Behind them, dirt rattled on the lid of the coffin as men began to fill in the grave.

Colonel May, who had prosecuted the case against McCall, came alongside Charley and said, "I'm sorry to have failed, Mr. Utter, but I give you my word that I will continue to seek justice in this matter. If not here in Deadwood, then elsewhere."

"Do what you got to do, Colonel," Charley replied in a dull, exhausted voice. "I hate to say it, but I reckon in the end it don't really matter. Won't nothin' bring back Bill."

"No, of course not, but McCall must be made to answer for his crime. And not by vigilante justice, either, but by true law." May hesitated. "You weren't considering avenging this heinous crime yourself, were you, Mr. Utter?"

Colorado Charley laughed, but it was a hollow, humorless sound. "Colonel, if I figured on doin' that, by now McCall would be either full o' lead or swingin' at the end of a rope. No, I'm gonna leave him to the law, and if that don't work out, I'll leave it to the Good Lord to set things straight."

Preacher Smith was close enough to hear that comment, and he nodded. "That's the best attitude to have, brother," he said. "Sooner or later, the Lord will always set things straight."

AL Swearengen leaned back in his chair and grinned in self-satisfaction. "That's it, then," he said. "Hickok's in the ground, McCall's a free man, and we don't have to worry about Varnes anymore. We don't have to worry about a damned thing."

"I'd feel better if McCall was dead, too," Laurette said. "Maybe you better kill him like you killed Varnes."

Swearengen held up his hands. "I never said I killed Varnes."

"You said we didn't have to worry about him anymore. I worry about anybody who's a threat to me unless they're dead."

"Let's just say that I don't think it's likely Johnny Varnes will ever show his face in Deadwood again. He swore to me, though, that McCall didn't know a thing about you and me bein' involved in the plan to get rid of Hickok."

"You figure he was tellin' the truth?" Laurette asked sharply.

"He was too damned scared not to."

She shrugged. "All right, then. We'll leave it at that. I reckon we got lucky."

"Any sign of that Bridges kid?"

"Not a damned one," Laurette said with a frown, "and it still bothers me the way he up and disappeared like that. He's still a loose end. He knows we wanted Hickok dead."

"But he can't prove there's any connection between us and McCall," Swearengen pointed out. "I tell you, we're in the clear on this."

Laurette still didn't look completely convinced, but she said, "Maybe. Now we can start figurin' out what to do about that damned preacher."

She had come up the back stairs of the Gem and into Swearengen's office earlier in the evening so that they could compare notes on the day's events. August 3rd, 1876 had been momentous in Deadwood. First there had been the trial of Jack McCall for Wild Bill Hickok's murder, and then the funeral for the Prince of Pistoleers his own self. This had been perhaps the biggest day in Deadwood's history.

"Smith won't be a problem," Swearengen said. "He's always trampin' off to preach in the other camps. We'll just have somebody follow him and bushwhack him while he's away from the settlement. If whoever guns him hides the body well enough, nobody will ever know what happened to him. It'll be like he disappeared into thin air."

"Just like Bellamy," Laurette said.

Swearengen's forehead creased in a frown. "You think somebody killed the kid and hid the body?"

"It's possible. That would explain why we haven't been able to find him."

"Who'd do that? Who had a grudge against him?"

"Maybe nobody had a grudge against him," Laurette said. "Maybe somebody just cut his throat and robbed him, something like that."

Swearengen nodded slowly. "Yeah, you could be right. Things like that happen all the time in Deadwood. It doesn't really matter, though."

"No," Laurette said. "I suppose it doesn't."

In her heart, however, she was still puzzled by Bellamy's

disappearance, and although she didn't like to admit it, she sort of missed the young man. She had been hoping to take him into her bed again. She hadn't realized until that night with Bellamy that she still enjoyed having a man now and then.

To get her mind off that, she asked, "Who are you gonna have bushwhack the preacher?"

"I don't know," Swearengen replied with a shrug. "It shouldn't be hard to find somebody, though. If it comes down to it, I'll tell Dan Dority or Johnny Burnes to do it. Hell, I might even do it myself."

Laurette's eyes narrowed. "You'd kill a preacher, a man of God?"

Swearengen laughed and said, "You're not gettin' a damned conscience, are you? You were the one who was so anxious to get rid of Smith. He's always bothered you more than me, even though I don't have any use for him, either."

"No, Al, I'm not gettin' a conscience. I just like to know what sort of man I'm partnerin' up with."

"You're plannin' to stay partners with me after this? I thought you hated my guts."

"I do," Laurette said without hesitation. "But Varnes opened my eyes. We can accomplish more together than we can by fightin' with each other. Give us a year or two and we'll own this whole damned end of town. After that . . ." Her shoulders rose and fell eloquently. "We'll see."

"Open season, in other words."

Laurette just smiled, but didn't say anything.

"You may be on to something there," Swearengen went on. "But if we're gonna keep on workin' together, we really ought to be friends . . . or at least pretend to be."

"I can be civil if you can."

"I was thinkin' maybe you'd like to come over here and suck my cock . . . partner."

Laurette smiled. "Why, sure, partner. I can do that. I better warn you, though . . . sometimes I get a mite carried away and I . . . bite."

Swearengen held up a hand, palm out. "On second thought, why don't we just have a drink?"

"Now you're talkin'," Laurette said.

But although she stayed there in Swearengen's office for a while, drinking and plotting, her thoughts kept straying back to the mystery of Bellamy Bridges. . . .

THE past forty-eight hours or so had been pure hell. Dan hadn't gotten much work done during that time, or much sleep. He was afraid to leave Bellamy alone with Ling. The girl was in love with him, and that might lead her to make a bad decision, like untying him. If that ever happened, Bellamy would run off and probably head straight back to Deadwood. Sometimes when he was out of his head he raved about having a showdown with Wild Bill Hickok. He was still bound and determined to get himself killed.

And Dan was just as determined to keep him alive.

So he tried to stay inside the tent as much as possible while Bellamy was awake. Only when the youngster fell asleep, exhausted from all his raging, did Dan venture outside to do a little work or to take care of the camp chores.

Bellamy refused to eat or drink. Dan didn't fight him on that. When he got hungry enough or thirsty enough, he would come around. First he had to get the sickness out of his system. For days before Dan had grabbed him, Bellamy had been living pretty much on whiskey, to the point that his body craved it more than anything else. In his soldiering days, Dan had seen men like that, men who got into fights while they were on a binge and were thrown into the guardhouse for a week or so, and during that week they suffered the torments of the damned. Bellamy did, too, although not as severely as some of the men Dan had seen. He hadn't been drunk long enough for that. But he still thrashed and writhed, and demons that only he could see assaulted him so that he screamed as if the flesh were being torn off his bones. He threw up until there was nothing left in his stomach, and then he had the dry heaves. He pissed his pants. He drenched himself in cold sweat so that the rest of his clothes were soaked.

And all the while he cursed them, screaming about what he would do to them if he ever got free. Ling blanched at some of the things Bellamy said, and Dan made the mental observation that it took an awful lot to make a whore turn pale. If Bellamy ever came back to his senses—no, *when* Bellamy came back to his senses—he was going to be mighty ashamed of himself for some of the things he had said. Assuming he remembered any of them, that is.

Dan had Ling sit at the opening of the tent and keep watch up and down the gulch. Whenever any prospectors came along the creek, Dan stuffed the gag back in Bellamy's mouth to shut him up. He didn't want anybody to hear the crazed shouting coming from inside the tent. If they did, they would think he had a lunatic in there. And for the first couple of days, that was pretty much the truth.

Then, on the second night, Bellamy fell into a deep sleep that lasted for six or seven hours. He was so still Dan began to worry that he had slipped into unconsciousness, rather than a natural sleep. Along toward morning, though, not long before dawn, Bellamy began to stir. Ling was sound asleep, stretched out on some blankets on the other side of the tent, but Dan was sort of awake, sitting cross-legged on the ground beside Bellamy, his head nodding and his chin resting on his chest as he dozed from time to time. He came fully awake and lifted his head as Bellamy moved around as much as the bonds would allow. Bellamy's eyelids fluttered open. He looked around wildly for a few seconds. The interior of the tent was dimly lit by a single candle. His gaze touched Ling's motionless form, then lifted to stare at Dan. He opened his mouth and tried to talk, but his lips and tongue were so dry he couldn't get any words out.

Dan leaned toward him and asked, "You want some water, kid? Something to drink?"

Bellamy's head jerked in a spasmodic nod. Dan dipped a cup in a bucket of creek water and put his other hand behind Bellamy's head, lifting and supporting it as he brought the cup to the young man's mouth. He trickled a little of the water between Bellamy's lips and then moved the cup away.

"M-more!" Bellamy managed to gasp.

"Wait a minute first," Dan said. "If you drink too much too

soon, you'll just heave it right back up. You got to be patient, Bellamy."

After a minute, he gave Bellamy a little more water. Gradually, Bellamy's mouth grew moist enough so that he could talk without too much trouble.

"D-Dan, what am I . . . doing here? Is this . . . your claim?"

"Our claim," Dan said. "You don't remember being here for the past two days?"

Weakly, Bellamy shook his head. "Don't remember anything . . . except bein' in Deadwood . . ." Suddenly, his eyes widened. "You . . . hit me!"

"Yeah, and then I brought you out here. That was two and a half days ago."

Bellamy closed his eyes for a moment and shook his head again. "Don't . . . remember."

Briefly, Dan considered the possibility that Bellamy was faking, trying to get him off his guard. He decided that wasn't the case. The confusion he saw in Bellamy's eyes was too genuine for that. Gaps in the memory were common in people who were in such bad shape, as Bellamy had been.

Dan gave him another swallow of water and said, "Listen, you've been sick, real sick. But I think you're getting better now. Why don't you just lie there and rest, and maybe after a while you'll want something to eat."

Bellamy let out a groan. "I don't think . . . I'll ever be hungry again."

"You'll be surprised," Dan said with a smile.

Bellamy turned his head to look over at Ling again. She was facing the other way, so he couldn't see anything except her back and the long, smooth black hair. "Wh-who's that? Looks sort of like . . . Ling."

"That's who it is. She's been helpin' me take care of you. She's mighty fond of you, Bellamy."

He sighed. "I know. Don't . . . deserve a girl . . . like her . . . I'm not good enough."

Not many men would say they weren't good enough for a mining camp whore. Bellamy was still filled with hate, but most of it was directed at himself now, Dan thought.

A few minutes later, Bellamy dozed off again. His face

was pale and gaunt, but it looked better than it had earlier. He was on the road to recovery. At least, Dan wanted to believe that was true.

Later in the morning, after the sun was up and Ling had awakened and been told the good news, Dan fried some bacon and cooked some flapjacks. The smell of the food cooking must have roused Bellamy. He stirred around for a minute, then opened his eyes to find Ling looking down at him, a smile on her face.

"Good morning," she said. "I hear that you're feeling better."

"I reckon," he said. "Still not sure about . . . everything that's happened."

"Don't worry about any of that," Dan told him. "You feel up to havin' some food and coffee?"

Bellamy licked his lips and then nodded. "You know . . . I believe I do. Can you . . . untie me so I can eat?"

Dan exchanged a glance with Ling. She said, "I think it would be all right."

Dan hoped Bellamy wasn't trying to pull some trick. "All right," he said. "Let's get you sitting up."

After a few minutes, he had Bellamy sitting up with his hands free, but he left the youngster's legs tied just in case, and he made sure there wasn't a gun or any other weapon within reach. He handed Bellamy a tin plate with a couple of flapjacks and some strips of bacon on it. Bellamy began eating hungrily.

"Lord," he muttered, "seems like it's been a week since I had anything to eat."

"Almost that long," Dan said.

"I sure am confused," Bellamy said with a shake of his head. "And I stink to high heaven, too."

"We can do something about that. Got a creek full of nice cold water out there where you can take a bath and wash your clothes."

Bellamy nodded. "After I eat. You said something about coffee?"

"Pot's on the fire outside. I'll go get a cup for you."

He stepped out of the tent, trusting that Ling could handle Bellamy now. Dan didn't expect any trouble. He knelt beside the small cook fire where the coffeepot was boiling and poured a cup for Bellamy.

The sound of a horse's hoofbeats made him look down the gulch toward Deadwood. He couldn't see the settlement from here, but he saw a rider coming toward him.

Quickly, Dan went back inside the tent and handed the cup of coffee to Bellamy. "Somebody's comin'," he announced.

Ling looked up at him, then glanced anxiously at Bellamy, who seemed puzzled by her reaction. "What is it?" the young man asked.

With a tight smile, Dan said, "You've been out of your head while you were here, Bellamy. I've made it a habit to gag you whenever anybody comes by, so they won't hear you yellin'. You reckon I don't need to do that this time?"

Bellamy looked down at the ground, shame on his face. "I won't raise a ruckus," he said quietly. "You've got my word on it, Dan."

"Good enough for me," Dan said with a nod, and he hoped that turned out to be the case.

He ducked back through the tent flap. The rider was only about fifty yards away now, and Dan recognized him as Phin Gordon, who had a claim about half a mile on up the gulch. Gordon raised a hand in greeting and called, "Howdy, Dan."

"Hello, Phin," Dan said as the visitor drew rein. "Haven't seen you in a while."

"I been to Deadwood." Gordon leaned his head in the direction of the settlement. "Rode down there a few days ago to pick up some supplies, and then with all the commotion, I stuck around to see what was goin' to happen."

"Commotion?" Dan repeated with a frown. "What commotion?" He hoped Gordon wasn't talking about his kidnapping of Bellamy. Had somebody besides Ling seen what happened?

"You ain't heard about it?" Gordon asked, sounding amazed. "Hell, I thought everybody in the territory knew by now that Wild Bill's dead."

Dan stiffened. "Hickok's dead?" he asked hollowly.

"Yep. Some drifter name of McCall gunned him down in the Number Ten. Damnedest thing. Just came up behind him and shot him."

Dan felt numb. He hadn't known Hickok all that well, but they had gotten along all right the few times they had met. And Hickok was a legend on the frontier, of course, the sort of bigger-than-life character who it seemed should have lived forever.

Obviously, though, Wild Bill had turned out to be just as mortal as the next man.

"That ain't the damnedest thing about it, though," Phin Gordon went on. "The folks in Deadwood got together a judge and jury and put McCall on trial yesterday mornin'."

"They hang him?"

Gordon shook his head. "Nope. Let him go."

Dan stared at the man. "You mean they found him not guilty?"

"That's right. McCall claimed Hickok had killed his brother a while back and threatened to kill *him,* so I reckon they figured it was self-defense. I hung around for the trial and then went up to the graveyard to watch 'em bury Wild Bill. It was a nice service. Colorado Charley Utter put up a marker for him."

All of this was hard to believe, but Dan had no doubt Gordon was telling the truth. Nobody would make up such a wild story.

This changed things, too. Now there was no danger of Bellamy going back to Deadwood and getting into a gun-fight with Wild Bill.

Hickok wasn't the only gunman in the settlement, though. Bellamy might just set his sights on somebody else.

"Thanks for letting me know, Phin," Dan said. "You want to light for a spell and have some coffee?"

"No, I been away from my claim for long enough already. I couldn't tear myself away from Deadwood, though. I fig-ure I was watchin' history unfold, right in front of my eyes."

Dan nodded. "I reckon so." The death of a man like Wild Bill Hickok probably *would* go down in history.

Gordon rode on up the gulch as Dan went back into the tent. Bellamy looked at him, hollow-eyed and pale. "You heard?" Dan said.

Bellamy nodded. "I heard. Hickok's dead. I remember now . . . I was gonna try to fight him."

"Yeah, and it would've been a damned stupid thing to do, too. He would've killed you."

Bellamy smiled, but the look in his eyes was bleak. "That was just what I wanted. Just what I deserved."

Ling said, "Bellamy, no! You cannot mean that."

"You don't know. . . ." Bellamy shook his head. "You just don't know all the things I've done."

Dan hunkered on his heels so he could look Bellamy in the eye. "Listen to me, kid. The past is over and done with. Everybody's done things they're ashamed of, things they think are so bad they can never atone for them. But that ain't the way it is. Every mornin' when the sun comes up, it's a new day, a new chance."

"You can't change the past," Bellamy said. "Nobody can."

"That's right. But you don't have to let the past control what you do in the future, either. There's nothing to say you can't follow a new trail." Dan reached out and grasped the young man's shoulder. "I been to see the elephant in my time, kid, and if there's one thing I've learned, it's that there are a lot of different ways to get there."

Bellamy looked at him, and tears shone in the young man's eyes. "You really think . . . it's not too late to change?"

"I know it's not. I'll help you. So will Ling. You got a chance, Bellamy. Take it."

Bellamy covered his face with his hands for a moment and took several deep breaths. When he lowered his hands, his eyes were still wet but his face was composed. "You're gonna have to untie my legs," he said. "I can't dig for gold while I'm trussed up like this."

Dan grinned. "You mean . . ."

"I mean this is still half my claim, or at least you keep tellin' me it is. We'd better get to work on it if we ever intend to be a couple of rich men."

Chapter Fifteen

ALTHOUGH the killing of Wild Bill Hickok was the biggest thing to hit Deadwood since the founding of the camp more than six months earlier, life went on for its citizens, and their interests soon turned elsewhere. There was a race coming up, and everybody liked a race. The town was pretty well split in its support between Colorado Charley Utter's Pioneer Pony Express and August Clippinger's Frontier Pony Express. And seeing as how there were quite a few folks in Deadwood who liked to gamble, plenty of wagers were made in the week following Wild Bill's funeral. There was a lot riding on the outcome of this race.

One postscript to Hickok's killing occurred a few days after the burial. Following his acquittal, Jack McCall had decided to remain in the settlement. He was well aware that some folks considered him a murderer and a craven coward, but still, he was the man who had killed Wild Bill Hickok. That was good for a drink every now and then, because there was usually somebody who wanted to hear him talk about how Hickok had killed his brother and how he had settled that blood debt. He spun the yarn so many times that after a while he almost began to believe it was true, even though he knew it was really a load of horseshit.

He wondered what had happened to Johnny Varnes. The gambler must have left town. That was a shame, because McCall knew that he owed his life to Varnes. Without that story Varnes had told him to tell at his trial, he'd be up there in the graveyard with Wild Bill by now. He'd have been strung up for sure.

But Varnes was gone and McCall didn't have any idea where he went, so that was that. If they ever crossed trails again, he would thank the gambler then.

McCall was walking down Main Street one morning, several days after the trial, wondering who he could cadge a drink off of next, when he looked up with bleary eyes and saw a large figure in buckskins striding toward him. Despite the heat, the man wore a bearskin coat. He had a black hat pulled down low over his eyes . . . deep-set eyes that smoldered with rage. Instantly, McCall recognized the craggy, bearded face.

California Joe.

At first McCall had worried that Colorado Charley would come after him, since Utter was supposed to be Hickok's best friend. But Charley seemed to be willing to abide by the jury's decision, whether he liked it or not, and besides, he was still mighty busy getting ready for that race.

California Joe was a different story, though. Joe had a reputation as something of a wild man, and he and Hickok had been good friends, too. McCall thought he remembered hearing something about them scouting together for ol' Yellow Hair Custer. And right now, as he stomped along the street, Joe definitely had blood in his eye.

Nervously, McCall glanced around. Plenty of people were in sight, but he didn't think the presence of witnesses would keep California Joe from doing whatever he wanted to do. For a second McCall thought about turning and running, but that might just provoke Joe into hauling out a hogleg and plugging him in the back. With uncharacteristic courage, McCall decided it would be better to face him and meet whatever Joe had in mind head-on.

Both men came to a stop. About ten feet separated them. California Joe said, "You're that McCall fella, ain't you?"

McCall nodded. "I am."

"You know who I am?"

Again McCall nodded, this time without saying anything.

"I been out o' town," Joe went on. "If I'd been here a few days ago, things would've turned out a heap different."

McCall swallowed, but still didn't say anything. There was no argument he could make. He was just glad California Joe hadn't gone to shooting yet.

Of course, that might be because the big man intended to kill him with his bare hands. . . .

Instead, Joe glared at him for a few seconds and then said, "The air up in these hills is mighty thin for a snake-blooded bastard like you, ain't it?"

McCall's heart leaped with hope. Maybe Joe wasn't going to kill him outright. He nodded and said, "I . . . I reckon."

"Then if I was you, I'd get on my horse—you got a horse?"

McCall's head jerked in the affirmative.

"I'd get on my horse," California Joe went on, "and I'd get the hell outta Deadwood. Might even get outta the Black Hills altogether."

"That . . . that sounds like a mighty fine idea," McCall ventured.

California Joe just glared at him in silence for a long moment. McCall got the idea.

He turned and lit a shuck out of there.

In less than ten minutes, he had gathered what little gear he owned, saddled the sorry pony he had taken in lieu of wages after doing some work at the livery stable, and ridden out of Deadwood, headed south toward God knows where. Anywhere that California Joe wasn't. All Jack McCall was interested in at the moment was putting some distance between himself and that grim-faced frontiersman.

He never came back to Deadwood.

* * *

THE race between the competing Pony Expresses was set to begin on August 10th, a week after the trial of Jack McCall and the burial of Wild Bill Hickok. Dick Seymour had little to do during that week except wait, and he hated waiting. Without something to occupy him, his mind inevitably turned back to the tragic deaths of his wife and children, and the desire for vengeance on Talking Bear that still burned inside him.

But he couldn't deaden his senses with liquor, couldn't distract himself by trying again to find some solace in the arms of a soiled dove. All he could do was wait, and try not to think too much.

Luckily, he had friends in Deadwood, and he spent as much time with them as he could. But Jack Anderson's romance with Jen took up a lot of time, of course, and Leander Richardson was still moping around about Wild Bill's murder, as was Calamity Jane. Dick couldn't blame any of them for feeling as they did. He missed Bill, too. He had known the legendary gunman for several years. He had even gone East along with several other men who had delivered a small herd of buffalo to William F. Cody for use in Cody's theatrical productions, and that was when Wild Bill had been part of Buffalo Bill's troupe, along with that other famed plainsman, Texas Jack Omahundro. Those had been good times, and Dick had enjoyed visiting the East again, where things were more civilized. Not the same as England, of course, but still a welcome change from the frontier.

But he had wound up back out here anyway, too fiddle-footed, as the Americans put it, to stay in any one place for too long. Now he had a job in Deadwood, and quite a few friends, and he realized that once again, he was in the process of putting down roots, just as he had done with Carries Water and their children.

He couldn't allow that, he decided as he was eating breakfast by himself in the Grand Central Hotel's dining room on the day before the race. A man who settled in one place, a man who surrounded himself with friends and even loved ones, ran a terrible risk.

The risk of having it all ripped away from him, leaving

him little more than an empty husk of a man whose only real feeling was pain.

He couldn't stand that. Not again. Soon he was going to have to move on. But not until after the race, of course. He owed Charley his best effort. That was why he wasn't allowing himself to become sodden with drink.

After finishing his breakfast, he went outside and paused on the porch of the hotel. His eyes narrowed slightly as he watched a stranger ride past. Long dark hair hung down to the man's shoulders under a flat-brimmed black hat. He glanced at Dick without interest, but that brief flick of dark eyes was enough to make the Englishman stiffen. He had looked into the eyes of killers before and seen the icy menace there, and the gaze of this newcomer to Deadwood was just as potent.

But then the man rode on and Dick turned away, already forgetting the stranger as his own concerns crowded back into his mind. He walked toward Colorado Charley's camp.

Charley was in his tent, writing letters to merchants in Cheyenne, trying to drum up business for the freight line he was putting in, too, in addition to the Pony Express. Dick pulled up a stool and sat down. Charley glanced up from the table where he was working and asked, "Somethin' I can do for you, Dick?"

"No, not really. I'm just killing time."

Charley grunted. "Sounds to me like you need a poker game . . . or a woman."

Dick grimaced. "I think not, especially the latter."

Charley put his pen back in its holder and corked the bottle of ink. "You know, Dick," he said, "you ain't ever been one to talk much about yourself. I know you come from England, and I know you used to be a buffalo hunter and a Injun trader, but that's about all."

"That's really all there is to say," Dick responded with a shrug. "I've led a very uninteresting life."

Charley snorted. "Now, I know that ain't true. A fella who's spent as many years on the frontier as you have is bound to have done some things and been some places. You want to talk about it?"

Dick hesitated. In a way, it would feel good to spill his guts. Telling his story might have a purgative effect. From his poverty-stricken boyhood in London's slums, his acting career, the debacle that had led to his banishment from England, all the way to his marriage to Carries Water and her murder at the hands of Talking Bear and the other members of the Sioux war party . . . It was quite a story, all right, the stuff of a penny dreadful. No doubt Charley would be entertained by it. To Dick, though, it wasn't an entertainment. It was his life. And most of the memories it brought with it were painful ones.

He shook his head. "No, Charley, I'm afraid you'd be terribly bored." He put his hands on his knees and pushed himself to his feet. "I can see you're busy, so I'll shove along. Sorry to have kept you from your work."

"Don't worry about it. You're always welcome here." Charley smiled sadly. "Hell, us friends o' Wild Bill got to stick together, don't we?"

"I suppose so," Dick said, but even as he spoke, the feeling inside him was stronger than ever. It was time for him to move on. By the time the race was done, it would be past time, but he could wait that long, he supposed. One last thing . . . for the memory of Wild Bill.

So Wild Bill Hickok was dead. Titus was surprised by the news when he heard a couple of men talking about it in the first saloon he came to. His trail hadn't crossed that of Hickok for years, not since Hickok had been marshal in Abilene. Titus had come up the trail from Texas with a herd of his brother's cattle, helping to drive them across Indian Territory from the ranch on the Brazos. That was when Titus had decided that he'd had enough of being a cowhand and working for his little brother. When the rest of the outfit went back to Texas, he stayed behind in Abilene, figuring he'd make a living for a while as a gambler. He had been on the street that night when Wild Bill shot Phil Coe and then gunned down his friend Mike Williams. It was quite a thing to see.

Unfortunately for Titus, he wasn't a good enough gambler to support himself. But he had always been good at hunting, and he was a crack shot with both a rifle and a handgun. He didn't mind killing, either. The war had taught him that, first at Fredericksburg, then in that damned Yankee prison camp, and finally riding with Mosby in the Shenandoah Valley. So, thinking that a man was a fool not to use his natural talents, he became a manhunter. Lots of men had bounties on their heads, and most were payable whether the hombre in question was dead or alive. Dead was usually simpler.

The Grand Central was the best hotel in town, but it was full up. Titus settled for a tiny room in another hotel. After he had cached what little gear he had there, he set out to find a drink and something to eat. That was when he'd heard about Wild Bill's murder. He was in a place called the Gem Theater. Despite the name, and an area where some chairs were set up in front of a tiny stage that was empty at the moment, the place wasn't really a theater. It was a saloon and whorehouse and gambling den, and a pretty successful one, from the looks of it. All the tables were occupied, men were lined up at the bar, and there was a steady procession of whores and their customers up and down the stairs to the second floor.

Titus shoved his empty glass across the hardwood to the bartender, a bulky, bearded man in a stained apron. The bartender picked up a bottle, but hesitated about refilling the glass until Titus dug out a coin and dropped it on the bar. Then and only then did the man splash more whiskey into the glass.

As he picked up the drink, Titus said, "A man'd think you didn't trust him, friend."

"You're a stranger in Deadwood, mister," the bartender said, "else you'd know that the man who owns this place don't have many friends."

"That'd be you?"

"Not hardly. Al Swearengen owns the Gem. Maybe you've heard of him."

Titus smiled thinly and shook his head. "Nope."

"Well, he's not a man to cross, and he likes to have cash on the barrelhead from strangers. If you stick around Deadwood for a while and we get to know you, might come a day when you can run a tab. Until then . . ."

"I probably won't be here that long." Titus downed the whiskey.

"Come here to look for gold, have you?"

Titus set the glass on the bar. "Do I look like a damned prospector to you?"

"Well, come to think of it . . . no, I don't reckon you do. I won't ask you your business. Wouldn't be polite."

"No. It wouldn't." Titus looked around the room. "Can I get something to eat here?"

"Sure, if you're not lookin' for anything fancy. There's a pot o' beans on the stove in back, and some cornbread."

Titus saw a table open up as a couple of men staggered out of the Gem. "Send a big plate of it over to that table," he instructed the bartender. "And right now give me a beer."

The bartender filled a mug and handed it to him. Titus carried the beer over to the table and sat down to wait for his dinner.

He hadn't been there more than a couple of minutes when a short woman with tightly curled blond hair sat down in one of the empty chairs. She wore stockings, garters, and a shift that was unlaced at the top so that it hung open enough to reveal the cleft between her breasts. "Howdy," she said. "I'm Tit Bit. They call me that 'cause I'm so small, but if you want to nibble on my tits, I don't mind that, neither, as long as you ain't too rough about it."

"Hello, Tit Bit," Titus said. "I don't recall askin' you to join me."

She shrugged, which made her breasts move under the shift. "You looked like you could use some company."

"What you mean is, I looked like I might be willin' to pay to take you upstairs and fuck you."

She frowned and said, "Well, you don't have to make it sound so dirty. If you didn't know what goes on in a place like this when you came in, you'd have to be pretty damn stupid."

"You're right," Titus said as he inclined his head in acknowledgment of her argument. "You want a drink, Tit Bit?"

"Sure."

When a waiter gal brought his food, he ordered a drink for the whore. "Hope you ain't in a hurry," he said to her. "Been a long time since I ate, and I'd like to fill my belly before I take you upstairs."

She reached across under the table and cupped a hand over his groin, squeezing. "You just go right ahead and eat, honey. I like my men to be at full strength. Wouldn't want you passin' out from hunger while you were ridin' me."

While he ate, she kept up a steady stream of talk, but he ignored most of it. He wasn't interested in anything she had to say. He had loved only one woman in his life, and he had married her. Then she had betrayed him and wound up dead—not by his hand, mind you, although for a while there he had been so crazy he might have killed her. But that had been enough romance for him. Now he bought a little time with a woman when he had to have one, and that arrangement seemed to work out just fine.

When he was finished with the beans and cornbread and the beer, he got to his feet. Tit Bit stood up, too, and took hold of his right hand. "You ready to go upstairs, honey?" she asked.

Without making a big deal of it, he took his hand back from her. A man in his line of work couldn't afford to have somebody clinging to his gun hand, not even a pretty little whore. He put his left arm around her waist instead and said, "Come on, darlin'."

As he started up the stairs with her, he reflected that he could have made a pretty penny in Deadwood. Here in the Gem alone, he had already spotted three men who had reward dodgers out on them. They probably had friends, though, and he'd have to kill them, too, if he wanted to take the wanted men, and he hated to work when there was no profit in it. Then there would be the problem of getting the bodies back to Cheyenne or somewhere civilized so he could collect the bounties on them. The corpses would stink like shit by the time he got there. No, it was better to stick to one job at a time, to go after the one man he had come to Deadwood to find. He'd take the bastard alive if possible. Under the circumstances, that might be best.

"Here we go, right down here," Tit Bit said as they reached the balcony. She led him to a door and opened it, revealing a narrow, cramped room with no furniture except for a bed with a sagging corn-shuck mattress and a rickety table with a basin of water on it. No chair, no pictures on the wall, no window. He'd seen jail cells with more charm and personality. But he supposed the room would serve its purpose.

After she had closed the door, Tit Bit reached down, grasped the hem of her shift, and peeled it up and over her head, leaving her nude except for the stockings and garters. The thick bush between her legs sort of surprised Titus. It was blond like the hair on her head. She stretched out on the bed and spread her thighs.

"Wash your pecker off before you stick it in, all right, honey?"

Titus figured he was in more danger of catching something from her than vice versa, but he didn't argue. He took off his hat and duster and hung them on one of the bedposts at the foot of the bed. He unbuckled his gun belt and coiled it on the table next to the basin. His boots, shirt, and trousers went into a pile on the floor. That left him in his socks and the bottom half of a pair of long underwear. He unbuckled the fly and took out his erect penis.

"That's a nice one, honey, nice and big," Tit Bit said. "Gonna make me feel real good, I'll bet."

He knew she said that exact same thing twenty or thirty times a night. It didn't bother him. He wasn't going to delude himself into thinking that this meant any more than it really did, which was nothing except a little physical release. When he was ready, he climbed onto the bed, positioned himself between her legs, and entered her. She gasped as if she had never experienced such a thing before.

Then she started clutching at him and pumping her hips and moaning softly, and he knew damned good and well she was just trying to get him to finish off in a hurry so that she could go downstairs and bring some other horny bastard up here. She had already wasted enough time on him by waiting while he ate his supper. She had probably done that only because she was tired and wanted to rest for a few minutes. When they were done, she was likely to try to charge him for that time, too.

He had a contrary streak in him, always had, ever since he was a kid. The harder the whore tried to make him come, the more he was determined to make it last as long as possible. The going rate was always so many dollars a fuck, no matter how long it took. He wasn't going to pay her for sitting with him downstairs, either. She was going to have to earn her two or three dollars this time.

"Oh, it's so good, so good!" she gasped. "Finish me off, finish me off!"

Titus kept humping. He barely heard her words of simulated passion. He let his mind roam backward instead, thinking about his boyhood on the farm in Virginia, how he had enjoyed wandering through the woods and hunting, just him and his rifle and sometimes a good dog. Sure, he had felt the stirrings of wanderlust even then, and he wasn't all that fond of farming, but he probably would have spent the rest of his life there anyway if the war hadn't come along and changed everything. Ruined everything. Like a lot of other Confederates, he had seen that it was going to be impossible to stay there and live under the thumbs of the hated Yankees. So he had come West with the rest of his family and drifted into bounty hunting. He hadn't seen his mother or any of his brothers or his sister for more than five years. That was just fine with him, too. It had been a long time since he had felt truly close to any of them.

"Damn it, ain't you ever gonna come?"

The exasperated question burst out of Tit Bit. Titus grinned coldly as he drove into her. "You want me to come, you gotta answer a question," he told her.

"What?" she grated, clearly angry now.

"Is there a preacher in Deadwood?"

The question shocked her. She stopped pumping her hips and stared up at him. "A preacher?" she repeated in astonishment.

"Yeah. Tall, skinny fella, maybe with a beard. Might call himself Smith."

"That's Preacher Smith. He's here in Deadwood, all right. Makes a damned nuisance of himself standin' on the street with all his sin-shoutin'. Us girls can't even walk outside without him callin' us harlots and tellin' us we need to repent and give up our wicked ways."

"That's just what I . . . uh! . . . wanted to know," Titus said as he thrust into her one last time and emptied himself.

It had been a long search, but he had found what he was looking for.

Chapter Sixteen

A banner stretched across Main Street from false front to false front, tied in place with ropes. In big letters it had painted on it THE GREAT PONY EXPRESS RACE. Below that, in smaller letters, was written *Deadwood, Black Hills, Dakota Territory—1876!* The race itself would start from a point directly under that banner, and it would finish there as well, because the first man to return and ride under the banner with fifty copies of the Cheyenne *Daily Leader* would be the winner, and the Pony Express he represented would become solely responsible for the mail route between Deadwood and Fort Laramie.

Dick Seymour felt excitement coursing through him as he stood next to the long-legged bay gelding that would carry him on the first leg of the race. Charley and Steve Utter, the Street brothers, Jack Anderson, and Leander Richardson all surrounded him, slapping him on the back and wishing him good luck. "Take it easy, boys," Dick told them with a grin. "You're going to knock all the fight out of me before the race even starts."

"I doubt that," Charley said. He had a big smile on his

face. Though he was still mourning Bill Hickok's death, he wasn't one to live in the past. This race represented a great deal to him, Dick knew. That was one reason he wanted to win. Charley had been a good friend.

And he had promised a sizable bonus if Dick won, as well. That money would allow him to travel elsewhere, now that his time in Deadwood was coming to an end.

The street was thronged with people. Some of them had gotten a brass band together—Lord knows where they had found the instruments—and the musicians were playing badly but loudly, trying to make up with enthusiasm what they lacked in talent. The betting was still going on as well; wagers on Dick and on Jed Powell flew fast and furiously.

Calamity Jane forced herself through the crowd and came up to Dick, taking him by surprise as she threw her arms around him and planted a big kiss on his mouth. Sort of like that brass band, Calamity tried to overcome her natural shortcomings with enthusiasm. She tasted like whiskey and tobacco and smelled of sweat and bear grease, but Dick had to admit that her kiss had a certain passion and intensity about it. He was surprised to find himself reacting to it.

But then, thankfully, she pulled back, grinned at him, and smacked a fist against his upper arm hard enough to leave a bruise. "Good luck, you goddamn Englisher!" she said, raising her voice to be heard over the blatting of the musicians and the hubbub of the crowd.

"Thanks, Calam," Dick told her. "I'm sure I'll need every bit of good fortune I can muster."

"Naw, you'll win. That skunk Powell don't have a chance."

Dick hoped she was right, but somehow he doubted it. Powell was a ruthless competitor, and Dick knew that Clippinger would have urged him to do whatever was necessary to win. He expected a few dirty tricks along the way.

General Dawson climbed onto a podium that had been erected in front of the Grand Central Hotel, underneath one end of the banner. He held up his hands for silence, but no one paid any attention to him. He tried to shout, but couldn't overcome the noise of the crowd. Finally, he motioned Seth Bullock up onto the podium with him and said something into

Bullock's ear. Bullock nodded, drew his gun, and thumbed off two quick shots into the air.

The twin reports finally succeeded in quieting the crowd. They weren't silenced completely, but the noise died down enough for the General to raise his arms again and bellow, "Ladies and gents, we're almost ready for the start of the big race!"

That brought cheers and whoops and applause. This time when the General signaled for quiet, the crowd cooperated and Bullock didn't have to shoot into the air again.

"Representing Colorado Charley Utter and the Pioneer Pony Express is that well-known frontiersman, former buffalo hunter and scout . . . Bloody Dick Seymour!"

That introduction stretched the truth somewhat, Dick thought as he waved his hat over his head in acknowledgment of the cheers from the crowd. He had never been a scout for the Army. But of course it didn't really matter.

"And riding for August Clippinger and the Frontier Pony Express, the stalwart Jedidiah Powell!"

More cheers went up. Clippinger and Powell had their supporters in Deadwood. Powell waved his hat in the air as he stood next to his first mount, an ugly, hammer-headed roan. Looks didn't matter in a race, though, only speed and stamina. Dick suspected that the roan had plenty of both of those qualities.

Powell turned and glared at Dick as he clapped his high-crowned hat back onto his head. Dick just smiled faintly. He wasn't interested in getting into a staring contest with Powell. This competition would be settled elsewhere, in the hills and on the plains between Deadwood and Fort Laramie.

"You all know the rules," General Dawson went on. "Each man will ride from here to Fort Laramie, where he will pick up fifty copies of the Cheyenne *Daily Leader*. First man back here with all his copies of the newspaper will be declared the winner!" He looked down at Dick and Jed Powell. "Are the riders ready?"

Dick just nodded curtly, but Powell shouted, "Goddamn right I'm ready! Ready to win this race!"

That brought more cheers from his supporters. The General waved them down, then turned to Seth Bullock, who still stood beside him on the podium. "Mr. Bullock, if I might borrow your firearm . . . ?"

"Sure thing, General," Bullock said as he drew his gun and handed it over.

Charley grasped Dick's hand and pumped it hard for a second. "Good luck, Dick," he said. "I know you won't let me down."

"Thanks, Charley. I'll do my best."

The General bellowed, "Riders in their saddles!" and Dick and Powell swung up onto their mounts. The General waved an arm. "Clear the street! Clear the street!"

The crowd split and moved back, creating an opening more than wide enough for two horses. The bay was skittish under Dick's saddle. He tightened his grip on the reins. The horse was ready for this race to start . . . and so was he.

The General thrust the revolver into the air. "Ready, gentlemen! On my signal . . ." He squeezed the trigger, and the gun cracked sharply. "Go!"

The two horses lunged forward, and the race was under way.

Side by side, the roan and the bay thundered down Deadwood's Main Street, past the Langrishe Theater and Nye's Opera House, past the Bon Ton Restaurant and the Senate Saloon and Shroudy's Butcher Shop, past the tin shop and Bullock & Star Hardware, past the Bella Union and the No. 10 and the Academy for Young Ladies and the Gem. The drunks and the gamblers and the whores had turned out to watch the beginning of the race like everyone else in Deadwood. They whooped and cheered as the riders flew past. One of the whores took her breasts out of her dress and shook them up and down. On past the Badlands and Chinatown and then into the sweeping curve as the trail turned south. Dick glanced over at Powell and saw that for now at least, the man was concentrating on his riding. Powell wouldn't try anything this close to Deadwood, Dick told himself. But he was still watchful and prepared if Powell tried to swerve his horse into the bay or attempted to slash him across the face with his quirt. Dick wouldn't put anything past the man.

Deadwood fell behind, and now it was just the two of them, riding hell-bent-for-leather through the hills. The trail twisted back and forth, taking the path of least resistance as trails usually do. The bay took the turns tightly, obeying the gentle tugs on the reins and the slightest pressure from Dick's knees. He was a good horse, not the best that Dick would ride in this race, but not the worst, either. Dick had picked the bay because he knew the animal would give him a chance for a good start.

The settlement was completely out of sight now, but the trail led beside scattered camps set up by miners working their claims. When the men heard the drumming hoofbeats, they stopped their work and came down to the trail to cheer the riders on. Some waved their hats over their heads while others fired guns in the air and whooped. Everybody in the vicinity of Deadwood had heard about the race. It was news as far away as Cheyenne, maybe even beyond that.

The bay began to pull ahead slightly. Dick felt a surge of excitement, even though he knew the competition had barely gotten under way. It would take at least three days to reach Fort Laramie. Dick's common sense overcame his enthusiasm and forced him to pull back on the reins. He slowed the bay, and Powell went past, still riding hard.

Leaving Deadwood at a gallop was fine. That was what the crowd expected, and enough showmanship had rubbed off on Dick from his time with Wild Bill, Colorado Charley, and Buffalo Bill for him to know that. But the race would be won with steadiness as much as speed. He pulled in the reins even more and brought the bay down to a rhythmic, ground-eating lope. Powell increased the lead. He looked back over his shoulder and leered at Dick as he pulled away.

The man was a fool, Dick told himself. He was going to ride that poor roan right into the ground.

Powell gradually pulled ahead until there was a gap of at least two hundred yards between him and Dick. Unworried, Dick kept going at the same speed. After half an hour, Powell's roan began to slow. The gap between the two riders lessened. Dick didn't try to catch up, however. He was content to hang back and save some of his mount's strength. They were in this for the long haul.

The race had started at approximately ten o'clock in the morning. It was a little after noon when Dick rode into the mining camp known as Lead, where he would change horses for the first time. By now Jed Powell was only about fifty yards ahead of him, and the roan was staggering. Dick felt a surge of anger when he saw the condition the horse was in. Powell hadn't accomplished a damned thing by pushing his mount so hard except to possibly break down the animal so that it would never be any good again.

Dick reined in and swung down in front of a pole corral where a bearded old-timer waited for him, along with a couple of young Mexicans. "Get that saddle off and onto the black," the oldster snapped at the hostlers, who hurried to carry out the order. The old man shook hands with Dick. "Clippinger's rider is ahead of you," he said.

"Not enough to matter," Dick said, "and he's ruined his horse. The bay will be ready to go again if I need him on the return trip."

"Yeah, I reckon that's right enough. Don't you be dawdlin', though. I got money bet on you, son. And Colorado Charley's an old friend o' mine, so I want him to get that mail route."

"I'll do my best," Dick promised. The hostlers had his saddle on a leggy black now. They finished cinching it into place and moved back. Dick grasped the horn, put his foot in the stirrup, and stepped up onto the horse. He had the animal trotting along Lead's only street almost before his rear end hit the saddle.

As quick as the transfer had been, though, Powell had changed horses just as quickly. Once again the two men and their mounts were almost side by side. Powell looked over and sneered. "You don't have a damned chance," he called, unwittingly echoing what Calamity Jane had said earlier about him.

Dick didn't waste any breath replying.

Powell appeared to have learned his lesson. He held his

horse in this time instead of letting it race all out. This time it was Dick who pulled out to a small lead, although he wasn't pushing his mount at all. Powell had to be really holding back. Either that, or he had miscalculated badly in picking the horse he rode now. By the time an hour had passed, Powell was so far back Dick couldn't see him anymore.

That was when he began to worry.

This was the main trail to Fort Laramie, the one used by wagon trains traveling to Deadwood and also by the regular riders of the competing Pony Expresses. But there were other trails, and some of them that Dick wasn't aware of might be known to Powell. Chances were that other trails wouldn't be any faster than this one, but there was no guarantee of that. Powell might know a shortcut.

That wasn't the only worry. Powell could be trying to get around his opponent so that he could set up some sort of ambush.

That thought had just gone through Dick's brain when he heard the whipcrack of a rifle shot. The black leaped wildly under him and screamed in pain. Instinctively, Dick tightened his knees and his grip on the reins and struggled to bring the horse under control. He saw a crimson streak on the black's shoulder where the bullet had creased it.

Another shot blasted. The bullet kicked up dust near the horse's rear hooves and made it lunge forward. Dick knew his best chance might be to let the horse run. When it tired itself out, then he could get it to settle down. So he gave the black its head, drew his gun, and searched for the source of the shots.

A thickly wooded ridge rose to his left and ran for about a hundred yards. He figured that would be a good place for the bushwhacker to hide, and he watched for a telltale plume of powder smoke as he waited for another shot.

That third shot didn't come. Dick turned his attention back to the trail in front of him. At the far end of the ridge rose a bald, rocky knob, its steep slopes littered with boulders. The trail went right past a looming shoulder of that knob.

Movement atop the rise caught Dick's eye. A rock a couple

of feet in diameter began to roll down the slope, picking up speed as it did so. It slammed into another small boulder and started that one rolling, too. In a matter of seconds, several other boulders were moving, knocked loose from their precarious perches by the rocks dropping down on them from above.

Dick stiffened in the saddle. The rock slide that was developing on the knob would sweep down over the trail and cover it. And the black, crazed by the pain of the bullet crease on its shoulder, was stampeding right into the path of the small but potentially deadly avalanche. The horse ignored Dick's efforts to rein it to a halt. Horse and rider flashed ahead, and the rocks tumbling toward them picked up steam.

Dick considered jerking his feet from the stirrups and leaving the saddle in a dive, but at this speed that might prove fatal, too. Another thought that flashed through his mind was that the bushwhacker had to be Jed Powell. Powell had deliberately creased the black and fired around its hooves to stampede it. Then he had hurried over to the top of the knob and started that first rock rolling. He'd probably had it poised and ready to fall.

It was a friendishly clever plan, Dick thought. If the boulders caught him and the horse, they would be crushed, but when their bodies were dug out of the rock slide, no one would be able to find any bullet wounds on them. The crease on the horse's shoulder would be overlooked as part of the damage from the falling rocks. No one would ever be able to lay the blame for what happened at the feet of Jed Powell.

He wasn't going to let Powell put him out of the race with such a dirty trick. Not on the very first day, not ever. Dick jammed his gun back in its holster, lashed the horse with the reins, leaned forward, and raked the animal's flanks with his spurs. The black, too caught up in its frenzy to be halted or even veered from the trail, responded by stretching out and galloping even faster.

Clouds of dust had begun to billow up from the rock slide. Seconds stretched out and seemed to become minutes. Dick urged every bit of speed he could get out of the black. A large rock slammed into the trail in front of them, bounced high in the air, and rolled off to the side. Other rocks, fist-sized or smaller, pelted down around them. One hit the horse on the rump and made it leap forward even more frenziedly. From the corner of his eye Dick spotted a boulder coming at him from the left and leaned far forward over the horse's neck. The boulder missed them, barely. Dust clogged Dick's mouth and nose and stung his eyes.

Then, suddenly, they were past the knob. Rocks still thundered down, but the boulders fell behind horse and rider now. They were clear.

And the black was tiring, just as Dick had thought it would. The horse stampeded full out for another hundred yards or so and then began to slow. Dick hauled back on the reins, and this time the horse responded. He wheeled the black around and looked back at the trail where it was now blocked by a pile of boulders. The dust was settling slowly.

Not wanting to carry the extra weight, Dick hadn't brought a rifle with him, only a handgun. Powell had had a Winchester sheathed in a saddle boot, he recalled. He was more convinced than ever that Powell was behind this attempt on his life. His eyes scanned the knob and the wooded ridge beyond it, looking for any sign of movement. He didn't see anything, and no one took any more shots at him.

Powell must have been bitterly disappointed when he saw his quarry outrun the rock slide. He didn't want to openly gun Dick down, though, because a killing like that might come back to haunt him. It might turn people against his employer, August Clippinger, too.

So, clearly, Powell had no compunctions about killing him, Dick thought—he just wanted to make it look like an accident.

If that was the way Powell wanted to run this race, then so be it. Dick wasn't going to stoop to his level and become a bushwhacker himself. If Powell made another try for him, though, Dick intended to fight back, and if Powell wound up dead, that was just too damned bad.

"Come on, horse," he said as he turned the black to the south again. "Let's see how much sand you've got left."

Chapter Seventeen

THE beginning of the race had drawn more men than usual into Deadwood, and that meant more business than usual for the Academy. One thing was certain any time you got a bunch of fellas together: At least some of them were going to want to get laid. So Laurette had her girls working hard that evening. She had told them to get their customers off as quickly as they could, so that they could move on to whoever was next. She stopped short of checking the rooms to make sure the girls were following her orders, but she spent the evening in the parlor and kept a pretty close eye on the comings and goings, so to speak. Traffic was brisk, just the way she liked it. Get 'em in, get 'em off, get 'em out.

No whorehouse could function for very long without having somebody around to keep trouble under control. Fletch had taken care of that chore for a while, until he'd gotten all high-and-mighty on her; then Bellamy Bridges had taken his place. Since Bellamy had disappeared, Laurette had been forced to find somebody else. She had settled on a man named Fontaine, a hulking Creole from New Orleans. Like most Frenchmen, he would back down if he was pushed hard enough, but his size and his glowering countenance kept most men from pushing him. He worked cheap, too. He was more interested in guzzling wine and getting his cock sucked than he was in being paid. Like a lot of men who spent most of their time in Deadwood's Badlands, he had come to the Black Hills to look for gold and then discovered how hard that work really was.

Laurette was in the parlor and so was Fontaine when one of the girls came hurrying in from her room. She was breathless and had a stained sheet wrapped around her nudity. She said, "Miss Laurette, the fella in my room's gone crazy! You gotta do somethin' about him!"

"I told you, hon, some gents like to stick it up a gal's ass. You'll get used to it," Laurette assured her.

The girl shook her head. "It ain't that. I wouldn't mind that. He's drunk, and I'm afraid he's gonna slap me around!"

Laurette frowned. That did present a dilemma. A whore had to expect a certain amount of rough treatment every now and then. It went with the territory, because some men figured if they were paying for it, they had a right to handle the merchandise however they wanted to. Laurette could understand that point of view.

On the other hand, a whore with her teeth knocked out, or with so many bruises that paint and powder couldn't cover them up, wasn't going to get as many customers and wasn't going to make as much money. *That* was unacceptable.

"Fontaine, go have a talk with the fella," Laurette ordered. "Tell him to take it easy or he'll have to leave."

"Oui, madame," Fontaine said with a bob of his shaggy head. He followed the nervous whore back down the hall.

A few moments later, a shot rang out back there and somebody yelled. "Shit!" Laurette said as she hurried toward the scene of the disturbance.

When she threw the door open, she found the whore huddled in a corner, Fontaine backed against the wall, and a drunken, bearded miner with his pants down and a gun in his hand. As the barrel swung toward her, she held her hands up, backed off, and said, "Whoa, partner! Put that hogleg down, and won't nobody get hurt."

"I am already hurt!" Fontaine cried. He had a hand clapped to the side of his head. Blood welled brightly between his fingers. "This pig has shot my ear off!"

Fontaine had a gun of his own on his hip, but he hadn't drawn it. Big surprise there, Laurette thought.

"I wasn't gonna hurt her," the miner protested. "I just like to squeeze a gal's neck a little when I'm with her."

Laurette had seen more than one whore choked to death under just those circumstances. She didn't blame the girl for not wanting any part of that. She said, "Look, mister, why don't you pull your pants up and come on out to the parlor with me? We'll have ourselves a drink, and maybe you can find yourself another gal who ain't so skittish."

The miner waved the pistol around, trying to point it at the whore in the corner, who sniffled in terror. "Don't want no other gal! I want this'un! And get that goddamn Frenchy outta here. I ain't a-scared o' him. Since that kid gunman o' yours went back to minin', you ain't got nobody here I'm a-scared of."

Laurette frowned. "What did you say?"

"I said I ain't a-scared—"

"No, about that kid who used to work here. You've seen him?"

The miner snorted. "Hell, yeah! He's workin' a claim up Deadwood Gulch with his old partner. I seen him up there a day or two ago. Saw that little Chinese whore who used to work here, too. Damn, she was a good'un. Had one o' the tightest pussies I ever—"

The derringer Laurette had slipped out of the sleeve of her dress barked just then, and the .32-caliber ball hit the miner in the right eye and jerked his head back as it bored on into his brain. The gun in his hand roared as his finger clenched involuntarily on the trigger. The bullet went into the floor at Fontaine's feet and made him jump and yelp. The whore screamed. The miner arched his back and tottered there for a second while his bowels let go explosively. Then he fell backward and landed in his own shit, twitching a couple of times as he died.

"*Madame,* you . . . you killed him!" Fontaine said.

"Hell, yes, I killed him," Laurette said. "The way he was wavin' that gun around, he might've shot any of us. He might've shot *me*." Calmly, she tucked the derringer back in her sleeve. "Haul him outta here and clean up the mess."

"But what . . . what should I do with him?"

Laurette grimaced in frustration. Here she had some important thinking to do, and she had to take the time to explain the simplest chores to this Frenchman.

"There's a bunch of deep ravines all over these hills. Do I have to draw you a damned picture, Fontaine?"

He shook his head. From the look on his face, he was scared she might decide to shoot *him*. "No, no, *madame*. I will attend to it immediately."

"See that you do," Laurette snapped. To the still-frightened whore, she added, "There's customers in the parlor. Go get you one."

Laurette went back to her office, walked over to the desk, leaned on it. Her pulse pounded in her head. She wasn't bothered all that much by killing the miner, although she had known a second of fear when she thought he might jerk the gun toward her before pulling the trigger. But that was over now, and she could think about what the man had said before he died.

Bellamy had gone back to the claim he had shared with Dan Ryan. He had abandoned her and all her plans and returned to prospecting, and he had taken Ling with him.

That son of a bitch! Did he honestly think she was going to let him get away with that?

Tomorrow she was going up the gulch to pay a visit to that claim, and Bellamy had better have a damned good explanation for what he had done, she thought. If he didn't, he was going to be one sorry bastard. He was going to regret ever coming to the Black Hills.

Hell, he was going to regret ever being born!

THE Reverend Henry Winston Smith lugged an empty wooden crate along the alley. He had just found the crate in back of the Bella Union and planned to take it out to Main Street, set it up in a good place, climb on top of it, and start spreading the Word. He was always on the lookout for a suitable box he could use as a pulpit. After he stood on them for a while, the boards usually began to crack, or they got so dirty from being placed in the street, with all its animal waste, that he had to throw them away and start over fresh.

Just like people had to throw away their sins and start fresh, he thought. Perhaps he could use that comparison in one of his sermons.

A grunting sound caught his attention. He looked over at the rear door of the Academy for Young Ladies and saw someone backing through it into the alley. Whoever it was had bent over and was dragging something. Smith stepped closer and asked, "Can I help you with your task, brother?"

The man jumped and let out a yelp. *"Mon dieu!"* he exclaimed as he turned toward Smith. His hand went to the butt of the gun on his hip. He stopped the motion without drawing the weapon. He stared into the shadows and asked, "Who's there? Is that you, Padre?"

"Yes, it's me," Smith said. He recognized the man now. "How are you, Brother Fontaine?"

"Merde, I almost shot you," Fontaine muttered. He turned back to whatever he had been dragging. Smith moved to one side to look past the Frenchman, and he stiffened as he saw the man lying half in and half out of the Academy's rear door.

"Is that man ill?" he asked.

"No, Padre, he's not feelin' a thing," Fontaine said.

"He's . . . dead?"

"Oui."

"What happened?"

"Better for you not to know." Fontaine bent and grasped the dead man's legs. "Now excuse me, Padre, I got to tend to this."

"But . . . but where are you taking him? He has to be buried properly. There should be a service for him. . . ."

"No offense, but he don't deserve bein' fussed over. I'll take care of him, don't worry."

"Everyone deserves to have their immortal soul commended to God when they pass from this earth," Smith said. "I insist—"

"Forget it, Padre," Fontaine said, and his tone didn't allow any argument. "Go on about your business, and I'll go about mine." He started dragging the corpse down the alley.

Smith just stood there, unsure what to do. If there had been a lawman of some sort in Deadwood, he would have gone to see the man and reported this. But General Dawson was the closest thing to a legal official in the settlement, and Smith knew he wouldn't do anything about it. Murder—if indeed that crime had been committed—was no concern of the federal government, the General would say.

Fontaine and his grisly burden were almost out of sight in the shadows now. Smith sighed. He had no choice but to go on about his business, as the Frenchman had advised. But this incident was going to weigh heavily on his heart. He would have to pray that he had made the right decision.

He had just turned toward the street when a voice said out of the darkness, "Howdy, Preacher."

Smith stopped. He couldn't see the man who had spoken, but the voice was unfamiliar to him. "Who are you?" Smith said. "Where are you?"

A low, cold chuckle sounded. "Reckon you could call me your guardian angel. I been keepin' an eye on you. If that fella had pulled his gun, I would've dropped him."

"I appreciate the concern, brother. Step out of the shadows where I can see you, and we'll talk."

"You mean you'll preach at me. I don't think so. I sort of like it here where it's dark."

"The darkness holds many foul, unclean things," Smith said.

"And here I thought you didn't know me," the stranger gibed.

Preacher Smith wasn't a man who gave in to fear readily. He had the strength of the Lord on his side. But at this moment, talking to this unseen stranger, he felt the stirrings of unease inside him. He licked lips that had suddenly gone dry and said, "Are . . . are you the Devil?" It seemed unlikely to him that Satan himself would visit Deadwood in human form, but one never knew what sort of tricks that prince of demons might get up to. He had invaded the Garden of Eden disguised as a simple serpent, after all.

Again the stranger chuckled. "No, Preacher, I ain't the Devil, although some folks have said I'm as mean as he is. I'm just a man . . . a man who's been lookin' for you."

Feeling that he was on a little firmer ground now, Smith asked, "What do you want of me?"

"You recall a man named Tarrant? Gerald Tarrant?"

Smith frowned. "No. No, I don't believe I do."

"You ought to. You killed him."

The words shocked Smith to the very core of his being. He took a step back as if he had been physically struck. "You're wrong, brother," he forced himself to say. "I never killed anyone."

"The law back in Massachusetts says different. It says a fella named Henry Smith is wanted for murder, for killing a man named Gerald Tarrant. Seems he blamed this man Tarrant for the deaths of his wife and son."

"I . . . I know nothing of this." Smith's voice nearly broke from the anguish in it.

"I'm sure the state of Massachusetts, or the common-wealth or whatever the hell they call it, would like to have you back and put you on trial for Tarrant's murder, Preacher, but that ain't why I'm here. Seems that Tarrant was a rich man. His family put a whole lot bigger bounty on his killer than the state ever would . . . and they don't care whether he's brought in dead or alive."

"You're mistaken, my friend. I tell you, you have the wrong man."

"I don't think so."

Smith's bearded chin lifted in uncharacteristic defiance. Normally the meekest of men, he was actually growing angry.

"If you feel that strongly about it," he snapped, "why don't you just shoot me and be done with it? You'll see, though, when you try to collect your blood money, that you were wrong."

The man in the shadows didn't say anything for a long

time. Smith just stood there, staring toward the place he thought the man was. Finally, the stranger said, "You know, Preacher, I'm almost tempted to believe you."

"You should believe me. I'm a man of God, and I'm telling the truth."

"You wouldn't be the first sky pilot to lie about something. Reckon I'll have to think about this."

"If you think I'm a killer, why aren't you afraid that I'll run away?"

"Where are you gonna go? You don't have a horse. You walk all over these hills. There's nowhere you can run that I can't find you and bring you back, anytime I want."

"Obviously, you *have* been watching me. You . . . you know that I try to do good works, even though as the Good Book says, it's by faith we are saved, not works."

"I put my faith in two things, Preacher . . . cold cash and hot lead."

"Then I truly feel sorry for you," Smith said softly. "Would you at least tell me your name, brother?"

But there was no answer from the darkness this time. Smith stood there for a long moment, wondering if the man had gone. Smith hadn't heard anything. The stranger would have had to move awfully quietly to depart without making a sound.

After a few minutes, though, Smith was forced to conclude that was exactly what had happened. The man had vanished into the shadows.

With a sigh, Smith picked up the crate he had set down earlier. Even though the past quarter of an hour or so had been very disturbing, first the encounter with the man dragging the corpse out of the Academy and then the unseen stranger talking about things that upset Smith, he still had his work to do, the task that the Lord had appointed him to.

Someone had to spread the Gospel in Deadwood. As long as there was breath in his body, Preacher Smith would continue to do so.

WHAT the hell was the matter with him? Titus asked himself that question as he emerged onto Main Street and paused in front of the No. 10 Saloon, where Wild Bill Hickok had been gunned down. It was already a famous place, but Titus didn't really pay any attention to where he was. He was too busy wondering why he hadn't walloped that damned preacher with the butt of his gun and taken him prisoner. That was what he would have done to any other fugitive he planned to take back for a reward. That is, unless he had a good excuse to shoot the son of a bitch. But he couldn't do that, he reminded himself, because this was one of those cases where the reward wasn't "dead or alive." Tarrant's family wanted Smith alive, so that he could stand trial.

Titus was sure he had the right man. He had seen the wanted poster. Smith wasn't even using a false name. He was still going by the same one he had used back in Massachusetts, back when he had a wife and a kid, before he had come West and started preaching.

All that sin-shouting was just a way for Smith to cover up his own guilt, Titus thought. Some men were that way. If they killed somebody, it ate away at their guts until they couldn't stand it anymore. They had to pretend to be something they weren't, something better, even righteous. Like they thought if they could cover up what they'd done wrong with enough holier-than-thou bullshit, it would go away.

Things didn't work that way. Dead was dead, and once a man had blood on his hands, it never washed off. Titus believed that was as true for him as it was for anybody else.

Lucky for him he just didn't give a shit how many men he had killed. Somebody like Smith, though, he would torture himself for the rest of his life, even if he had been justified in his actions. Titus didn't know about that. He hadn't cared to dig into the details. All that mattered was that there was a five-thousand-dollar bounty on Smith's head, and he intended to collect it.

So why hadn't he taken the first step to doing that? It was unlikely he would have a better opportunity.

He raised his left hand, scratched at his bearded jaw. What he had told the preacher was true—there was no place he could run that Titus couldn't find him. Titus intended to keep an eye on him, and when he was good and ready, he would take Smith into custody, haul him down to Cheyenne, throw him in a jail cell there, and send a telegram to Massachusetts. He wondered if Tarrant's family would insist that he bring Smith all the way back there before the bounty was paid. It was possible, but Titus hoped not. He had no desire to go back East, or even as far as Chicago. It was right outside Chicago that the Union prison camp had been located. . . .

He shoved those bad memories out of his brain. The damned Yankees liked to carry on about Andersonville, but conditions had been even worse at Camp Douglas. It didn't pay to think about it.

Turning, he walked into the No. 10. In the days since Wild Bill's death, the place had gotten back to normal. Men stood at the bar, and a card game was going on at the very table where Hickok had been sitting when he was shot. The only visible reminder of the incident was a dark stain on the planks of the floor. Once blood set in, it was mighty hard to get out.

The bartender came over, eyes narrowed warily. Titus generally had that effect on folks. "What'll it be?" he asked.

"Whiskey."

The bartender poured the drink and slid it across the bar after Titus put a coin down to pay for it. Titus picked up the glass and downed the whiskey. As he put the glass back on the bar, he asked, "You know that fella who stands around in the street, preachin'?"

"Preacher Smith?" The bartender nodded. "Sure I know him. I reckon just about everybody in Deadwood who's been here more than a day or two knows him. The preacher is usually the first one to speak to folks when they come into town."

That hadn't been the case with Titus. But he had ridden in while the hoopla for that Pony Express race was going on, so he supposed it was no surprise Smith had missed greeting him.

"Seems like all that sin-shoutin' would get on folks' nerves."

"Naw, the preacher means well," the bartender said. "Besides, anytime anybody needs help, he pitches right in. Maybe he gets under the skin of some people, but I'll betcha there ain't a fella in Deadwood who's better liked than good ol' Preacher Smith."

Now there was a practical reason for biding his time, Titus told himself. A man ran a risk when he tried to take a prisoner who was well liked. The citizens of Deadwood might spring to the defense of the preacher, and Titus couldn't fight the whole settlement. It would be better to wait until Smith was on one of his jaunts into the hills. Then Titus could grab him and light out for Cheyenne without having to worry about an angry mob trying to stop him.

The bartender regarded him with eyes that had narrowed slightly with suspicion. "Just what's your interest in the preacher, anyway, mister?" he asked.

"No particular interest," Titus said. "I've just seen him preachin' in the street and wondered how folks felt about him."

"He's a good friend to just about everybody. That's how folks feel about him."

"Well, maybe I'll be his friend, too," Titus said with a faint smile.

Right up until the time I have to take him back to face a hang rope.

Chapter Eighteen

THERE was nothing like hard work to sweat all the meanness out of a man. The first few days were rough; the craving for whiskey could come on Bellamy without any warning, as did the almost overwhelming feelings of grief and remorse. Memories of Carla and of Fletch haunted him. Of all the things that folks left behind when they died, the body was the easiest to bury. The rest lingered and tormented the mind—the things left undone and unsaid, the things that never should have been done and said, the hasty actions, the thoughtless words, the fabric of life itself that once woven can never be changed, no matter how much a person might desire to do so. Bellamy struggled with all of that, and sometimes the only way to dull the pain in his soul was to work until the pain in his body overwhelmed it. He swung a pick and wielded a shovel until blisters rose on his hands, burst and bled, and scabbed over. He hunkered in the icy waters of Deadwood Creek until all feeling was gone from his feet and calves and his thigh muscles shrieked. He worked from dawn to dusk, from can to can't, day after day, and at night he slept only fitfully, plagued by dreams. Even when they weren't actually nightmares, they were so vivid as to be disturbing. At least once a night he cried out in his sleep and woke himself up.

But when that happened, Ling was always there to hold him and tell him that everything would be all right. They hadn't made love since they had been here at Dan's camp, but they had spent long hours clinging to each other, Bellamy drawing on the strength that she had to share with him.

Dan was always around, too, to put a strong hand on Bellamy's shoulder when he had the shakes, to talk to him quietly and calmly, to make him feel that if he didn't give up, eventually everything would be all right again. Bellamy wanted desperately to believe that.

Sure enough, slowly he began to feel human again. The hard work, the isolation, the unwavering friendship and love of Dan and Ling . . . all that had an effect on him. Bellamy realized, early one morning, that the worst of it was now behind him.

And then he stepped out of the tent and saw the horse-drawn buggy coming up the gulch.

Bellamy's breath caught in his throat and his muscles stiffened as the vehicle rolled toward him and he recognized the woman at the reins. Laurette wore a bottle-green dress and a hat of the same shade perched on the red curls piled atop her head. She handled the horse and buggy skillfully. The trail alongside the creek wasn't really meant for a buggy, but Laurette seemed to be having no trouble following it.

Dan came out of the trees up the slope of the gulch. He must have already been at the shaft they were sinking into the hillside, despite the early hour. For that matter, Bellamy was surprised to see Laurette up and around this early. She usually slept until at least noon, he recalled. It took something urgent to bring her out before then.

Something urgent—like finding him. As he watched the buggy approach, he had no doubt that Laurette had come for him, and maybe for Ling, too, if she knew the Chinese girl was here.

Dan saw her coming and hurried down to the tent. He asked quietly, "Are you all right, Bellamy?"

Bellamy swallowed and managed to nod. Just the sight of Laurette stirred up too many memories and unwanted feelings, but he told himself that he was strong enough to overcome them. He had to be.

"I'm fine," he said. "Don't worry, Dan."

"Hell, kid, worryin's what I do."

Bellamy had to smile a little at that. Dan had a point. His years as a sergeant had taught him to worry all the time. If he hadn't, chances were more of the men who had served with him would have wound up dead.

Behind them, Ling poked her head out of the tent. She said, "What's going on?", then gasped softly as she saw Laurette's buggy, which was now only about fifty yards away. "Oh, no."

Bellamy turned and extended a hand to her. "Don't worry," he told her as he helped her to her feet beside him and Dan. "Nothing's going to happen. That part of my life, and yours, is over."

Ling nodded, but she didn't look convinced. Her fear of Laurette had come back and had her in its grasp.

Laurette brought the horse to a stop. Dust swirled up from the buggy's wheels. Laurette tied the reins to one of the posts that supported the black canvas cover over the buggy seat and then said, "Hello, Bellamy. Hello, Ling. I was beginnin' to wonder if I'd ever see you two again."

Dan started to speak, but Bellamy stopped him, stepping forward a little as he did so. "What do you want, Laurette?" he asked.

She put a smile on her face. "Why, I want you and Ling to come back to work, of course. The Academy just ain't been the same without you two."

Bellamy shook his head. "We're not coming back. We've put all that behind us."

The smile remained on Laurette's face, but it looked a bit more strained now. She laughed and said, "Shoot, son, you can't change who you are. The two of you belong back there, and you know it."

"Don't call me son," Bellamy snapped. "You had a son. He's dead."

Laurette's tight control slipped a little more. "You ought to know," she said. "You killed him."

"That's enough, damn it," Dan said. "Mrs. Parkhurst, you're not—"

Again Bellamy stopped him, this time by raising his voice and saying to Laurette, "I thought I was saving your life. If I had known then what I know now, I might have let Fletch shoot you."

"It hurts me when you say things like that, Bellamy. You know I never done nothin' to you. Or maybe I should say . . . I never done nothin' to you that you didn't want me to do."

Bellamy's jaw tightened. He didn't like being reminded of his depravity, but it was an inescapable fact. The day might come when he would burn in hell for his sins, but until that day came, he would just have to learn how to live with the consequences of his deeds.

"It doesn't matter what you say. Ling and I aren't coming back to the Academy."

"You're speakin' for her, too, are you?" Laurette looked at Ling. "What about it, girl? Don't you want to come back and work for me again? Didn't I always treat you right? You had plenty to eat and a good place to sleep, a roof over your head and pretty dresses. You made money. Ain't that better than sharin' a damned tent with a couple o' prospectors and lettin' 'em fuck you for free?"

Bellamy moved in front of Ling and said angrily to Laurette, "Shut your filthy mouth—"

Ling stepped around him, angry herself now, too mad, in fact, to remember that she was scared of Laurette. "No one's fucking me, you cold-hearted bitch, and the next time somebody does it'll be because I want him to!"

Laurette couldn't conceal her surprise at what she heard. She stared at Ling in silence for a couple of seconds, then said, "I'll bet you could talk good English all along, you little slut."

Bellamy's hands began to tremble. "Get out of here," he said. "You're not wanted here. You don't belong here. Go back to your filthy whorehouse and leave us alone."

"Don't get high-an'-mighty with me, boy," she shot back at him. "Wasn't but a few days ago that you were just as bad as anybody in Deadwood, guzzlin' whiskey and fuckin' whores and gettin' into gunfights. You got no right to start actin' like you're as pure as that goddamn preacher."

Bellamy put an arm around Ling's shoulders, and Dan stepped in front of the two young people. "Look, Mrs. Parkhurst, Bellamy and Ling have made it plain. They're not interested in goin' back to Deadwood, and they sure as hell don't plan on goin' back to work for you. So you might as well leave. There's nothing here for you."

Laurette stared at him angrily for a long moment, but finally she nodded. "I'll go," she said, "but only if I can talk to Bellamy for a minute alone, first."

"I don't reckon that's a good idea."

Bellamy said, "No, Dan, it's all right. If it'll get her to leave, I'll do it."

Dan turned to him with a frown. "You sure, kid?"

"Yeah," Bellamy replied, nodding. "Don't worry, Dan. She's not going to change my mind."

"What do you think, Ling?" Dan asked the girl.

She clearly didn't like it, either, but she said, "Bellamy is much stronger now than he was. When that woman leaves, he will still be here."

"All right, then." Dan took Ling's arm. "We'll go up to the shaft and leave them alone. But Bellamy, you give a holler if you need anything."

The two of them walked up the slope into the trees, leaving Bellamy standing there looking at Laurette with a level stare. He told her, "Whatever you've got to say, get on with it."

"You know what I've got to say, Bellamy. It ain't just me that needs you to come back to Deadwood."

"You're talking about Swearengen and Varnes."

"Varnes is gone," she said, "but Al and me are still workin' together, for now. One of these days, though, he's gonna try to double-cross me. We both know that. If you're not there when he does, he's liable to kill me."

"If I was Swearengen, I'd worry more about what *you're*

going to do. You're about as trustworthy as a—" He stopped before he said "snake." Such a comparison probably wouldn't be fair to the snake. He went on. "You don't need me. Hickok's already dead."

Her eyes narrowed. "You didn't say anything to Ryan about what we planned . . . ?"

"He knows about it."

"You damned little fool."

"I suppose you and Swearengen paid that fella Jack McCall to kill Wild Bill?"

Laurette shook her head emphatically. "I swear, Bellamy, we didn't know a thing about it until after it happened. Bringin' McCall in was strictly Varnes's idea."

"Where's Varnes now?"

She hesitated. "I don't know. He left Deadwood, right after Hickok was killed, before McCall was put on trial, even."

He had the impression that she really knew more than she was saying, but he didn't press her on it. Varnes didn't really matter.

"So what is it you and Swearengen want from me now?"

"That preacher is still drivin' folks away from both of our places. Something's gotta be done about him."

"A lot more people come into the Gem and the Academy than Preacher Smith runs off. Can't you just leave him alone?"

A cunning look came into Laurette's green eyes. "Maybe we could. I want you to come back anyway, so you can keep the peace in the Academy. The gent I got handlin' that job now ain't worth shit at it. I had to shoot the last troublemaker myself."

Bellamy shook his head. "Sorry. I just can't do it."

"Because of Carla? Because of Fletch?"

"Just because," Bellamy said curtly. "That's all the answer you're going to get."

She regarded him somberly for a long moment and then sighed. "Shit. You're not gonna change your mind, are you?"

He shook his head. "No."

"Well, then, I guess there's nothin' I can do." She untied the reins. "I reckon I'll be seein' you, Bellamy."

"Not likely."

Laurette flapped the reins and clucked to the horse. She turned the animal around and started it back toward Deadwood. Bellamy stood there watching the buggy dwindle in the distance.

Dan and Ling must have been watching from the edge of the trees. They came down the slope to join him. "Well, at least she's gone," Dan said.

"Thank God for that," Ling added.

Bellamy nodded.

But despite that, and despite everything that had been said, he had the uneasy feeling that he had not seen the last of Laurette Parkhurst. When she wanted something, she wasn't the sort of woman to give up easily.

And God help him, for whatever reason, she still wanted him.

DICK saw the log buildings of Fort Laramie ahead of him, scattered around the parade ground. He urged the horse forward and looked over his shoulder. There was no sign of Jed Powell, who had started falling back earlier in the day when his horse's strength began to fail. Once again, Powell had handled his mount badly, pushing the animal too hard and not conserving enough of its strength.

For the past two and a half days, Dick and Powell had jockeyed back and forth, first one leading and then the other. Most of the time they had ridden roughly parallel courses, not getting too close to each other. After the rock slide had almost killed him, Dick supposed that Powell was afraid to get too close. Powell might think that Dick would open fire on him if he got the chance. And in truth, Dick would have been tempted, although he knew he wouldn't have actually started any gun trouble.

The rock slide hadn't been the last of Powell's dirty tricks. During one of the times when he was ahead of Dick, he had fouled a waterhole. That wasn't much of a problem; water wasn't all that scarce in this part of the country, although Dick and his horse had been forced to go an extra five miles—a thirsty five miles—before they came to a creek. In another place, Powell had strung a thin rope across the trail, tied to a tree on either side, in hopes of tripping up Dick's horse and causing the animal to break a leg. That ploy hadn't worked, though, because Dick had spotted the rope in time to stop. While he hadn't actually seen Powell do either of those things, he was confident that his opponent was responsible for them. Nobody else had any reason to want to stop him, or even to slow him down.

Now Fort Laramie was in sight at last, and Dick was going to get there first and claim his fifty copies of the Cheyenne *Daily Leader*.

He poured on the speed, and several minutes later he reached the fort. One of the lookouts must have seen him coming and spread the word, because a large group of soldiers were waiting for him on the parade ground, cheering and waving their caps. Anything that broke the monotony of life on a frontier post like this one was welcome.

The fort's commanding officer, Colonel Stilwell, was waiting on the porch of the headquarters building. He lifted a hand in greeting as Dick pulled the sweating horse to a stop in front of the building. "Welcome to Fort Laramie, Mr. Seymour!" Stilwell called. He slapped a bundle tied with rope that sat on a small table beside him. "Got your papers right here!"

Dick swung down from the saddle as Army hostlers hurried forward to switch the rig to another mount. On legs that trembled a little from weariness, he climbed the steps to the porch and shook hands with the colonel.

"Do you have time to stay a while, maybe have something to eat?" Stilwell asked.

Dick shook his head. "Unfortunately, no, Colonel, as much as I'd like to. I don't know how close behind me my competitor is—"

"Another rider comin'!" a trooper bawled from the parade ground.

"Well, I'd say there's my answer to that question," Dick said with a grim smile. He picked up the bundle of papers from the table. Another bundle just like it still sat there, waiting for Jed Powell to claim it.

The hostlers had Dick's saddle on a fresh horse by now. Dick tied the bundle of newspapers behind the saddle and then checked the cinches for himself. It wasn't that he didn't trust the soldiers; he just preferred to see for himself that everything was as it should be.

Powell reached the parade ground just as Dick started away from the headquarters building. Powell was swaying in the saddle from exhaustion, but he stiffened and sat upright as he spotted Dick riding toward him. Dick tried to give him a wide berth, but there were too many soldiers crowded around. He couldn't veer away from Powell.

Suddenly, Powell gave a hoarse shout and spurred his horse, making the animal lunge forward. He turned the horse so that it almost collided with Dick's mount. As Dick tried to get out of the way, Powell left the saddle in a diving tackle. His long arms went around Dick, and the men fell heavily to the hard-packed dirt of the parade ground.

Powell's attack had taken Dick by surprise, but as the impact broke them apart, he regained his wits enough to roll away, putting some space between himself and Powell. He didn't think Powell would give up this fight easily, and as he came up onto his knees, he saw that he was right. Powell had scrambled upright first and was coming at him, swinging a booted foot in a vicious kick.

Dick twisted aside and reached out to grab Powell's leg. He heaved hard on it, throwing Powell off balance and upending him. Powell crashed down on the ground again. This time the breath was knocked out of him, so that all he could do for a few moments was to lie there gasping for air.

As Dick got to his feet, Colonel Stilwell pushed through the crowd of yelling, excited soldiers. Even more than the arrival of the Pony Express riders, a fight was a welcome distraction, so the troopers were setting up quite a clamor. Stilwell finally silenced them by bellowing, "Quiet! Quiet, damn it!"

Dick stood a short distance from Powell, his muscles

tense and his hands clenched into fists. He didn't know if Powell would continue the fight or not, but if he did, Dick was ready.

"Powell!" the colonel barked. "What the hell do you think you're doing?"

Powell pushed himself onto hands and knees and shook his head as if trying to clear cobwebs from it. He glared up at Stilwell and said, "Stay outta this, Colonel. It ain't any o' your business."

"The hell it isn't! This is my fort."

"But I'm a civilian, and so's Seymour. You ain't got any jurisdiction over us." Powell struggled onto his feet. "This is between him and me."

Dick said, "We're supposed to be racing, not brawling. But I suppose, considering the things you've already done, that you're not interested in a fair competition."

"You damned Englisher!" Powell's breath was laden with whiskey fumes, proving that he hadn't been swaying in the saddle entirely from exhaustion. He probably had a flask tucked in his saddlebags. With a snarl, he leaped at Dick, swinging a balled fist and ignoring Stilwell's shouts. "Nobody beats me!"

Ducking, Dick let the roundhouse punch go harmlessly over his head. Powell was bigger and stronger, with a longer reach. But Dick was faster, and his life on the frontier had given him some hard muscles of his own. He stepped in and hooked a swift right into Powell's midsection, then followed it with a left to the jaw. Powell was jolted back a step, but he shook it off and came at Dick again, this time with a flurry of shorter, faster punches that were harder to avoid. One of them landed cleanly on Dick's breastbone and sent pain shooting through him as it knocked him back. Another blow sunk into his ribs, and a third grazed his head. If they had been in a boxing ring, rather than an open parade ground, he would have been on the ropes by now. He caught himself, blocked another of Powell's punches, and launched a desperate counterattack. A right and a left drove Powell back and gave Dick a little much-needed breathing room.

He knew he couldn't stand toe-to-toe with the man and slug it out. Powell could absorb too much punishment for that. Dick had to rely more on his quickness. To that end, he fell back more than he needed to as Powell charged him again. Sensing an advantage, Powell roared angrily and bull-rushed even harder. Dick grabbed his arm, twisted at the waist, and bent over as he turned Powell's own strength and weight against him. The wrestling hold sent Powell flying up and over to land on his back with devastating force.

Dick pounced on him, pinning him to the ground with a couple of knees in his chest. Once, twice, three times Dick slammed a punch into Powell's face, until the bigger man lay there limp and senseless, barely conscious. Dick might have hit him again if a couple of the troopers hadn't grabbed his arms and pulled him off.

"Settle down, Dick!" Stilwell ordered sharply. "It's over."

His chest heaving, Dick stood there in the grip of the soldiers for a long moment as his rage subsided. When he could speak again, he said, "You saw the whole thing, Colonel. Powell jumped me. I was just defending myself."

"Yeah, I reckon that's true enough," Stilwell said, "but I'm still tempted to throw both of you in the stockade until you've cooled off, civilians or no civilians."

Dick shook his head. "I have a race to run. Please order your men to let go of me."

With a disgusted grimace, Stilwell flipped a hand at the troopers. They released Dick and stepped back.

One of the men led his horse over to him. Dick picked up his hat, knocked the dust off it against his leg, and settled it on his head. He reached up, grasped the saddle, and found the stirrup with his left foot. A little awkwardly because he was already starting to ache all over from the pounding, he pulled himself onto the horse.

"I won't keep Powell here," Stilwell warned. "As soon as he comes to his senses, he can leave any time he wants. I can't interfere in the race."

"That's fine," Dick said. "I didn't ask for your help, Colonel."

"Fact is," Stilwell growled, "I may have one of the men throw a bucket of water in his face to bring him around."

Dick jerked his head in a nod. "Whatever you want to do."

With that, he heeled his horse into a trot. The soldiers moved out of the way to let him past. He rode away from the fort, headed north again toward Deadwood.

Chapter Nineteen

THE Hunton ranch, Sage Creek, Hat Creek, Bald Rock, Windy Hill . . . all the places ran together in Dick's brain as he rode on for the next two days, stopping during the day only to change horses, eating jerky and stale biscuits in the saddle, making cold camps at night so that a fire wouldn't attract the attention of the Sioux. He rolled in his blankets and slept the sleep of the dead, but only for a few hours each night. Then, well before dawn, once the sky had begun to turn gray in the east, he was up and in the saddle again, pushing on.

He hadn't seen Powell since leaving Fort Laramie. Maybe the man had abandoned the race and stayed there at the fort, or even gone back to Cheyenne. Or perhaps he had hung back and passed Dick during one of the nights. Maybe he was up ahead somewhere right now, gaining in the race. Dick's brain was so muddled from exhaustion that he didn't know what was possible and what wasn't. All he knew was that he would continue on until he reached Deadwood and hope for the best.

If he won, then Charley Utter would have the mail business

to himself and wouldn't have to worry about Clippinger anymore. The riders for the Pioneer Pony Express wouldn't have to maintain this killing pace while on the regular run. But that wouldn't have anything to do with Dick, because he would be gone by then. He was still determined to leave Deadwood and hope that he could find peace elsewhere, even though he knew how unlikely that was.

Glancing at the sky, he saw that the sun had dropped a considerable distance toward the western horizon. It would be dark in another hour. He hoped to reach Jack Bowman's ranch before then. If he did, he would accept Bowman's inevitable offer of hospitality and get a few hours of sleep in a real bunk instead of on the ground. Then, tomorrow, he would make the last run to Deadwood. He and his mount would both be fresh. Would they be in time to beat Jed Powell? Dick didn't know, but at least he felt confident that he had done his best. No one could ask for more. Win or lose, his conscience would be clear.

That thought was going through his mind when a prairie chicken suddenly erupted from a clump of brush up ahead, next to the trail. The bird wouldn't have acted like that unless something startled it. Biting back a curse, Dick reined in and reached for his gun. So Powell *was* ahead of him after all and was going to try to ambush him again! This time Dick would settle things with the treacherous bastard, once and for all.

But before he could even draw his gun, someone leaped at him from the side and grabbed him, pulling him half out of the saddle. The attacker seemed to have come out of thin air, but the part of Dick's stunned brain that was still working told him the man had been concealed in the thin scrub just off the trail. Powell wasn't capable of such stealth.

But the Indians were. . . .

He heard a triumphant whoop as he felt himself falling. He got his hand on the butt of his gun, but then he hit the ground and the weapon slipped away from him. Moccasin-shod feet scuffed the dust around him. He rolled desperately as more whoops filled the air.

Kicking out, he felt his booted foot connect with something, drawing a grunt of pain. Dick got his hands under him and pushed himself up. He had to get back to his horse if he was going to have any chance of getting away.

Men surrounded him and strong hands closed on his arms, jerking him to a halt. The rancid smell of the grease with which they coated their hair filled his nostrils. He looked around wildly, saw that there were four or five of the warriors. Two of them had hold of him, and they were too strong for him to break loose. Another of the Sioux had caught his horse and held the reins.

They turned him so that he was facing toward the setting sun. A tall, powerful figure came striding out of the glare. With the sun behind the man, Dick couldn't make out his face, but when the Indian stopped, stared at him for a second, grunted and then spoke, he recognized the voice.

"The Englishman. Good."

"Talking Bear!" Dick gasped. "You bastard!"

The war chief moved aside enough so that Dick could make out his harsh, cruel features. He was smiling now as he said, "You should have died the other two times we met, Englishman. This time, you will not escape. You will die like your dog of a squaw and your puling half-breed brats."

Dick let out a scream of rage. He couldn't hold it back. Nor could he control himself as he pulled free of his captors with a sudden jerk, fury sending the strength of a madman into his muscles. He lunged toward Talking Bear, his hands outstretched to clamp around the arrogant murderer's throat.

Something crashed on the back of his head, driving him forward and down. He hit the ground face-first and tasted dirt in his mouth. That was the last thing he was aware of before the world faded out around him.

THE pain he felt on awakening told him that the Sioux hadn't killed him right away. That was a surprise in a way, but not much of one. It made sense, once Dick thought about it, that Talking Bear had wanted to keep him alive. Talking Bear hated him for marrying an Indian woman, even though Carries Water had been Kansa, not Sioux. He would want to take his time about killing this white man. He would want to enjoy it.

What Dick heard next, though, came as a total surprise to him. A voice hissed, "Wake up, Seymour! Damn it, you got to wake up and talk to these Injuns! They're gonna kill us!"

Dick's eyes flickered open. A harsh red glare stuck painfully against them and made him wince. Even that slight movement sent pain rampaging through his skull. Holding his head as still as possible, he forced his eyes open again and let them adjust to the light. Then and only then did he look over into the terrified face of Jed Powell.

The two white men were tied hand and foot and lay on the ground near a fire, close enough so that the heat from it was uncomfortably warm on their faces. Before the night was over, though, they would probably have a lot more to worry about than a little discomfort, Dick told himself. He heard the talking and the laughter from the members of the war party and knew that whatever they had planned for their captives, it wouldn't be anything good.

The Sioux, as a general rule, did not go in for torture as much as some of the other tribes, such as the Comanche and the Kiowa and the Blackfoot. Although he had never encountered them, Dick had heard that the Apache, out in Arizona Territory, were the worst of all about that. The Sioux were fierce fighters, but would usually kill their enemies outright.

There could always be special circumstances that would make them alter their usual behavior, though, and Talking Bear's hatred for him was one such circumstance.

"Seymour!" Powell whispered, seeing that Dick was awake. "You gotta do somethin'—"

"Shut up," Dick grated out. "What do you expect me to do?"

"Y-you can talk to these savages. You lived with 'em, had yourself a squaw. I heard the talk—"

"I didn't live with the Sioux. I only traded with them, and some of them didn't like me even then." Dick looked toward the group of warriors on the other side of the fire. He saw

Talking Bear watching him. "Including the leader of this war party."

Powell gave a low groan. "Oh, Lord, they're gonna kill us, sure as hell. . . ."

"More than likely," Dick agreed. Across the way, Talking Bear came to his feet. Quickly, Dick asked Powell, "How did they get you?"

"The red bastards came outta nowhere! There wasn't enough brush to hide a jackrabbit, let alone half-a-dozen Injuns. They jumped me and knocked me down, got my guns, and then tied me up. I saw they already had you. Thought you was dead at first, then I figured out you were just out cold."

Dick nodded. So Powell had come along after he'd been captured, probably not long after, because from the sound of it the Sioux had jumped him at the same place.

It appeared that the race was over and that both of them were going to finish last. That thought made the ghost of a smile flicker across Dick's mouth.

Talking Bear stood over them now. "White motherfuckers be quiet," he said. He spoke better English than Dick spoke Sioux, and obviously he had even picked up some of the white men's obscenities.

Dick looked up at him and said, "I thought Indians didn't curse."

Talking Bear spat on him. "White men deserve to have their own bad words used on them."

Dick ignored the spittle running down his cheek. With a calm he didn't really feel, he said, "Then I suppose that makes you as big a motherfucker as we are, Talking Bear."

For a second as he watched Talking Bear's face darken with rage, he thought the war chief might draw the knife at his waist, lean down, and cut the throat of this insolent white captive. Dick almost hoped that would be the case. Better to die quick than slow. But Talking Bear controlled his anger, and as if reading Dick's mind, he said, "You will die, Englishman . . . both of you will die . . . but not yet."

Again forcing himself to remain calm, Dick asked, "What did you have in mind?"

An ugly smile spread across Talking Bear's face. "You will scream for a long time before you die."

"Listen, Chief," Powell suddenly babbled. "You understand English. You know what I'm talkin' about when I tell you I ain't got nothin' to do with this man. Hell, I hate him as much as you do. Let me go and I'll even help you kill him."

Talking Bear turned toward him with a fierce glare. "Let a white man go to kill more of my people in the future? Let a white man go to ruin the land and the air and the water? Visions have spoken to me. They have told me to kill all the white men I find. Only by doing that will this land be as it once was. Only by doing that will my people ever be free. No white man ever kept his word. All white men who come here must die."

"You'll never accomplish that, Talking Bear," Dick said. "You don't know it, but you've already been defeated. There are too many enemies for you to ever win."

Talking Bear gave a short bark of laughter. "Tell that to Yellow Hair."

"Custer had only two hundred men. There are thousands upon thousands where he came from."

Talking Bear made a slashing motion with his hand and said, "Enough! You waste your breath, Englishman, when soon you will need it for screaming." He turned to the fire, bent, and picked up a burning branch. He blew the flames out, but that left the end of the branch still glowing red with heat. "Here is a taste of the pain you will know," he said as he thrust the branch against the breast of Dick's shirt.

The heated end of the branch burned through the fabric and into Dick's chest. His jaws locked together and his lips drew back from his teeth as he felt the searing pain. His back arched. He smelled something burning and knew it was his own flesh.

"Oh, Lord!" Powell cried, even though nothing had been done to him.

Talking Bear finally pulled the stick away from Dick's chest. Dick managed to roll onto his side and sort of curl up around the pain. This was the worst physical torment he had ever known.

But it still paled next to the emotional torture he had endured since the death of his family.

Talking Bear tossed the branch back into the fire. "The beginning, Englishman," he said. "That was just the beginning."

UNFORTUNATELY, Talking Bear was telling the truth.

Throughout the rest of that long night, he and the other members of the war party took turns inflicting pain on the two white captives. They were burned and slashed, kicked and struck with clubs. Nothing too bad, nothing that would kill them, just enough to keep them in constant agony. Dick endured the torture stoically, but Powell screamed until his throat was raw and he was too hoarse to make a sound. Dick took no satisfaction from the pain the other man was feeling, even though Powell had tried to kill him. He wouldn't have wished this on his worst enemy.

Except for the fact that Talking Bear *was* his worst enemy, and he would have gladly watched such torture carried out on the war chief, he told himself.

But even as the thought went through his mind, he knew it wasn't true. He would kill Talking Bear without hesitation, but it would give him no satisfaction. The only thing that could possibly do that would be to have his family back, and that was impossible.

Along toward morning, Dick passed out, whether from sheer exhaustion or because he had lost enough blood from the myriad of small cuts the Indians had made on his body, he didn't know. Perhaps it was simply his brain's way of escaping from the pain. As consciousness faded, he thought that he would probably never wake up again.

But once again, he had underestimated Talking Bear. Sometime later, water splashed in his face, jolting him out of the peaceful oblivion into which he had retreated. The ordeal wasn't over after all. He looked up into Talking Bear's ugly, leering face. . . .

And then gasped, because standing behind Talking Bear, peering down at Dick over the war chief's shoulder, was Carries Water, with a smile on her round, beautiful face.

Dick stared at his wife and babbled incoherently. It was impossible that she was here. Carries Water was dead. He had seen her bloody corpse with his own eyes. He had built her funeral platform with his own hands, along with those for their children. She could not be alive now.

Talking Bear laughed at him and straightened, evidently convinced that the hated Englishman had lost his mind. As he turned away, he stepped *through* Carries Water, and in that instant, Dick knew she wasn't real after all, knew she was just a figment of his fevered imagination.

But then why, he had to ask himself, did he *feel* the touch of her hand as she knelt beside him and reached out to him? Her fingertips stroked his beard-stubbled face, and they were cool and smooth and their very touch sent relief flooding through him. The pain that enveloped him didn't go away, but it eased, and any such respite was welcome.

Her lips didn't seem to move, but he heard her voice in his head. *My husband,* she said, *do not let him win. Do not give up. You can defeat him.*

Let me come to you, he pleaded in his mind. Let us be together again, just you and me and our children. . . .

It is not time. When the Great Spirit wills it to be so, it will be so. Until then, you must fight. You must win.

She started to fade from his sight. He gave a choked cry, unwilling to let her go, but nothing he did could stop her. At the very last, she leaned over him and brushed her lips against his, and he felt her kiss as surely as he felt the heat of the sun and the wind on his face. Then she was gone, and he cried, "Come back!"

Talking Bear stopped and turned to look back at Dick. "You speak to me?" he asked.

A huge rage and a determination stronger than any Dick had ever known suddenly filled him. "Yes, I speak to you," he said. "Come back and free me. Settle this with honor. You and me, Talking Bear. Man to man. Trial by combat."

Talking Bear laughed. "Why should I do this thing when you are already my prisoner?"

"Because you know that the others of your people will never speak of you in the manner you want unless you defeat me with your own hands. There is no honor, no glory, in killing a defenseless prisoner."

Talking Bear glared at him. "You speak in foolish circles. The death of an enemy is all that matters." He looked around at the other Sioux, as if expecting them to confirm his statement, but instead they just looked blankly at him. His scowl darkened.

"You know I speak the truth, Talking Bear," Dick went on. "Fight me, just you and me, and if I win, you let us go. Powell and I ride away and you don't bother us again." He knew Powell was still alive because he had heard the harsh rasp of the man's breathing. Powell seemed to be unconscious, though. He had passed out from the torture, just like Dick had.

"And if you lose?"

Tied up as he was, Dick could manage only a semblance of a shrug. "Then I reckon I'll be dead, so it won't really matter to me what else you do."

Talking Bear looked at his warriors once more and then jerked his head in a curt nod. "We will fight, white man, if that is what you want. And I will kill you with my own hands, just as you say." He walked over to Dick, pulling his knife from its sheath as he did so, and knelt to cut the rawhide bonds on the white man's wrists and ankles. Dick winced as blood began to flow back into the numbed extremities.

Dick waited as long as he could, flexing his fingers to get feeling back into them, before he pushed himself unsteadily to his feet. "How do you wish to fight?" he asked. "Knives or bare hands?"

"Knives." Talking Bear put out a hand to one of his men. The warrior drew his knife and handed it to the war chief. Talking Bear flung the knife so that it stuck in the ground at Dick's feet. Dick didn't bend to get it just yet. He wanted to recover as much as he could before the battle began, even if it was just a matter of a few extra seconds.

Powell began to stir. "Wha . . ." he half-said, half-moaned.

"Take it easy, Powell," Dick told him. "We're going to get out of this."

Powell made a dubious noise, but Dick didn't look down at him. He kept his eyes focused on Talking Bear, alert for any treachery. He didn't think the war chief would try anything underhanded in front of his men like this, but Dick wasn't going to bet his life on that.

"Tell the others that if I win, Powell and I will be allowed to leave unmolested."

Talking Bear didn't care for the demand, but he spoke to the rest of the war party. Dick savvied enough of the Sioux tongue to know that Talking Bear had said the right things. The warrior who had provided the knife for Dick nodded solemnly. Say what you would about the Sioux, they were not treacherous or dishonest. Dick felt reasonably confident that the others would live up to the agreement that he and Talking Bear had made.

Finally, he was satisfied and knew that he couldn't postpone the confrontation any longer. He bent and grasped the handle of the knife that was stuck in the ground. He pulled it loose and straightened quickly . . .

But not quickly enough. Talking Bear was already lunging at him, the blade in his hand redly reflecting the dawn light.

Chapter Twenty

NOT knowing where he found the speed and strength to do so, Dick threw himself to the side to avoid the war chief's rush. He was not quite fast enough to get out of the way completely, though. The point of Talking Bear's blade tore Dick's bloodstained shirt and raked a fiery line along his ribs.

But what was one more little scratch when he had already endured a night of torture? Dick ignored the pain and slashed at his enemy. He felt a fierce surge of exhilaration as he saw the red gash his blade left behind on Talking Bear's left forearm.

With a grunt of pain, Talking Bear wheeled and came after him. Dick parried the chief's thrust. The knives rang together, and sparks leaped from the blades as they clashed. Then the two men sprang apart, studying each other for a second before they closed again.

Dick was operating largely on instinct and the rage that fueled him. He had fought with knives before, but it had never been his preferred style of combat. To tell the truth, he was basically a peaceable man, handy enough with fists or a revolver, a crack shot at a distance with a rifle, and no expert with a knife at all.

But a man backed into a corner and forced to fight for his life will often develop a seeming sixth sense that warns him of his opponent's next move and guides his own actions. Without that, he usually dies—quickly, painfully, messily.

Dick didn't intend to die. To do so would be to let Carries Water down, and he couldn't allow that again. He had already failed her once. Never, never again.

And as Talking Bear used all the swiftness and power at his command, only to see the hated white man avoid his thrusts again and again—even worse, to suffer the wounds that the white man's flickering blade dealt out—the knowledge dawned in the war chief's eyes that his simple hatred was no match for whatever it was that drove this slender, mild-looking Englishman. Panic began to gnaw at Talking Bear's nerves, and as always, panic betrayed him. He overcommitted, found himself off balance when a wild slash with the knife missed, and suddenly cried out as Dick's blade cut deeply across his wrist, severing the tendons. Talking Bear's hand opened and his knife fell from fingers that no longer obeyed his commands.

Dick stepped back. Talking Bear was crippled and disarmed. That was the end of it.

Only it wasn't. With the sort of furious roar that might have come from his namesake, the war chief threw himself forward with blinding speed and batted Dick's knife hand aside with a sweep of his left arm. He crashed into the white man and knocked him off his feet. Both men crashed to the ground. Talking Bear's weight pinned Dick down and kept him from drawing air into his lungs. He became aware that he no longer held the knife. He was disarmed now, too, and the fingers of Talking Bear's left hand clamped around his throat like iron bands.

Through the roaring of his own blood in his ears, Dick faintly heard Powell yelling at him, encouraging him. Powell had come around enough to realize that Dick was fighting for both of them, and that his life was at stake, too.

Like the tides of the ocean, a red-tinged blackness flowed

through Dick's brain and then ebbed momentarily. Before it could come back again, he drew his right leg up and managed to throw it in front of the Indian's torso, hooking it under Talking Bear's chin. When he heaved his back off the ground and straightened his leg, Talking Bear's grip was torn loose. The war chief was thrown backward.

Gasping for air through his raw throat, Dick somehow scrambled after his enemy. He clubbed his hands together and brought them down in Talking Bear's face, feeling the satisfying crunch as his nose broke. Blood spurted from the pulped nose. Talking Bear couldn't use his right hand, but his left swept around and crashed into Dick's head, knocking him to the side. Dick rolled, and Talking Bear came after him. The war chief snatched up a rock with his good hand, and Dick knew that if he got a chance, Talking Bear would use that rock to crush the white man's skull. He avoided the first blow, but he felt his strength deserting him. He was slowing down, and that could prove fatal. As both men came to their feet, Talking Bear swung the rock again. Dick ducked under it and lunged forward, grappling with the Sioux. He slid behind Talking Bear and locked his right arm across the war chief's throat.

Dick hung on for dear life. He gripped his right wrist with his left hand, strengthening his grip. Talking Bear staggered around the camp, at one point stepping blindly into what was left of the fire. He couldn't scream because Dick's arm across his throat cut off his air. He stumbled backward, picking up speed, and Dick realized that Talking Bear intended to throw himself over on his back, trapping Dick underneath him. Dick twisted his body and stuck a foot between Talking Bear's calves. Talking Bear fell, but he landed facedown with Dick on top of him. Dick rammed a knee in the small of his opponent's back and held it there. At the same time he heaved up with all his strength.

Talking Bear's neck snapped with the sharp crack of a branch breaking.

Several members of the war party cried out in horror and rage as they realized what had just happened. A couple of them reached for their knives and started forward, but the warrior Talking Bear had spoken to just before the combat began moved to intercept them. He spoke sharply to them, and although they were obviously reluctant to obey, they stepped back and contented themselves with glaring murderously at Dick.

He lowered Talking Bear's head and shoulders to the ground. The war chief lay motionless, his eyes slowly glazing over in death. Dick pushed himself to his feet, staggering a little as he got up. He had no idea if Talking Bear's second in command spoke any English, but he looked at the man and said, "You know the agreement Talking Bear and I made. Since I defeated him, the other white man and I will now go free."

Still lying tied up on the ground, Jed Powell began to sob in mingled relief and disbelief.

The Sioux warrior looked like he wanted to cut Dick's heart out, but he nodded and said gutturally, "You take other man . . . go."

"And you won't come after us," Dick said, driving home the point.

"You go. You live." The warrior struggled to maintain his control. "You never come back. You come back . . . you die."

"Fair enough," Dick said. He turned, picked up Talking Bear's knife, and used it to cut Powell free. Powell had trouble standing. He was covered with blood and bruises like Dick.

Sheer nerve was all that was keeping Dick going. Their horses were tied nearby. He led Powell over to them, both men hobbling. He had to help Powell get mounted. Then he pulled the reins loose and swung up into his own saddle. Leading Powell's horse, he turned his mount and heeled the horse into a walk. Slowly, they plodded away from the Indian camp. Dick expected to hear the bloodthirsty whoops and shouts of the war party coming after them at any second, but the warrior Talking Bear had left in charge managed to keep the other Sioux under control. Dick didn't dare look back until he and Powell had covered several hundred yards.

When he did, he saw that the Indians were gone.

The Sioux had left the bundles of newspapers tied on the horses. Probably they had had no idea what the bundles were or why the white men were carrying them. At the moment, however, the race was the last thing on Dick's mind. He and Powell were both in bad shape. They needed to have their wounds cleaned up and needed some rest as well. As Dick looked around, he spotted a rocky pinnacle in the distance that he recognized. The Bowman ranch was less than ten miles away. If he and Powell could make it there, Jack Bowman and his men would help them.

The sun rose and grew hotter. Dick looked back often, keeping an eye on their back trail, but he didn't see any dust rising in the air or any other signs of pursuit. The Indians were keeping Talking Bear's promise, or at least that appeared to be the case. Dick wasn't going to believe he and Powell were truly safe until they reached Bowman's place.

Powell seemed to have dozed off. He sagged in the saddle. Dick slowed his horse so that Powell's mount drew alongside his. If Powell started to fall, Dick wanted to be able to catch him.

He looked away and then caught a glimpse of movement from the corner of his eye. As he started to turn he saw Powell swinging a hamlike fist at his head. Dick tried to get out of the way but couldn't. The blow crashed against his skull above his left ear and drove him to the right, completely out of the saddle. He hit the ground hard and lay there stunned, still conscious but for the moment unable to move and hardly able to think.

Hearing the pounding of hoofbeats, he raised his head with an effort and peered in the direction of the sound. He saw Powell riding away, leading the riderless horse. The bastard had tricked him! Powell had pretended to be asleep so that Dick would let his guard down, and then he'd struck. Dick had saved his life by killing Talking Bear, but Powell was still trying to win the race, even if it meant leaving Dick out here to die. Anger welled up inside him, and Dick was able to push himself up onto hands and knees.

Then his strength deserted him and the world began to spin crazily around him and he fell again, unable to rise this time. Everything faded out around him as once more darkness claimed him.

* * *

SPUTTERING, he came awake. Water filled his mouth and choked his throat. He choked and gasped and coughed, and a strong arm lifted him and pounded him on the back. "Shit, partner!" a voice said. "You looked parched, but I swear I wasn't tryin' to drown you!"

Another bout of coughing wracked Dick for a few seconds, but then the choking sensation eased. He forced his eyes open and looked up into a rugged, bearded face shaded by a broad-brimmed hat. The man looked familiar. After a moment Dick recognized him as one of Jack Bowman's ranch hands, a man named Herron.

"C'mon, Dick, let's get you on your feet," the cowboy said. "You'll feel better then." He straightened and hauled Dick upright with him. Dick's head was still spinning, but Herron kept a steadying hand on his arm until the world started to settle down. "What were you doin' layin' out here all by your lonesome, anyway? I thought you was supposed to be racin' back to Deadwood."

"I was," Dick rasped. "It's . . . too long a story to tell now . . . Can you get me to Bowman's place?"

"Sure. My horse'll carry double that far."

Herron climbed into the saddle and pulled Dick up behind him. As they rode toward the ranch house, the cowboy explained that he had been checking Bowman's south range and was on his way in when he'd found Dick lying there unconscious. Dick wondered how long it had been since Powell had left him there, but there was no way of knowing.

"You look like you been waltzin' with a wildcat," Herron said. "I don't reckon I ever seen anybody quite as beat up as you look, Dick."

"The Sioux grabbed me . . . me and Powell both."

"Shit! Good thing you was able to get away 'fore they lifted your hair."

Dick just nodded tiredly. He still didn't have the energy to tell the whole story.

A few minutes later, they came in sight of the ranch house. Herron eased his six-gun out of its holster and blasted three shots into the air. That brought men out of the house and the bunkhouse and the cookshack. They gathered around as Herron rode up, and Jack Bowman and another man reached up to give Dick a hand down from the saddle.

"You're alive!" Bowman exclaimed, and that struck Dick as funny for some reason. He smiled thinly.

"Did you think I wasn't?"

"Powell said the Sioux got you! He said you were dead, and he barely escaped with his life."

"How long?" Dick asked. His voice was so hoarse that he had to repeat the question.

"How long since Powell was here?" Bowman said. "About half an hour, I reckon. I tried to get him to stay, but he said he had to get back to Deadwood."

"I need . . . a fresh horse."

"Damn it, Dick, you don't mean to say you're goin' after him?"

"Got to . . . got a race to win."

Bowman's face was grim. "Powell looked like he was on his last legs, and you look worse."

"That's what I told him," Herron put in. "Told him he looked like he'd been tanglin' with a wildcat."

Something occurred to Dick. "That . . . lineback dun of yours . . . is he rested?"

"Yeah, and you're welcome to him, of course, but Dick . . . you're gonna collapse any minute now. You can't ride to Deadwood in this condition."

"Got to. Promised Charley . . ."

Dick swayed a little, caught himself, took a deep breath. Powell had a half hour's lead on him, but he might be able to cut that down on the dun. The horse wasn't much for looks, but he had speed to burn, and plenty of sand, to boot.

"You're a crazy man, you know that?"

"If you really want to help me, Jack . . . have your men saddle the dun."

Bowman sighed and turned to his hands. "You heard the man! Get that rangy critter ready to ride!"

* * *

No hat, his face and arms and torso covered with dried blood, his shirt in tatters . . . Dick supposed he was about the most horrible sight anyone could imagine. Mothers could frighten small children just with his description. He was certainly a far cry from the dashing young actor he had once been.

But Dakota Territory was a far cry from the stately English countryside, too, or the bustling cosmopolitan city that was London, for that matter.

Time meant nothing now, so he had no idea how long it had been since he'd left Bowman's ranch. He was in the hills, following the twisting trail between wooded slopes. That cut down on the view; it was rare that he could see more than a couple of hundred yards in front of him, and often not that far. So there was no way of knowing if he was catching up to Powell or not. All he could do was keep moving and hope.

That was pretty much true of life itself, he thought grimly. All anybody could do was keep moving and hope. . . .

The dun had responded magnificently. The horse was ugly as sin and would take a bite out of anybody's hide if they were unwary enough to turn their back on him, but Lord, he could run! And it took a special kind of horse to maintain any sort of speed in this rugged terrain. Dick didn't know how good a mount Powell was on, but he would have been willing to bet that the animal was no match for the dun.

The only question was whether or not there would be time to catch up before Powell reached Deadwood.

Suddenly, Dick saw a flicker of movement in front of him as something or someone went around a bend in the trail up ahead. He leaned forward in the saddle, urging more effort from the dun. By the time he reached the same bend and rounded it, whatever he had seen was gone. Two more turns, though, and there it was again, a man on horseback, riding hell-for-leather along the trail that followed a narrow, bubbling creek.

Powell! Dick recognized the man, and before Powell went out of sight around another bend, he even caught a glimpse of the two bundles of newspapers tied on behind the man's saddle. The bastard planned to ride into Deadwood with all one hundred copies of the Cheyenne *Daily Leader*!

Well, they would just see about that.

Dick didn't have to lash the dun with the reins or rake the horse's sides with his spurs. All he had to do was lean forward again and say, "Run, you son of a bitch, run!" and the dun responded. The wind tore at Dick's bruised, bloody face as the horse raced along the trail.

How far were they from Deadwood? He tried to focus on landmarks, but he was too exhausted and his brain too stunned by everything that had happened. All he knew was that they were still on the trail, and he had the dun to thank for that.

Horse and rider swept around another bend. Dick saw Powell again, now less than a hundred yards ahead of him. Powell threw a wild glance over his shoulder and spurred madly, but his mount was already giving him all it had. Slowly, Dick began to close in.

Another turn, and suddenly Dick knew where they were. The trail sloped downward. Before them, in the distance no more than half a mile away, lay Deadwood. Within minutes they would reach the settlement and the race would be over.

Even over the frantic pounding of hoofbeats, he heard Powell shouting and screaming at his horse. Dick drew nearer. The dun's head was even with the hindquarters of Powell's horse. Hooves flashed with blinding speed. The dun surged forward. The horses were running almost side by side now on the trail.

Dick reached over. He grabbed the rope holding one of the newspaper bundles together and pulled. It wouldn't come loose. He needed a knife to cut the rope, but even if he'd had one, he probably couldn't have managed under the circumstances. The hurricane deck of a galloping horse was no place for delicate work.

Powell bellowed a curse and hipped around in his saddle, striking at Dick. Dick ducked under the blow. Surely if he reached Deadwood first, even without the newspapers, he would be declared the winner of the race once he explained Powell's treachery.

But Dick was stubborn enough so that he wanted to win fair and square, with no explanations required, just a clear-cut victory. He leaned out again and grabbed the rope and pulled, and this time the bundle of newspapers came loose. With it swinging from his hand, he veered the dun away from Powell's horse, putting a little distance between them.

Now the turn that led into Main Street was just ahead. Dick and Powell were still side by side as they rounded into it, but then the dun called on his last reserves of strength and pulled ahead. Hearing the rataplan of hoofbeats, people ran out of the buildings to see what was going on, and their excited shouts filled the air as they recognized the two contestants in the great Pony Express race. Men waved their hats over their heads and jumped up and down. The street cleared ahead of the riders, giving them an open path to the finish line. Dick kept his attention centered on the banner that ran across Main Street and didn't even look at Powell anymore. He knew he was in the lead.

What he didn't realize until he flashed under the banner and finally glanced back was that he was a good three lengths in front. Powell's horse had finally given out, and the dun's last burst of speed had left it in the dust.

Dick eased up on the reins and let the dun slow to a halt at its own pace. Men gathered around them, whooping and cheering and applauding. Colorado Charley Utter fought his way through the crowd and beamed up at Dick when he reached the dun's side. "You did it!" he shouted as he grabbed Dick's free hand and pumped it. "You won! You won!"

"Here are . . . the papers," Dick said as he extended the bundle to Charley, who took it and danced around in triumph. Several men in the crowd were so excited they took out their guns and began firing into the air. If this kept up, it would rival the Fourth of July celebration Deadwood had thrown the previous month.

He felt a pounding on his leg and looked down to see the grinning, pleasantly ugly face of Calamity Jane. "Damn it, Dick, I knew you'd beat that bastard!" she enthused. "But what the hell happened to you? You look like shit!"

Dick opened his mouth to tell her that he felt like it, too, but the words never came out. Instead, in what was becoming a distressingly frequent occurrence, he passed out, tumbling from the saddle and never even feeling it as he fell into the arms of the crowd.

Chapter Twenty-one

"ARE you sure we can't talk you outta this, Dick? God-damn it, you're the best rider I got!"

Dick pulled the saddle cinch tight on the dun. He smiled and said to the flamboyantly dressed little man beside him, "I'm sorry, Charley, but my mind is made up. Since leaving England, I've never stayed in one place for too long, you know. I'm just too restless. Fiddle-footed, as you Westerners say."

Colorado Charley shook his head. "There ain't nobody in Deadwood—hell, in the whole Dakota Territory!—who's more of a Westerner than you, Dick. It don't matter where you come from, your home's on the frontier now."

"There are all sorts of frontiers," Dick said quietly as he lowered the stirrup. He patted the dun's shoulder. Word had come from Jack Bowman's ranch that Dick was to keep the gallant horse, and he was very grateful for that. The two of them made a fine team. A winning team. They had won the great Pony Express race, hadn't they?

The end of the race was three days in the past. Dick had slept for most of that first day in Colorado Charley's tent.

That was a measure of how grateful to him Charley was, since he didn't share his sanctum easily. Doc Peirce had cleaned up Dick's wounds, and Charles Wagner had fed him for free in the Grand Central Hotel's dining room. Plenty of rest and three meals a day prepared by Aunt Lou March-banks had gone a long way toward restoring Dick's strength. He felt good enough now to make good on his plan to leave Deadwood.

Colorado Charley wasn't the only one who had tried to talk him out of it. So had California Joe, Calamity Jane, Jack Anderson, and Leander Richardson. But as he had looked around at his circle of friends, Dick had been struck by how odd it seemed that Bill Hickok was no longer one of their number. The group had never had a real leader, but if it had, that man would have been Hickok. It had lost something when Wild Bill was killed. He was the glue that had held them together, and without him they were starting to drift apart. The White-Eyed Kid had already begun talking about leaving the Black Hills, him and Jen, so that the two of them could make a new start elsewhere. Joe and Calam were natural-born drifters, too, and it wouldn't surprise Dick at all if they moved on soon. He didn't know Richardson well enough to speculate on what the young man might do. Charley seemed to be the only one putting down roots here, what with his freight line and his Pioneer Pony Express.

But it wasn't just them, Dick realized as he took one last look around at the settlement. Short though it might have been, an era had ended with the death of Wild Bill Hickok. Deadwood would never be the same. It was still a tough place, of course, but never again would it be the wild, brawling mining camp it had been for the first few months of its existence. The pounding of hammers had gradually done away with a place that had probably been as much myth as reality to begin with. In defiance of government treaties and danger from the Indians and rugged terrain and freezing cold in the winter and blistering heat in the summer, civilization had come to the Black Hills. Since he had been back, Dick had even heard talk that someone might start a stagecoach line between Cheyenne and Deadwood. What was next? The railroad?

Yes, Wild Bill Hickok's death was the exclamation point that should have ended the story. But life, of course, was not that neat. It went blithely on its way, in cheerful ignorance of dramatic structure. The hammers kept pounding, and the walls went up.

"Dick? You look like you went a million miles away from here for a second."

Charley's words pulled him out of his reverie. He looked around at his friends, smiled, and said, "A million miles or a million years . . . it's all the same, isn't it?"

Calamity Jane grunted. "You really are a crazy damned Englishman, you know that?" She threw her arms around him and hugged him hard. "You take care o' yourself, you hear?"

"I will," he promised. He shook hands with all the others in turn and hugged Jen, as well. Then he put his foot in the stirrup and swung up onto the dun. Lifting his hat for a second, he said, "Good-bye, my friends." He wheeled the dun and rode north. He had decided to head that direction because he had never seen Canada. It was part of the British Empire, after all, so it was time he took a look at the place. Perhaps it would remind him of home. . . .

"He'll be back," Colorado Charley said as he stood with the others watching the Englishman ride away. "You just wait and see. One o' these days, ol' Bloody Dick Seymour will come ridin' right back into Deadwood."

But he never did.

AL Swearengen growled, "Place is gettin' too damned civilized."

Laurette Parkhurst snorted in disgust. "Tell me about it! You want another drink?"

"Sure." Swearengen leaned forward in his chair and shoved his empty glass across the desk.

They were in Laurette's office in the rear of the Academy for Young Ladies. It was early evening and quiet, quiet enough so that if they listened hard, they could hear the droning voice of Preacher Smith as he exhorted the faithful and the not-so-faithful out on Main Street.

Swearengen threw back the whiskey that Laurette poured for him and then said, "Somethin's gotta be done about that preacher. He's just gettin' worse and worse. He was outside my place for four or five hours last night, raisin' hell. No tellin' how much business I lost because of him."

Laurette took a sip of her drink. "I've been thinkin' on that. Figured we might be able to kill two birds with one stone, as the old sayin' goes."

Swearengen raised his bushy eyebrows. "What are you talkin' about?"

"When Bellamy went off to work on that minin' claim, he left his rifle here."

"So?"

She smiled. "So what if somebody was to shoot Preacher Smith while he was walkin' over to Crook City tomorrow to hold services, and Bellamy Bridges' rifle was found close to the body?"

"You know Smith's gonna be goin' to Crook City?"

"He told one of the fellas who was in here earlier that was what he planned to do. Said the folks in Crook City needed to have the Gospel spread to them, too. Smith's tramped all over these hills, visitin' every little camp he can find."

Swearengen nodded slowly. "Yeah, he does that, all right. But you think people would really blame the kid for killin' him, just because his rifle was found nearby? Seems unlikely to me."

"You forget that Bellamy doesn't have many friends around these parts. Hell, Ryan and Ling are probably the only ones who'd have anything to do with him. He was pretty much a bully and an asshole while he was workin' for me."

Swearengen chuckled. "Yeah, he was, that's true enough. I wanted to kill him a time or two myself."

"I'd rather see him strung up as a murderer," Laurette said tightly. "Serve him right for turnin' his back on me."

"Anybody who turns his back on you is a damned fool," Swearengen said, a quirk of his eyebrows adding meaning to the statement. Laurette just smiled coldly in response. Swearengen went on. "All right, say you plan to frame the Bridges kid for killin' the preacher. You've still got to have somebody to pull the trigger and actually get rid of Smith."

Laurette picked up the bottle and splashed more whiskey in her glass. "I was sort of figurin' on handlin' that part of it myself. You don't know this about me, Al, but maybe you should. . . . I'm a hell of a shot with a rifle."

Swearengen looked at her for a long moment and then said, "No, I didn't know that. You really think you can do it?"

"I'm damned sick and tired of countin' on somebody else to take care of things for me," she snapped. "Comes down to it, I trust me more'n I trust anybody else. A whole hell of a lot more."

Swearengen held out his glass for a refill. "All right, then. Tomorrow we get rid of the preacher, and when folks find out what happened, they'll lynch Bridges, if all goes accordin' to plan." He lifted the glass after Laurette poured more whiskey into it. "Here's to gettin' rid of obstacles."

She clinked her glass against his. "To gettin' rid of obstacles," she agreed.

And both of them wondered just how long it would be before the other one was nothing but an obstacle that had to be removed from the trail.

LEE Street, one of the narrow streets that crossed Main, became nothing but a set of wooden steps as it climbed Forest Hill on the northern edge of the settlement. At the top of the steps was a small cabin. It had been sitting there empty when H.W. Smith arrived in Deadwood, and no one had objected when the preacher had moved into it.

On a night such as this, when he had been preaching for several hours, the climb to his home was tiring, but Smith ignored the leaden feeling in his muscles. He watched the shadows nervously, thinking even as he did so that giving in to such anxiety was in its own small way a sin. He was supposed to trust in the Lord. Whatever happened was according to divine plan, so there was no need to be concerned.

Surely, after all his years of selfless service to God and mankind, the Lord would not allow him to be taken back, returned to the presence of his enemies, locked away for a crime he had not committed, no matter how much he might have wanted to.

And, God help him, he had *wanted* to kill Gerald Tarrant. He had wanted it so very badly.

The memory was as fresh in his mind as if a single day had passed instead of a decade. *The carriage being whipped down the street by its driver, the man inside the carriage shouting for more speed because he was late for a meeting with a business associate, the vehicle careening around a corner just as the woman with the helpless infant in her arms stepped out into the street to cross it . . .*

They had looked so small and fragile and broken, lying there on the cobblestones like that, while Gerald Tarrant spared them not even a glance. He was too busy complaining to the policeman about the delay. And then, of course, he had been allowed to go on his way. The accident had been unfortunate, even tragic, but Tarrant lived on Beacon Hill and owned part of a bank and a shipping line and a mill. The woman and child who had died under the wheels of his carriage had only been the wife and son of a near-penniless Methodist minister.

Smith's grief had been so terrible that it had almost shaken even *his* faith. Almost. But in the end he had triumphed over it with the help of the Lord, and he had been ready to go on with his life. That was when his brother had shown up at his house one night, the house he had shared with the two who were now gone, the house that now seemed so achingly vast and empty despite its smallness. Ezra's eyes had been wild with fear and anger and shock at what he'd done. The hands that gripped Henry's shoulders and shook him were stained with blood. In haunted, disjointed words,

Ezra had explained how he had gone to Gerald Tarrant's fine mansion on Beacon Hill and slipped inside. Tarrant was a widower, so he was alone in his bedroom when Ezra Smith confronted him and demanded justice. That had so often been the way, Ezra, the older brother, standing up for Henry, the younger, the gentle soul who wouldn't harm anyone, not even to take vengeance on the man responsible for the deaths of his wife and son.

And then, when Tarrant had put up a struggle, Ezra, who had never quite understood what strong drink did to him, had beaten the man to death with his bare hands.

Ezra had a family of his own and a business. He had never done anything like this before, despite a few tavern brawls. But he had looked into his brother's eyes and seen the horrible pain there, and he had known that Henry would never do anything about it himself. So he had gone to teach Tarrant a lesson and instead had killed him, and now Ezra Smith was a murderer and terrified of what would happen to him.

It had taken Henry quite a while to calm him down and find out everything that had happened. Once he had heard the story, once he was sure that no one had seen Ezra entering or leaving Tarrant's house, he had known right away what he had to do.

"If I run away, everyone will blame me," he had said to his brother, speaking in low, urgent tones so that he would get through to Ezra. "If you stay here and talk about what a terrible thing it is and how you never dreamed that your brother would commit such a crime, no one will harm you."

"But . . . but you'll be a fugitive!" Ezra had protested. "You'll be wanted for murder, and you'll be on the run for the rest of your life!"

"There's nothing to keep me here," Henry had said with a sad smile. "You shouldn't have done what you did, Ezra. Vengeance is mine, sayeth the Lord. But it's done, and I'll not see you punished for it when you were only thinking of me. Stay here in Boston. Live your life. Love your family. That's all I ask."

Go, and sin no more, Jesus had said. Preacher Smith

prayed every day that his brother had followed that advice.

Meanwhile, the law had jumped to the conclusion that he was guilty when he disappeared from Boston, just as he had known they would. But the frontier was so far from Massachusetts, it had seemed to him that he would be safe there. He could never reclaim the life he had lost on that cobblestoned street, but he could build another life, a life filled with the same sort of good works he hoped he would have done if the tragedy had never occurred. After so long a time, the authorities would stop looking for him.

But Tarrant's family had a long memory, and the bounty they had placed on his head was large enough to extend its seductive power hundreds of miles, all the way to the Black Hills of Dakota Territory. It had brought the bounty hunter here.

But why hadn't he tried to take his quarry back and collect that blood money? What was he waiting for?

Smith didn't know, but despite his faith, he watched the shadows. Worry gnawed at his vitals. He had known this day might come, the day when he would have to run again.

But not tonight. Tomorrow. He had let it be known around town that tomorrow he would walk up the gulch along Whitewood Creek that led to Crook City in order to preach to the miners there. He even planned to leave a note on the door of his cabin to that effect, saying that he would return to Deadwood that afternoon.

But that was a falsehood. A lie. A sin. He would never return to Deadwood, and he told himself it was necessary that he mislead anyone who might try to follow him. God would forgive him for that, surely. . . .

He reached the top of the steps and the little cabin that waited for him. Pausing, he turned and looked down at Deadwood. Most of the buildings were dark now, but in the Badlands, lights still burned. Places like the Gem and the Bella Union and the Academy for Young Ladies never closed, and it wouldn't really matter if they did. The sinners would just find somewhere else to commit their iniquities. The struggle was never-ending.

But he wouldn't give up. He would fight until breath no

longer remained in his body. Not here, perhaps, but some-where else. Somewhere he was needed. The Lord would give him the necessary strength.

Feeling a little better, Preacher Smith straightened his back, opened the door of his cabin, and went inside. Tomor-row he would bid farewell to Deadwood forever.

Chapter Twenty-two

❧❧

DAN and Bellamy were in the mine shaft, working, when they heard Ling call out to them. "Someone's coming!" the Chinese girl said, and there was a note of alarm in her voice.

They dropped pick and shovel and hurried to the shaft's entrance, squinting against the brightness as they stepped out into the glare of the morning sunshine. It was Sunday, August 20th, and even though Dan felt a little guilty about working on the Sabbath, the gold was waiting for them, there in the rock, and it was impatient to be let out. The Good Lord would understand that, but just to make sure of it, when he and Bellamy struck it rich, Dan planned to find a church somewhere and make a nice donation to it. Or maybe he'd just give the money to Preacher Smith, if Deadwood didn't have a real church by then.

First, though, they had to deal with whoever the visitor was before they could get back to work. Both men wore holstered Colts, and Dan had picked up the Winchester that leaned against the rock wall at the mouth of the shaft. They started down the slope toward the camp.

Ling hurried up to meet them. "A rider," she said. "I think it is the one called Dority, the man who works in the Gem Theater."

Dan frowned. That was odd. Dan Dority didn't have any reason to be coming out here. Maybe he was on his way somewhere else and was just passing by their claim. But as they walked on down to the camp, he saw that wasn't the case. The visitor was Dority, all right, and he had reined in and thumbed back his hat as he waited for them.

"Mornin'," Dority greeted them.

Dan had never had many dealings with the man. He had hauled Bellamy out of the Gem when they first came to Deadwood and Bellamy had gotten sick drunk on some of Swearengen's whiskey. That was about it.

"What do you want?" Dan asked curtly.

Dority nodded toward Bellamy. "Came to talk to the kid there, mainly."

Bellamy said, "I'm not interested in anything Al Swearengen has to say, Dority."

The man took off his hat and wiped sweat off the inside of the band. "I ain't here on behalf o' Al," he said as he replaced the hat.

"Bullshit. You don't even take a crap until Swearengen says it's all right."

Dority's face darkened with anger. "You got no call to talk to me like that. I'm riskin' trouble by comin' out here, you know that? That Parkhurst woman's a bad one to have for an enemy."

Bellamy frowned in surprise. "What's Laurette Parkhurst have to do with this?"

Dority rested his hands on the saddle horn and leaned forward. "She's gonna have Preacher Smith killed today."

Ling exclaimed, "No!" while Dan and Bellamy stiffened.

"How do you know?" Bellamy asked.

"Heard about it from one o' the whores. The fella who's supposed to do it let somethin' slip about it while he was with her, and she got upset about it and told me later. None of us particularly like the preacher, but damn it, you hadn't ought to go around bushwhackin' a man o' God!"

Dan looked over at Bellamy. "Do you know what he's talking about?"

Bellamy nodded, a grim look on his face, and said, "Laurette's wanted to get rid of Preacher Smith even longer than she had it in for Wild Bill Hickok." To Dority, he asked, "Do you know who this bushwhacker is?"

Dority shook his head. "I didn't see him myself, and the whore who told me about it said she'd never seen him before. Probably some gunnie who just drifted into town. Look, kid, all I really know is that the preacher's gonna be ambushed while he's on his way up to Crook City today, unless somebody can stop it."

"Why tell *me*?"

"Because I heard from Al that you and the Parkhurst woman had a fallin'-out. Thought you might like to scotch her plans for her. Besides, there's no real law in Deadwood. They call Ike Brown the sheriff, but he ain't worth shit when it comes to real trouble. It was just luck he grabbed Jack McCall. Seemed to me like maybe you could handle a chore like this."

Bellamy and Dan exchanged another glance. "Do you believe him?" Bellamy asked.

Dan didn't answer directly. Instead, he asked Dority, "How come you decided to double-cross your boss and tell us about this?"

"I ain't double-crossin' Al," Dority replied with a vehement shake of his head. "He's got no part in this. It's all the Parkhurst woman's doin'."

"He's been talking to her about getting rid of the preacher," Bellamy said accusingly.

"Just stringin' her along, that's all. Al Swearengen is a lot of things, kid . . . but he don't go in for bushwhackin' preachers."

Ling put a hand on Bellamy's arm. "Preacher Smith is a good man. If you can help him . . ."

"I don't know," Bellamy said. "I don't know who to believe."

"Hey, I told you about it," Dority said with a shrug. "What

you do about it is up to you." He turned his horse as if to ride back to Deadwood.

"Wait a minute!" Bellamy called. "When is this supposed to happen?"

"I don't know for sure," Dority said over his shoulder. "From what I heard, Smith was plannin' to leave sometime this mornin' to walk up to Crook City."

"All right," Bellamy said, reaching a decision. "Dan, will you ride with me? We'll see if we can find him, and we'll go to Crook City with him. No one will bother him if we're along."

"Yeah, sure," Dan said without hesitation. It would mean losing a day's work, but they could spare that to help out the preacher, who had been the first man to greet them when they reached Deadwood.

"So long, then," Dority called with a wave of his hand. He rode off down the gulch.

Bellamy turned to Ling. "Will you be all right here by yourself?"

"I'll be fine," she assured him. "Just leave me a pistol."

Bellamy nodded. His thoughts were whirling. He couldn't believe that Laurette was going to go through with her plan to have Smith killed. It was cold-blooded murder, with just about the most innocent victim anybody could imagine.

On the other hand, he had learned that Laurette would stop at nothing to get what she wanted, so he wasn't all that surprised.

He just hoped he and Dan would be in time to save the preacher's life.

SMITH came out the door of his little cabin and closed it behind him. He had a carefully lettered card in his hand, and using a nail that he took from his pocket, he pinned it to the door. The card read simply: *Gone to Crook City to preach and, God willing, will be back at three o'clock.* Carrying his Bible, he started down the steps that led to the street.

When he got there, a couple of prospectors were passing

by. They hailed him, and one of the men asked, "Where you headed today, Preacher?"

"Crook City," he replied. "The people there are waiting to hear the Gospel."

"That ain't such a good idea," the second miner said. "There's talk around town that somebody spotted some Injuns up that way yesterday. You don't want to run into any o' them Sioux. Bloodthirsty savages, the whole lot of 'em."

Smith smiled and held up the Bible in his hand. "This is my protection."

"That's all well an' good," the first prospector said, "but if it was me, I'd rather have me a good cap-an'-ball revolver to deal with them Injuns."

"The Lord's Word has never failed me yet," Smith said, "and I am not afraid to put my trust in it now."

"Well, keep your eyes open, anyway, Preacher."

The miners went on their way. Smith smiled after them. In their own rude way, they were good men. Most of the inhabitants of Deadwood were. Crude, unrepentant sinners, of course, obsessed with gold and the pleasures of the flesh . . . but there was still a spark of goodness in them, deep though it might be buried.

He was going to miss them.

Determinedly putting that thought behind him, he strode toward the trail that led to Crook City.

TITUS stepped out from behind the thick trunk of the pine where he had been standing as he watched Smith leave the cabin. He had overheard the preacher's conversation with the two prospectors. Now Titus's long legs carried him up the steps to the cabin, where he quickly read the note Smith had left tacked to the door.

This was the perfect opportunity, Titus realized. He could grab Smith and have him well away from Deadwood by nightfall, without any chance of the townspeople interfering. He still had his doubts about whether or not Smith was really guilty of the crime he had been charged with. He had been keeping an eye on Smith for days now, and it was amazing how well liked, even loved, the man was. It just didn't seem possible that such a gentle fella could have beaten somebody to death with his bare hands.

But that was for a court to decide. Titus's only concern was the five-thousand-dollar bounty. That money was going to be his. Smith's ultimate fate was in other hands.

Titus walked toward the corral where he had left his horse. He had bought another horse and saddle from the liveryman, since he would need a mount for his prisoner. He didn't get in a hurry.

He wanted Smith to be well away from Deadwood before he moved in to grab him.

SWEARENGEN was loading his rifle when the knock sounded on the door. "Come in," he said.

Dan Dority stepped into the office. He took his hat off and said, "I done just like you told me, Al. I rode out to that camp and told the kid that the Parkhurst woman was havin' the preacher bushwhacked today."

Swearengen levered a round into the Winchester's chamber. "What did the little bastard say?"

"He's gonna try and stop it, him and that partner of his who used to be an Army sergeant."

Swearengen nodded. "Good. You did just fine, Dan. If this works out, there might even be a little bonus in it for you."

"Thanks, Al," Dority said with a grin.

"There's just one more thing I need you to do this morning."

"What's that?"

"Go saddle me a damned horse."

LAURETTE had left the buggy in a clump of trees, well out of sight of the trail, and had tied the horse's reins securely to a pine trunk. Then she had hiked up here onto this rocky slope, cussing all the way because her tight, high-buttoned shoes weren't made for clambering around the Black Hills. She needed a good vantage point above the trail, though, and from where she sat with her back pressed against a rock and another one in front of her where she could rest the barrel of the rifle, she could see a good hundred yards along the well-worn path. When Smith showed up, she could draw a bead on him and kill him with ease.

It was a damned shame she had to do this herself. She had always believed that a pretty gal shouldn't have to do any real work other than flattering some stupid man and letting him stick his dick in her every now and then. But what she had told Al Swearengen was true—she *didn't* trust anybody else to take care of this chore. She couldn't ask Fontaine to do it, that was for damned sure. He'd just foul it up and she would somehow wind up getting blamed for whatever happened. Swearengen hadn't volunteered to do it himself, and Bellamy had gone and gotten religion on her. She would have trusted Fletch, if he was still alive, but of course he never would have agreed to it. For somebody who had done some of the things he had, Fletch sure had been quick to get on his high horse when it came to bushwhacking a trouble-some preacher.

No, when you came right down to it, if you had some-body who just had to be killed, it was better to do it yourself.

But she had started to worry a little about the fact that once it was done, Swearengen would have something to hold over her head. The citizens of Deadwood didn't care all that much about murder, by and large, but they wouldn't like it when the preacher was killed. Laurette was counting on that in her plan to frame Bellamy. Stringing him up would satisfy the town's appetite for rough justice—but if they found out later that Bellamy had been innocent and Laurette was really the one who had killed the preacher . . .

Well, it wouldn't be pretty, that was all. And in order to make sure it never happened, she might have to go ahead and get rid of Swearengen, too. Maybe even today, when she went back to Deadwood to tell him that everything had gone well and the preacher was dead. But was she really up to two killings in one day?

She smiled, knowing the answer.

Hell, yes.

DAN and Bellamy had to walk to Deadwood, and by the time they got there, the preacher was already gone. Dan bit back a curse as he read the note Smith had left on the door of his cabin.

"All right," he said, taking command as easily as he had on the many patrols he had led into hostile territory. "We've got to get hold of some horses, so we can catch up to him. Come on."

They hurried back down the steps to Main Street. At the livery corral, Dan asked the old-timer who ran it about renting a couple of mounts.

"Seems like ever'body wants hosses this mornin'," the oldster complained. "Like to work a fella to death."

"Do you have any horses or not?" Bellamy asked impatiently.

"Hold on, young fella. Don't get your bowels in an uproar. O' course I got horses, and rigs, too. I can fix you up."

"We don't have any time to waste," Dan said.

A few minutes later they rode out of Deadwood on mounts that were definitely below average in quality. It was only eight miles to Crook City, though, so it didn't really matter how good the horses were as long as they would hold up for that far.

"Is there any other trail to Crook City?" Bellamy asked anxiously as they trotted along the path that followed the course of Whitewood Creek. Like all the trails in the Black Hills, it was pretty crooked.

"This is the only one I know of," Dan replied. "Don't worry, Bellamy, we'll catch up to the preacher in time."

"You can't know that for sure."

"I can have faith that we will. Seems appropriate, considerin' what we're tryin' to do." Dan paused, then asked, "What are we gonna do about Laurette Parkhurst?"

"Even if we save Preacher Smith, we can't let her get away with this," Bellamy said. "Somebody's got to put a stop to what she's doing."

"Hard to do when there's no real law in Deadwood."

"Maybe Deadwood needs some law of its own."

"You mean like vigilantes?"

Bellamy nodded. "If that's what it takes."

Doubtfully, Dan said, "I don't know, kid. That sort of thing gets out of hand mighty easy. It might be better to see about getting a real sheriff, somebody with some legal authority."

"That'll be too late to stop Laurette."

"You've got to wonder," Dan mused, "what makes her think she can get away with murder."

"Has anybody stopped her up until now?"

"Well . . . no."

"That's why she thinks she can get away with it," Bellamy said. "Somebody who's evil doesn't stop what they're doing until they're forced to."

Dan suddenly stiffened in the saddle and put out a hand. Both men reined in sharply. "I saw something up ahead," Dan said. "Looked like the sun glinting off something."

"A rifle barrel?"

"Could be. Come on!"

They kicked their horses into motion again. The trail twisted so much Dan lost track of where he had seen the glint of sunlight reflecting off something. Anyway, he told himself, it might not have anything to do with Preacher Smith and the grim errand that had brought them out here. But he didn't really believe that.

They swept around a bend, into a section of trail that ran relatively straight for a hundred yards or so before twisting back to the right at the base of a rocky bluff. About fifty yards along the trail stood the tall, distinctive figure of Preacher Smith. His head was turned so that he could look back at them. Clearly, he had been striding along the path when the sound of the horses galloping up behind him had made him stop and look back.

And a short distance beyond the preacher, unseen by him

so far, a bearded figure was stepping out of the trees along-side the trail, rifle in hand, ready to kill.

"It's the bushwhacker!" Bellamy yelled. "Look out!"

Then he yanked the pistol from its holster on his hip and started firing as he drove his horse straight toward the preacher and the gunman.

WHO the hell—! Titus thought as he brought the Winchester to his shoulder. Then the answer came to him. More bounty hunters—that was who the two men had to be. They were after Smith just like he was.

Well, they weren't going to get him. That five thousand dollars was his!

With the ease born of natural talent and years of experience, he centered the rifle's sights on the chest of the blond youngster who was galloping toward him, yelling and shooting, and fired.

WHAT the hell was going on down there? Laurette had been just about to squeeze the trigger when Smith had stopped suddenly and turned look back along the trail. Then a second later two riders had come charging around the bend, and a man she'd never seen before walked out of the trees, and—

Son of a bitch! That was Bellamy, shooting and hollering about something. The man Laurette didn't know brought his rifle up. There was going to be a shoot-out, right there on the trail.

And Preacher Smith was right in the middle of it. Laurette smiled as she lowered her head and nestled her cheek against the smooth wooden stock of the rifle and drew a bead on the tall, black-clad figure clutching the Bible. This was working out just fine for her. When Smith wound up dead, everybody would figure he had been struck by a stray bullet. She wouldn't even have to bother framing Bellamy, because he was already here. All she had to do was pull the trigger, smooth and steady, just like when she was a girl back in Ohio. Her ma had tried to tell her that it wasn't ladylike for a

gal to go huntin', but Laurette didn't care about that. Her ma
was just a dirty old whore and didn't know anything—
except that men would pay not only to fuck her, but also to
fuck her daughter, even though Laurette wasn't hardly old
enough, and out there in the woods, with a rifle in her hands,
when she was shooting at a squirrel or a rabbit, she could
pretend that it was her ma's face she saw over the sights, or
the face of one of the men who laid on her and tore at her
and slobbered on her, and it always felt good to squeeze the
trigger and hear the roar of the shot. . . .

She heard it now, but it was odd, because she didn't think
she had pulled the trigger yet. That was all she had time to
think before something smashed into her back and drove her
forward against the rock. The sun was hot, but a heat much
more fierce suddenly filled her. She opened her mouth but
no sound came out, only a trickle of crimson.

Whore or not, her ma had been right. Bad things happened to little girls who went into the woods.

DAN saw smoke and flame geyser from the barrel of the
stranger's rifle and cried, "Bellamy!" as the youngster lurched
in the saddle. Bellamy toppled off his horse. Rage filled Dan
as he reined in and jerked his own rifle up. He knew better
than to try to fire from the back of a running horse. He drew
a bead on the stranger who had just shot Bellamy and began
cranking off rounds as fast as he could work the Winchester's lever, hoping that the preacher had the good sense to
get down and stay the hell out of the way.

PREACHER Smith wanted to cry out as the roar of shots assaulted his ears. He didn't, though, nor did he drop to the
ground or run for cover. He recognized the man who had
come from the woods—the bounty hunter, the man who was
determined to take him back to face justice . . . unjust though
it might be. And trying to stop him were young Bellamy
Bridges and his friend Sergeant Ryan. Bellamy, who had
sunk into a morass of depravity but who appeared to have

somehow pulled himself out of it, with the Lord's help to be sure.

And then Bellamy went tumbling out of the saddle as blood flew in the air, and Smith did cry out at this. If Bellamy was mortally wounded, then his death could be laid at Smith's feet, because it was the preacher's life he was trying to save when he was shot. Not another death, Smith thought. Not another innocent soul struck down senselessly. Shaking, his Bible clutched tightly in his hand, he turned and raised his arms and lifted his face to heaven and cried out, "No more, please, God, no more!"

The answer came from above, but not from heaven. The shot that rang out, mixing with all the other shots that filled the air, came from the bluff above which soared a beautiful blue sky dotted with white clouds. Smith's gaze was fixed on those clouds as the hammer blow struck him in the chest, staggering him but not knocking him off his feet. He caught himself and stayed that way for a second, swaying slightly, and then he fell slowly to his knees. His head dipped forward. He saw the crimson drops falling in the dust of the trail. He felt a surge of pain and disappointment, but he also felt relief. Peace at last, he thought. After all this time, he would finally have peace. He would be reunited with his lost loved ones, his wife and his beautiful son. He was going home. . . .

As he fell forward, he twisted so that he wound up lying on his back at the edge of the trail. That way he could look up into the sky and think for the last time that truly God worked His wonders in mysterious ways.

TITUS ducked back into the trees with lead singing around his head. Whoever that stocky son of a bitch was, he could shoot. And Titus wasn't going to stand around and get killed for nothing.

Because that was what it would amount to, he told himself bitterly. He had seen the way the bullet had torn through the preacher's body, had known from the way Smith folded up and fell that he was a goner. Just like that, five grand had been snatched out of Titus's grasp, because the reward posters hadn't said anything about dead or alive. Dead, Smith wasn't worth a damned penny.

At least those other two wouldn't get the bounty, either.

As he ran for his horses, Titus wondered briefly who had shot the preacher. He knew it hadn't been him, so it must have been the bastard who was with the kid. A ricochet, maybe. For a moment he had thought he heard a couple of shots from somewhere higher up, but that seemed mighty unlikely.

Anyway, it didn't matter now. He reached the horses, jerked their reins loose where he had tied them, and vaulted into the saddle of his mount. The shooting seemed to have stopped for the moment, but he didn't care. He just wanted to get out of here.

And if he never came back to Deadwood, that would be just fine with him.

DAN threw himself off his horse and ran to Bellamy's side. Still holding the rifle, he went to one knee beside the fallen youngster. The stranger had run off into the woods, and the sudden flurry of hoofbeats Dan heard told him that the man probably wasn't coming back. Still, he kept one eye on the trees as he rolled Bellamy onto his back.

The splash of red on the young man's shirt gave Dan reason for hope. The bloodstain was on the right shoulder. The bullet had drilled Bellamy there, rather than through the body. Either the stranger wasn't a very good shot, or maybe Bellamy's horse had stumbled a little at just the right time to throw off the man's aim. Dan didn't care; he was just glad to see that Bellamy was still alive.

Not only alive, but regaining consciousness. His eyelids fluttered open. His face showed pain and confusion as he gasped, "Dan? Dan?"

"Take it easy, kid," Dan told him. "You're hit, but I think you'll be all right. We just need to get you back to Deadwood as fast as we can." He tore a couple of strips off Bellamy's shirt and bound up the wound as best he could, hoping to slow down or maybe even stop the bleeding.

"The . . . the preacher . . . ?"

Dan glanced at the black-clad form lying motionless at the side of the trail. The Bible was still clutched in Smith's hand.

"He didn't make it, Bellamy."

Bellamy closed his eyes and moaned. "No! She's going to get away with it!"

Dan didn't know what to say. He had been watching the stranger closely. Hell, he hadn't taken his eyes off the man while he was shooting at him! And he would have sworn that the stranger *hadn't* shot Smith.

But if that was true, then who had killed the preacher? Dan didn't want to think any of his shots could have gone that wild, but that was the only explanation that made any sense. His jaw tightened. Lord help him, it looked like he had done the very thing he and Bellamy had raced out here to stop.

Hashing that out would have to wait. Right now, Bellamy needed medical attention. As gently as possible, Dan hauled the youngster to his feet, led him over to his horse, and got him into the saddle. Bellamy grunted in pain several times and his face was washed out and drawn, but he was stubbornly hanging on to consciousness.

"Can you stay in the saddle?" Dan asked him.

"Yeah. I can ride."

Dan swung up on his own mount. "Let's get you back to Deadwood, then."

"What about . . . the preacher?"

Dan glanced a final time at the still shape. "Somebody will have to come back out here for him." He grasped the reins of Bellamy's horse. "Come on."

"She's going to . . . get away with it," Bellamy said again, pain in his voice.

Maybe for now, Dan thought, but not forever. In the long run, nobody got away with anything. All of a man's sins, even his innocent mistakes, they all caught up to him sooner or later.

Justice might be delayed . . . but it could never be denied.

* * *

WELL, Al Swearengen thought as he slid the rifle back into the saddle boot on the rented horse he had ridden out here, that had worked out just dandy. He wasn't quite sure who that stranger was or why the gunfight had broken out, but he had taken advantage of the circumstances, as he always did. He had planned for Bellamy Bridges to be on hand to see Laurette shoot the preacher. That way, at the very least Laurette would wind up dancing at the end of a hang rope. Hell, the kid was so hotheaded he might have shot Laurette himself, after he saw her murder Smith.

That wasn't how things had played out, but Swearengen was nothing if not adaptable. He had seen his chance and seized it. One shot in Laurette's back, one shot in the preacher's chest, and he was rid of two problems. Simple. And with all the bullets that had been flying around down there, nobody would ever blame him for anything. Nobody would ever know that he was even here.

He put Laurette's body in the buggy and then drove the vehicle over to the edge of a nearby ravine. After turning the horse loose, he put his shoulder against the back of the buggy and shoved. It took him a few minutes of grunting and straining, but eventually the buggy went over, crashing to the bottom of the thirty-foot drop. Swearengen had picked the place well. A few more minutes of work and he had the bank ready to cave in. He had to get his rifle and use it as a lever to start the biggest rock moving, but then as he stepped back, a couple of tons of rock, dirt, and debris slid down on top of Laurette's body and the wrecked buggy. Let her disappear. Folks would wonder where she had gone off to. . . .

But hell, whores were always pretty undependable, now weren't they?

Feeling better than he had in a long time, Al Swearengen rode back to Deadwood. His town, he thought.

And as he rode, he began to whistle a merry little tune.

Epilogue

~~~

DAN took Bellamy straight to Doc Peirce's barbershop, and while Peirce was cleaning and bandaging the wound—which he assured Dan was not life-threatening—several riders came galloping into town, shouting that they had found Preacher Smith's body out on the Crook City trail. The preacher, they said excitedly, had been killed by Indians.

It was a logical conclusion. Sioux had been spotted in the area the day before.

And as Dan heard the talk, he rubbed a hand wearily over his face and then turned to look at Bellamy. "Hear that?" he said. "Preacher Smith's been killed by Indians."

Bellamy frowned, obviously confused, but then, slowly, he began to nod. No one knew for sure whose bullet had really ended the preacher's life. It was just simpler all around to blame it on the Sioux.

When Bellamy had been patched up, Dan took him back up Deadwood Gulch to the claim. Ling cried over him when she saw that he was hurt, and of course she fussed over him for days while he was healing. His shoulder mended all right, but he would never be a fast draw again. His arm was too stiff for that.

Preacher Smith was buried in Deadwood, in the grave-yard where he had prayed over so many departed souls. Pretty much the whole town turned out, as well as many of the miners. The General said a few words, as did Mayor E.B. Farnum. A.W. Merrick took notes for the story in his paper. Colorado Charley Utter concluded the service by reading from a paper that had been found in the preacher's pocket. Most folks thought it was the text he intended using in the sermon he planned to deliver in Crook City. Charley's voice rang out over the wooded slopes as he read, "Many ways there are in which we may assist in spreading the story of the Cross . . . by whom we have received grace and apostleship, for obedience to the faith among all nations for His name."

And the crowd said, "Amen." Probably not all of them knew what they were amen-ing, but they said it anyway, and they meant it.

Calamity Jane blew her nose on her bandanna and wiped away tears from her eyes. "That was a mighty pretty service," she said to Charley as they started back down the hill with the others. "There's been too many funerals in Deadwood, though."

Nobody could argue with that.

WHEN Laurette Parkhurst disappeared, the Frenchman called Fontaine who had been working for her tried to keep the Academy going for a while, but he was no businessman. Billy Nuttall paid him off to leave town and took over the building. It would make a nice addition to the Bella Union once some of the walls were knocked down. The whores who had worked for Laurette had to find other employment, but that wasn't difficult. Not in Deadwood. Several of them just walked across the street to the Gem Theater and went to work for Al Swearengen.

It wasn't long before the Academy for Young Ladies was pretty well forgotten, along with the woman who had run it.

But then businesses, like people, were always coming and going in a place like Deadwood.

"You sure I can't talk you into staying?" Dan asked.

Bellamy smiled. "I'll be back, don't worry about that. I . . . I just have to go home for a while. I want to see my family and . . . and try to forget everything that happened here."

Dan saw the way Ling winced slightly at Bellamy's words. Bellamy didn't see it, though. The boy had never felt about Ling the way she felt about him, and despite his fondness for Bellamy, Dan could have given him a thrashing right about then.

Still, it might be better for him to go. He had been broken, and he wasn't fully mended yet. He might never be. Bellamy had been forced to look inside himself and see with his own eyes the depths to which he was capable of sinking. That had shattered something inside him, and he was still too young to realize that everybody had those depths. Everybody was capable of doing things that they didn't want to look at afterward. Everybody cried out for forgiveness at one time or another, knowing full well that they didn't deserve it and could only hope and pray that it would be granted anyway. . . .

Bellamy shook hands with Dan and hugged Ling and then got on his horse and rode away. The two of them stood together beside the creek watching him, and Ling said, "We'll never see him again, will we?"

Dan shook his head and said, "I don't know. Depends on how soon he grows up . . . or if he ever does."

A few days later, Dan Dority came into Swearengen's office and said, "Al, you remember that Chinese gal who used to work for the Parkhurst woman?"

Swearengen frowned. "The one who disappeared at the same time as the Bridges kid?"

"Yeah. She's back. I hear she's gone to work at a place down in Chinatown. Calls herself the China Doll now."

Behind the desk, Swearengen poured himself a drink. "And this is supposed to interest me because . . . ?"

Dority shrugged. "I hear the boys talkin' while I'm tendin' bar. She's supposed to be mighty good at what she does, Al. I just thought you might want to go down to see her and ask her to work here."

"Did you, now?" Swearengen tossed back the whiskey in his glass. "If she wants to work here, she can damn well come and ask *me*."

"Fine, fine." Dority started to back out of the room. "I didn't mean nothin' by it, Al. I just thought it might be fittin', somehow, after everything that happened, for her to work here."

"All that's over and done with," Swearengen said. He snorted. "Hell, it's been a couple of weeks. Everybody's forgotten about it already."

He reached for the bottle and thought about Bill Hickok, and Carla, and that damned Silky Jen and the White-Eyed Kid, and Calamity Jane and the preacher and Colorado Charley and that Pony Express race and Fletch Parkhurst and Laurette and Bellamy and all the others who came to Deadwood looking for something, looking for gold, sure, but looking for other things as well, things like love and redemption, vengeance and death, escape and peace. The lucky ones found what they sought.

The rest, sooner or later, all came to the Gem.

"Two weeks in Deadwood," Al Swearengen said with a shake of his head. "Ancient fuckin' history."

Author's Note

THIS novel, like the others in the series *Tales from Dead-wood,* is a mixture of fiction, fact, and speculation based on the historical records of the time, which are often contradictory. Many of the characters were actual citizens of Deadwood in the summer of 1876, and many of the events happened as described. The backgrounds and motivations of some of these historical characters, such as Dick Seymour and Preacher Smith, have been supplied by the imagination of the author. It is known, however, that Dick Seymour vanished from the pages of history after leaving Deadwood. How Preacher Smith really died remains a mystery. Some historians believe he was indeed killed by Indians while on his way to Crook City to preach. Other scholars lay the blame for his death at the feet of the same group rumored to have been responsible for the murder of Wild Bill Hickok. The writer of historical fiction has the luxury of picking and choosing which version to believe—and so does the reader.

After leaving Deadwood, Jack McCall made the mistake of bragging about being the man who killed Wild Bill, and that made it easy for the determined Colonel George May to catch up to him, accompanied this time by a federal marshal. McCall was arrested in Laramie, Wyoming, on August 28th, 1876, and charged with murder. He was tried in federal court at Yankton, Dakota Territory, found guilty, and on December 6th, 1876, was sentenced to hang for his crime. While in jail and during his trial, he claimed that he was paid to assassinate Hickok by a gambler named Varnes, who represented the criminal element in Deadwood. The fact that this mysterious Varnes had disappeared—and there was speculation about whether or not he even existed—made people disregard McCall's story. Whatever McCall's motive might have been, the sentence handed down by the court was carried out on March 1st, 1877, and he was hanged by the neck until dead.

In 1879, Wild Bill Hickok's body was moved from its original grave and reinterred in Deadwood's new Mount Moriah cemetery. His old friend Colorado Charley Utter was on hand for the ceremony. Wild Bill still rests in Mount Moriah today, overlooking the city of Deadwood, South Dakota.

SPECIAL thanks as always to Samantha Mandor and Kimberly Lionetti for getting this project off the ground and for their continued faith in the author. Thanks as well to all the historians and scholars whose work paved the way for this yarn spinner. Where I've taken minor liberties with the facts, I hope it was for good reasons.

Mike Jameson
Azle, Texas

MIKE JAMESON

Tales from

DEADWOOD

*The first in a new series of fictionalized
tales, based on real-life characters,
that show Deadwood as it really was—
and might have been.*

Deadwood is the infamous and lawless
cesspool where a man is as likely to strike
it rich as he is to lose everything.
Now, the legendary Wild Bill Hickok—
who has lost his eyesight—and
Calamity Jane are coming to start
their own trouble.

0-425-20675-0

MIKE JAMESON

Tales from DEADWOOD: The Gamblers

*Imagine a town with no law,
and you have Deadwood.
Second in the new series of fictionalized
tales based on real-life characters.*

The famous Wild Bill Hickok has come to
Deadwood to stake his claim—and some
of the town's gamblers worry that the
legendary lawman will clean up Deadwood.
For help, they call on the Gem Theater's
ruthless owner, Al Swearengen—who knows
a stone-cold shootist who can end Hickok's
wild days permanently.

0-425-20959-8

**Available wherever books are sold or at
penguin.com**